"This is it," shouted Marek. **"If they come aboard, we destroy the ship!"**

"Listen!" roared Connor. "I've met some of them. I don't think they're violent. They could have killed me, or dissected me—but they didn't."

"Look at the screen!" said Zella.

The main vision screen was pulsing with blue and yellow diagonal bands that rushed swiftly from corner to corner. Other colors appeared, and the angle changed. Simultaneously, a strange sound, like a distorted voice, echoed through the ship.

A fragment of multicolored picture seemed to melt and surge on the screen, and then, suddenly, it was brilliant and sharp. Nordstrom and Zella gave involuntary cries . . .

"We communicate," boomed a voice through the ship.

Ace Books by Wynne Whiteford

THOR'S HAMMER
BREATHING SPACE ONLY
SAPPHIRE ROAD
THE HYADES CONTACT

WYNNE WHITEFORD

THE HYADES CONTACT

ACE BOOKS, NEW YORK

Portions of this book previously appeared
in the anthology books *Envisaged Worlds, Other Worlds*
and *Alien Worlds*, all published by Cory & Collins.

THE HYADES CONTACT

An Ace Book / published by arrangement with
the author

PRINTING HISTORY
Ace edition / September 1987

ISBN: 0-441-35446-7

Ace Books are published by
The Berkley Publishing Group,
200 Madison Avenue, New York, New York 10016.
The name "Ace" and the "A" logo are trademarks
belonging to Charter Communications, Inc.
PRINTED IN THE UNITED STATES OF AMERICA

10 9 8 7 6 5 4 3 2 1

To Gwayne M. Naug
—who's always there when I get
back to Earth

1

From orbit it looked as though Connor's team had drawn the most promising planet in the system. Fourth from a star slightly whiter and hotter than the Sun, it looked strikingly Earthlike—blue and white, about the right size, with oceans, continents and forests. Even the air was breathable.

True, the axis was more oblique, there was no moon, and the "day" was under sixteen hours. But there would be cities here some day, thought Connor. The main center might be Connor City. Why not?

Harn, the biologist, was at first enthralled at the vista of a whole new world of species to classify, but after his first exploratory tour in the flier, he returned to their prefabricated base on the plateau very silent.

"Something wrong about the place," he said at length. "About the vegetation, the insect life. There are not enough species."

"What's wrong with that?" asked Connor. "Perhaps selection narrowed things down to a few successful types."

"No." Harn shook his blond, crew-cut head emphatically. "It hasn't worked like that. Look. See all that forest?"

From the north slope of the plateau a sea of vegetation flowed over the horizon, lapping the lower slopes of stark, granitic peaks.

"It stretches east to the sea, west for a thousand kilometers without any change—that's as far as I went. Judging from the photos from orbit, it goes halfway round the planet. South of here you have a river complex like the Amazon Basin."

"So?"

"In the Amazon jungles you find hundreds of species of plants. Here I found five."

"Five?"

"I noted four species in the first minute—and that was it. I've covered a linear distance of three thousand kilometers, sampling at fifteen localities ranging from coastal swamp to the limit of vegetation on the mountains. Everywhere, I found the same four species of plant—with a fifth confined to saltwater estuaries."

"What sort of plants are they, Charl?"

"One's a tall tree like a primitive pine. Another's superficially like an Australian tree fern. There's a ground-cover plant like dark blue ivy, and another thing like nothing I've ever seen—spiral yellow blooms. The fifth type grows in saltwater mud, rather like a lime-colored mangrove."

"And that's the lot?"

Harn nodded. "That's all the vegetation on the damned planet, as far as I can see. Highly organized plants, but unrelated."

Connor was looking through Harn's photographs. "But some of these look different. These things like stunted pines."

"They're on a high plateau—local modification of the tall trees. There are other variants, like these—see? Mineral deficiency, perhaps. This is an albino form of that. But it still gets back to five species. You see the implication, don't you?"

"How do you see it, Charl?"

"These things haven't evolved here. They've been brought here."

"How can you be sure?"

"Because I've seen something like it before. Where we've been converting a lifeless planet to one capable of sustaining life. We've begun by introducing a few tested species of plants so an oxygen atmosphere eventually develops. It doesn't take long, from a historical viewpoint, when the plants are free to multiply without natural enemies."

"And you think someone has . . . seeded this place?"

"Yes."

"But who?" Connor kept looking through the photographs.

"Could any of these be Earth vegetation, modified by the different environment?"

"No. The pines are something like Earth trees of a hundred million years ago—and the spiral things come from a different evolutionary line altogether. Even a different chemistry."

"Any clue where they could have come from?"

Harn shook his head.

The white sun was almost setting when Kosaka came in from his suborbital survey. He spread his large, grid-marked photos on the table in the planning module. Connor went over them carefully with a magnifier while they filled in Kosaka on the theory Harn had developed.

"That's strange," said Kosaka. "I'll show you something."

He turned over a number of photos until he found the one he wanted. "Ah! It was early morning there—the light was not the best. But look there."

On the right of the photo was the familiar forest, on the left a stony or gravelly desert. Kosaka ran his finger down the center of the sheet.

"The forest ends along that line. The few trees on the left are small, not fully grown. The thought hit me that the trees on the right had been—well, planted. The ones on the left have come from wind-blown seeds." He stood back, his dark eyes flickering from Connor to Harn and back again.

Connor looked through his magnifier. "Let's take a run out there tomorrow. Not that we're likely to learn much. Some of these trees are nearly a hundred meters high. Whoever seeded the place did it a hundred or more years ago."

"I would have said five hundred to a thousand years," said Harn, "except that the iso-drive wasn't invented then."

"Unless—" said Connor, but didn't finish the sentence.

"Unless what?" asked Kosaka.

"Nothing," said Connor. He shivered slightly, glancing up at the dark blue sky.

Next morning Connor and Kosaka took the flier on a journey around the planet. After they had covered 120 degrees of longitude, they made their third brief landing on a plain overshadowed by towering mountains.

"What was that?" said Kosaka suddenly.

"What?" Connor followed the direction of his pointing finger.

"A flash of light. Like sunlight glancing off glass or bright metal."

"Are you sure?"

"Yes. Below these peaks."

Connor took out the powerful binoculars and steadied himself against the flier, half kneeling. The red granite ridge showed sharp and jagged against the deep blue, with little sign of softening erosion.

"Give me the glasses. I can pick the exact spot." Connor handed them over. Kosaka grunted. "Can't see anything flashing now. But see those two peaks like fangs, just above the slanting fault line? The flash came from the notch, just where that dark spot is."

Connor took back the glasses. The magnification was high, the field narrow, and the peaks ten or twelve kilometers away. He looked over the glasses to get his bearings, then focused on the conspicuous fault line and ran slowly up the length of it to the two pinnacles.

"I've got the notch."

"Right. The dark spot."

"What dark spot?"

Kosaka did not answer. Connor turned, and they looked at each other. Silently Kosaka took the glasses and focused them on the notch below the peaks. Abruptly he lowered them and turned to face Connor. His normal tan coloring faded to a creamy pallor.

"It's gone." His voice rasped like a rusty hinge.

"What was it like?"

"Just a dark spot. I took it for a bush, a small cave entrance, the shadowed side of a boulder—could have been anything." He looked wide-eyed at the mountains, then back to Connor.

Connor felt suddenly cold. "I think we'd better get back to the base," he said.

"What do we do about . . . that?"

"Check it out on the photos taken from the suborbit."

At sunrise the following day Kosaka went out to check the magnetometer, which was located a kilometer away from the base to avoid interference. Connor took the opportunity to get Harn's feeling about Kosaka's sighting of the flash and the disappearing dark spot.

"He must have thought he saw *something*," said Harn. "The flash of light I can understand. A pinpoint flash of light is a common enough optical effect—superimposed on a landscape, it could seem the way he described it. But the dark spot—I don't know. You saw nothing you could take to be a dark spot?"

"No."

"Were you both looking in the same place?"

"I think so."

Harn walked up and down the room. "What do you want to do? Check it out?"

"Of course. But we're a hell of a long way from home, or from any help. We have no weapons of any kind. We don't want to start something that someone else finishes for us."

"What d'you intend to do?"

"One thing would be a suborbital scan with infrared, when that area's in the dark. Might pick up any heat source."

"Taking Jiro with you?"

"God, yes. He might think I'm questioning his reliability if I don't."

Later in the day they took off and circled around to the night side of the planet, beginning the infrared scan soon after reaching the terminator. Connor sat at the controls, while Kosaka operated the scanner.

"Pattern of heat from the forest," he said. "Lot of residual heat in the rock outcrops."

"Keep it rolling. We'll take a route right around to the far terminator."

"Over the sea now," said Kosaka, watching the monitor screen. "Should be over the other continent in a few minutes."

Connor watched the slow, majestic march of the stars upward from the black horizon ahead as they went around towards the middle of the hemisphere of night.

"Getting more vegetation—and more rock. We'll be over land for the next ten-thousand kilometers."

Connor was not sure of the exact moment when he became aware of the light below. He was watching the constellations, some of them distorted from an Earth viewpoint, as they swung up over the endlessly retreating horizon. At one point ahead, to the right, the horizon appeared to be notched by some great chasm, for one of the fainter stars showed below it.

Within seconds the realization came to him; no chasm could be as deep as that. For a moment he thought of a star reflected in still water, then his pulse rate quickened sharply.

"Jiro!"

"Yes?"

"What's that light down there?"

Kosaka took a long time to reply, although he evidently saw the light as soon as Connor pointed to it.

"Fire in the forest? Volcanic?"

"No," said Connor. "Look at the color of it."

"Almost white, isn't it? Tinge of violet."

Both shouted aloud at the same instant. The light was gone. Luminous flecks of aftervision danced for a few seconds against empty darkness.

"Try to get a bearing on it," said Connor.

"I was too late for a photo, but I took it anyway. All I've got is the star field, and blackness below."

"That might help a bit. We have our course on record, and the time. The stars should show the direction."

"All very approximate. Con?"

"Uh-huh?"

"Think they saw us?"

"I don't know. But I think they saw us yesterday—from that ridge."

"So do I. Did you think that I'd imagined that dark spot?"

"Imagined? Hell, no! Why d'you think we're out here now?"

"What's wrong?" asked Harn as soon as they returned to the base.

"We saw a light in the forest," said Connor.

"A light? What sort of light?"

"Single point source, as far as we could tell. We were at thirty thousand meters, and at least five hundred kilometers away, so it must have been bright."

"Was it focused? Like a searchlight pointed at you?"

"No. Just a spot of light, like a star."

"Anywhere near where you thought—where you saw the flash in daylight?"

"Let's look at the charts." Connor ran off a copy of the relevant chart and penciled a cross marking their position when Kosaka had seen the flash. Next he drew in their route across the dark forest.

"The position of the light would be approximate. I'd make it in here." He drew a long ellipse, extending away from their point on the route.

"I'd make it more like this." With a different colored marker Kosaka drew another ellipse, half overlapping Connor's.

"So there you are," said Connor. "At the least the light and the spot on the pinnacle were fifteen hundred kilometers apart. If they were made by one man—or whatever—either he had a vehicle of some kind or he was very quick on his feet."

For a long time there was no sound but the purr of the air conditioner. Connor walked to the door and stepped out, looking towards the sunset.

"If it were a man, why didn't he try to contact us?"

"Could be many reasons." Kosaka moved alongside him. "He might have been left behind from some other expedition. Stayed behind, maybe. Might be insane." He ran a hand through his black hair. "You said yourself, we're a long way from home."

Harn joined them. "We don't have much to go on, do we? We don't know whether it's he, she, or they. In fact, we don't even know if it's human."

"That's what's stopping me from rushing in," said Connor. "Let's look at the data. We've come farther towards the Hyades than any other expedition. Right?"

"As far as we know," said Kosaka.

"Sure, as far as we know." Connor gestured towards the forest. "Yet someone has been here before us, and forested the planet as part of a long-term habitation project."

"We know it's no one from Exdev," said Hern, "but there are plenty of settled planets between here and Earth. My guess is that it's a secondary settlement from one of them."

"I don't agree. The forest is too old, too developed. It dates back before the invention of the iso-drive." Connor spun to face Harn. "Another thing! It has absolutely no terrestrial trees. Any other planets where I've seen vegetation introduced, it's been mainly Earth vegetation."

"It boils down to this, doesn't it?" said Kosaka. "We've got to see him. Or them."

"Or it," said Connor. He looked up at the darkening sky, towards the section dominated by the stars of the Hyades Cluster. They were much nearer, brighter, more numerous than they appeared in the skies of the Earth, because this planet was nearly as far beyond Aldebaran as Aldebaran was distant from Earth, and in its moonless night sky the golden shower of the Hyades was bright enough to throw a blurred shadow.

"Perhaps something from there," said Connor.

Harn looked up at the swarm of suns. "Could be. Must be anything from a hundred to a thousand habitable planets in the solar systems of the cluster. Dry planets, wet ones, heavy, light, hot, cold, bright, gloomy, any combination you could think of. You might find any sort of life there."

"So," said Kosaka, "if they're humanoid, they could be tall or squat, depending on gravity."

"Not necessarily. Look at the range on Earth. The gazelle and the hippopotamus, the giraffe and the flatworm, the gorilla and the gibbon, they all develop in the same gravity. Which is normal?"

"Getting back to the point," cut in Connor, "which of us meets him? I'm going to call it 'him' until I know better."

"Why not all of us?"

"You know enough of our history to see why not, Jiro. For most of man's history a stranger was an enemy. If *he* thinks like that, it's better there's only one of us there."

"I'm the biologist," said Harn. "I suppose it's my field."

"Why not mine?" Kosaka stepped forward. "I'm the only one of us actually born on Earth, the original center of our culture."

"Wait!" Connor held up his hand. "Let's come at it from a different angle. Who's the most expendable?"

There was silence.

"I am," said Connor.

"But you're in charge of the expedition," objected Kosaka. "You're our engineer, pilot, navigator."

"But either of you can carry all those tasks by now. If I don't come back by the next sunset, or if anything you don't understand happens—take the landing module up into orbit and radio for the survery ship."

"This needs more discussion," said Harn.

"Well, let's sleep on it." Connor looked at his watch. Around the far side of the planet the dawn terminator was sweeping across the forest towards the place where the light had shone in the featureless dark.

They prepared a meal, each slipping silently into the few

simple procedures which had become almost automatic. Kosaka then went out to check the magnetometer and atmosphere controls. Connor walked outside.

At once he was certain what he wanted to do. After a single glance around, he strode over to the flier.

Within seconds, he was sitting at the controls, snapping switches to check the atomic batteries. He pressed the call button of the radio. The voices of the others came to him over the speaker.

"Emergency," he said briefly. "I'm making a trip above the area where we saw the light. Should reach the spot just after sunrise, local time."

This time he flew over the large continent at a much lower altitude, using ground-sensing radar to keep him only three hundred meters above the largest trees. The forest had looked flat from thirty thousand meters, but down here it rolled over undulating hills and sudden, unexpected valleys. Sometimes he swept over island-studded rivers, and swamps that looked like mangrove swamps photographed through a trick color filter that turned them lime green.

It was strange that the sheer alien quality of the vegetation had not struck him so forcibly before. He had seen barren planets transformed by plants before, made into a parody or sometimes a close copy of Earth. But this was different. This had been made into a copy of somewhere else.

Sometimes he lifted over saw-toothed ridges of red or purple granite, or rock similar to granite, which jutted through the introduced forest like the bones of dinosaurs. He checked his charts. Soon he would be entering the area of the penciled ovals where they had estimated the light had shone.

He cut his forward speed to a hundred kilometers per hour, then to fifty, and he took the altitude down to a hundred fifty meters, so that he was flying at less than twice the height of the upper treetops. Sweat began to trickle down his forehead and neck.

The ATRAN—the automatic terrain recognition and navigation radar—lifted him over a number of whaleback ridges, then brought him down over a broad plain covered with the dark blue, ivylike plants, with a few clumps of the things like tree ferns. The pulse hammered faster in his ears. He switched to manual control.

He nearly missed the thing he was looking for. A shallow valley opened off the plain to his right, and from the very corner of his vision he saw some far-off structure that was neither tree nor rock. Immediately he brought the flier almost to the ground, moving into the shelter of a dense belt of trees.

He switched off all its systems and let it rest on the firm ground, on a drift of gravelly rock where the blue ivy had failed to gain a hold. For a long time he sat at the controls. Finally he decided to risk a short radio contact with his base.

"I've found something. I'll keep my personal radio at low output and use the flier to beam you an amplified signal. Okay? You know what to do if anything goes wrong."

"Be careful, Con," came Harn's voice. "We'll keep the channel open."

"Good luck," added Kosaka.

"Connor sealed his lightweight suit, then climbed carefully out of the flier. He stepped up the microphone gain of the suit's audio equipment until he could hear the rustle of leaves in the wind with far greater sensitivity than with the unaided ear. Quietly as possible he began to walk forward, wincing at the amplified crashing of his feet on gravel and detritus. He neared the last of the trees and stopped, peering through their thinning screen at the open valley beyond, his breath rasping loudly.

He could see the structures clearly now, but did not understand them. They had the unreality of things seen in a mirage.

They looked like objects made of green metal, windowless, doorless, their edges ill-defined and wavering, like the edges of things immersed in clear water.

One was a truncated cone, the size of a large oil-refinery storage tank, mounted on three sprawling legs of flimsy-looking girder construction. Another was a featureless ovoid, the size of a large aircraft, suspended slightly above the ground without visible support. Far apart from these, a slim, triangular tower thrust a couple of hundred meters in the air, bearing at its apex something in such rapid, continuous movement that he saw it only as a spherical blur.

Connor watched for a long time, the blood pounding in his temples. His saliva tasted like metal.

He realized, now, that he had never really believed he would find anything other than a human being. He realized that he had even rehearsed little speeches to make as he walked up on the mining camp or biosurvey station, or whatever it turned out to be. "We wondered who you were. Half expected to find little purple men . . ."

But the joke had turned sour on him. This was one of the points where history could take a different track.

He couldn't see any of the inhabitants of the structures. And suddenly it came to him that he didn't want to. Not yet.

He moved carefully back to the flier, fighting an impulse to run. Had they seen him land? That blurred thing spinning at the top of the tower might be something analogous to a radar dish, with an incredibly rapid three-dimensional scan.

He climbed aboard the flier and sat for a long time at the controls before attempting to move it. He decided to put a thousand kilometers between himself and the things in the valley before he used his radio.

He took off and fled back across the plain and the undulating hills, with his ATRAN adjusted so that he almost clipped the higher trees. Only after he had crossed a substantial range of mountains did he increase his height and call the base.

Neither Harn nor Kosaka replied. Strange, because they had said they'd keep the channel open. No radio ever failed these days—unless his own transmitter had become influenced by something at the alien base.

It was still night on the plateau when he saw the lights of his own base. Something struck him at once as strange, even while he was still far away from it. Then he realized it. The buildings were unchanged, but the landing shuttle was gone.

They had lifted off without waiting for him. Without even making radio contact. Unless, of course, his receiver was out of action.

He circled the base at a distance, then made two low passes over it at speed. Nothing moved. A wedge of light spread from the open door of the radio room.

He landed near the laboratory, the door of which was slightly ajar. He called Harn and Kosaka, but was hardly surprised when there was no reply. A fitful gust of wind banged the door of the radio room.

"Jiro! Charl!" He shouted with hands cupped around his mouth, wondering at the same time why he bothered to call. The absence of the shuttle was evidence enough that he was alone here.

He found his hands were shaking as he went into the radio

room and switched on the long-range transmitter. He had no more response to his broadcast than to his shouts. He began listening, switching from wave band to wave band, and as he swept past on his way from one band to another, he heard a brief chirrup of sound on a frequency between the normally used bands.

Code? It was no voice, yet not Morse. Thinking it may be a compressed "bleep" he taped some of it, then relayed it at a lower frequency.

It was an intermittent signal on several close but distinct frequencies, a busy whistling and piping so different from anything he had heard over the air that the very sound made him uneasy. He tried a directional fix, half expecting it to come from the structures in the valley, but it came from a point in the sky.

He switched it off, and as he turned, something moved quickly away from the small window.

Connor stood perfectly still, trying to control the mounting panic that shook him. He had been trained for every conceivable emergency, as the experts had classified emergencies. Space had long been an arena where man pitted himself against the cold yet predictable forces of nature, assisted by his computers. But this was a situation not in the manual.

He had the impression that the thing outside the window had been bigger than a man, light-colored, lightning fast in its movements. He looked around the room for a possible weapon. All he could find was a tubular rod about a meter long, part of an aerial assembly.

He went silently to the door, peering out into the dark.

"Anyone there?" he called.

From somewhere in the dark came a strange, ululating cry that was different from anything he could identify. It was the most frightening sound Connor had ever heard.

He snapped off the light, but diffused light still streamed from the door of the laboratory a few meters away. He thought of running for the flier, then remembered the speed of the thing that had whipped away from the window.

From behind the radio room came a faint sound, as if something heavy had stamped soft-footed on the ground. The hair on the back of Connor's neck seemed to be trying to stand straight out from his skin.

Gripping the bar and raising it above his head, he tiptoed

along towards the corner of the building. A faint muffled tap sounded.

Deciding that surprise was his only chance, Connor sprang around the corner. Then several things happened to him within a single second.

He saw that there was no one in the vicinity—only a small stone rolling to rest on the ground. Then the upraised bar was torn *upward* from his hands with contemptuous ease. A deafening shriek, something like the cry of a puma, seemed to come from directly above him, momentarily paralyzing him with its heart-stopping suddenness.

An immense weight flung him to his knees, while a pair of inhumanly powerful hands gripped his arms and wrapped them around his bent-up legs.

He was stunned, bewildered, as something lifted him and ran with him past the laboratory. The streak of light from the door showed him a fleeting impression of supple arms covered with close white fur, like a cat's fur. He was aware of a strange smell, vaguely marine, then the voice of the thing screeched out a complex torrent of sound.

It flung him outward towards open ground. He tensed for the impact, but it didn't come. Instead a blinding flash of light locked him inside a shimmering lilac globe that shut out all external sound and sight. He tried to straighten out, but his hands and feet slid helplessly across the glowing interior surface of the globe. It did not feel solid, like metal or plastic. But his hands could not force their way into it for more than a centimeter.

His own rasping breath was the only sound he heard as he lost consciousness.

Connor awoke lying flat on his back under brilliant, lilac-tinged light that seemed to emanate from a glowing ceiling of mist. It reflected from curved walls of what looked like green metal.

His arms were at his sides, but when he tried to move them, something restrained them so that he could move them only a few centimeters. It was the same with his head and his legs—something held him straight and still.

He closed his eyes against the hard assault of light and tried to get the feeling of his bonds. No solid object touched him, yet when he tried to move a hand or foot outward, some force as insistent and pervasive as gravity forced it back again. When he tried to lift his leg above the horizontal, it felt unbearably heavy, until he let it fall to its original position.

He heard a flurry of movement near him, and a shadow flicked across his closed eyelids. There were quick, sharp sounds like the snapping of switches or couplings. In the background he could hear the rhythmical pulse of something like a pump, the hum of what might have been electric motors. Again he was aware of that unfamiliar smell, vaguely suggestive of the sea.

He opened his eyes. From two directions he heard brief hissings and chatterings of voices that were not like the voices of anything he knew.

With shocking suddenness, a tall, white figure bounded silently into his field of view.

At first glance it looked like an animated snowman—then he realized it was enclosed in a protective suit of material like nylon. It was manlike, yet there was something grotesque about it. It was long-limbed, huge-headed, thick-shouldered, with an effortless violence of movement.

Connor must have made some sound, for the figure spun to face him. A section of the suit across the upper part of the face was transparent. What Connor could see of the face did nothing to reassure him.

Gone, at one blow, was any hope that the thing might have been human. The great oblique, lime-yellow eyes explored his face with intense alertness.

He forced himself to keep looking up at the eyes, although their appearance was so alien that waves of primitive fear washed over him like chilled water. The black pupils were cross-shaped, with vertical and lateral slits dilating and contracting independently as they scanned his face.

A voice came to him, muffled by the fabric—a rapid blend of hissing, muttering, and whistling that carried no hint of meaning. Perhaps all he heard were the overtones of speech pitched in a different frequency range.

"My name is Connor," he said slowly. To his surprise his own words came back from some device nearby—they had been recorded and played back.

He heard the metallic sound of some apparatus being moved, and a brilliant light shone down on his face from close by. Narrowing his eyes against the glare, he saw a bulbous object like a large diving helmet with trailing wires being lifted above him by long hands in white, rubberlike gloves—hands which seemed to have too many fingers.

The helmet was slipped down over his head, completely shutting out his view of the room. As it was settled into place, hundreds, perhaps thousands of fine, needlelike probes slid inward to prickle his scalp. It was all done with bewildering speed.

A picture flashed in front of his eyes, bright and three-dimensional—the picture of a desolate sweep of beach, with rolling surf under a hot, orange sky streaked with clouds.

"What's that?" came a voice beside him. It was unmistakably Harn's voice.

"Charl!" shouted Connor.

"No," came the reply, but this time the voice was Kosaka's.

"What the hell's going on?"

"What's that?" asked Harn's voice again, and Connor realized that he was listening to a recording. The question was repeated again and again, and so was the picture. It was a moving picture which ran for four or five seconds, then with a sudden flicker repeated itself.

Connor felt numb and chilled. They must have captured both Harn and Kosaka and recorded their voices. Perhaps a dozen times the wave broke on the outlandish beach, and a dozen times Harn's voice asked, "What's that?" Then the picture changed and Connor found himself looking at the face of Kosaka. His eyes were wide, the whites showing all around the iris, and his mouth was open, as if he were shouting in horror and disbelief. "What's that?" said Harn's voice.

"Jiro!" said Connor involuntarily, and at once the picture vanished.

"Ah, thank you." This time it was Kosaka's voice, and it was followed by Harn's, saying "communicate" as if the word had been snatched from the middle of a sentence.

The pictures continued in an endless stream. Some were of things he could identify, others meant nothing to him. Each time the tireless repetition of the recorded "What's that?" accompanied the picture. Connor could see what they were trying to do, and eventually they wore him down.

"What's that?"

"A mountain."

"Ah, thank you . . . What's that?"

"I don't know. Something of yours?"

The interrogation went on and on. Pictures, pictures, an endless flood of them, coming faster and faster as he began naming the things he could recognize—things like rocks, ponds, trees, bridges. The bridges and buildings were not of human construction, but their function identified them enough for him to name them. Always, Kosaka's recorded voice would reply "Ah, thank you," in the never-changing tone.

The pictures came faster and faster, as if his interrogators didn't want him to have time to think between his answers. Each time he named some object, their response would come back like the crack of a whip, and the pitch of the recorded voices began to grow higher and higher as they ran the recording at increased speed.

He didn't remember how it ended. He awoke in an eerie green half light that at first gave him the feeling that he was under water.

"Con!"

The voice came from the left. He rolled over. It was not a recording this time—Harn was sitting against a wall a couple of meters away, and squatting cross-legged beyond him was Kosaka.

Connor looked down at the floor. It appeared to be of bare metal, but when he pressed his hand down, it encountered resistance a centimeter or two from the floor, as if he were pressing an invisible sheet of plastic foam. Harn chuckled.

"We haven't figured how it works, but you get used to it after a while."

Kosaka stood up with a single lithe movement, stretching his arms. "Hi, Con. How did they get you?"

"One of them jumped me from the roof of the radio shack."

Harn and Kosaka spoke together. "What?" "You mean you actually saw one of them?"

"Felt it before I saw it. The thing was quicker than a panther."

"Like a man?" asked Harn.

"Not much. Oh, it stood on two legs, but the general effect was more like a big-headed tiger crouching half erect."

"What was the face like?" broke in Kosaka.

"Only saw the eyes. Big and slanting, wide apart. Bright lime color, pupils like black four-pointed stars." Connor shivered. "You know the thing that shook me most? Its unpredictability. I felt that when I first saw their buildings."

"Buildings? What buildings?"

"Oh, of course. Near where we saw the light, I found—structures. I tried to radio, but couldn't reach you. Came back to base, and found you and the landing shuttle gone."

"The shuttle? How could they have moved that?"

Connor shrugged. "Whatever they did, it's gone. This damned thing must have been hanging around the base when I arrived. What irritates me is that it must have stalked me like a cat stalking a retarded mouse."

Harn grunted. "They got us separately—both in the open. A sort of instant cage of spinning rings of light that closed into a sphere. We had a theory they must have been all brain and no muscles." He made a gesture of resignation. "Think I'll give up guessing and just watch."

"What happens now?" asked Kosaka.

"Let's fit together what we know," said Connor. "We can wipe out the idea that these things are human, even remotely mutated human stock. They have no connection with the human race whatever. They're the peak of a different evolutionary pyramid."

"Scientifically they've come a long way—maybe further than us. Does that mean they're basically brighter? Or have they just been around longer?"

"Maybe both!" said Connor. "I had the impression of an intelligence that worked like lightning. Look—they didn't come here expecting to find anything like us—but you should have seen the equipment they'd assembled together. Jury-rigged, but effective. They actually talked to me with recordings of words you two had spoken."

The others were silent for a long time, absorbed. Muted sounds came occasionally from beyond the metal-walled room.

"I think they do a lot with plasma," mused Kosaka.

Harn was thinking along a track of his own. "You know," he said at length, "I think they may have an edge on us because they're better integrated."

"What makes you say that?"

"Your description, Con. The thing you described sounded to me as if it had evolved from some kind of carnivore. You mentioned a tiger and a panther, at different times. Right?"

"Well, it certainly had the speed, the power. A sort of controlled savagery it could switch on and off in an instant."

"Controlled . . ." Harn frowned, rubbing his hand along his jaw where bristles were emerging. "Look, it's been said that most human troubles come from the fact that the neopallium, the frontal lobes of the brain, evolved recently and quickly, so that their motives sometimes clash with those of the older, more primitive parts of the brain."

"So?"

Harn was warming up. "Now listen. Carnivores—lion families, tiger families, wolf packs—don't fight to the death within their own groups. It would be easy for a lion or wolf to kill any other by surprise in an instant—but they don't do it. They've evolved built-in inhibitions to prevent them killing their own species."

"Well?"

"We haven't the same physical weaponry. It's harder for a man to instantly kill another man, without using some weapon. So we haven't evolved the same powerful inhibitions against intraspecies killing that you have in a wolf pack or a pride of lions. So you have feuds, wars, hot wars, cold wars, back to the beginning of history. Two steps forward, then a step back—that's been our progress all along."

Connor looked up. "And you think these—these things, these people, whatever—you think they've been well enough integrated to move straight ahead? All steps forward? No wars or dark ages?"

Harn spread his hands. "Could be."

"Hey, wait!" Kosaka stepped forward. "Could this give us an advantage? We could be more used to struggle, perhaps?"

"Listen," said Connor. "You haven't actually met one of them. If you're thinking of a surprise attack, forget it."

"Look!" shouted Kosaka, pointing. Connor whirled. Behind him a doorway stood open in the metal wall.

Connor walked slowly towards the doorway. The room beyond was the laboratory where they had interrogated him. There was no one in it. He stepped through, and at once the door closed behind him, shutting off Kosaka's warning shout in the middle of a syllable.

Connor turned and slapped his hands against the smooth, unyielding surface of the door. It had closed so swiftly and silently that he had not even noticed from which side it had moved.

He walked slowly through the room, looking at the complex, glittering apparatus on the long benches—metal and crystalline devices linked with a maze of thin, insulated wires. The insulation was black, but identified at intervals with colored bands; some of these were vividly red, yellow, green, and other easily distinguished colors, but as many others were marked with dull blacks or purple blacks hardly different from the background color of the wires. Evidently they were the overtones or harmonics of colors the human eye could not see.

With no warning, out of what he had believed to be empty air, Connor was seized by the shoulders and thrust into a curving black chair that did not seem to have been designed for human use. A swift, cream-colored shape flashed past him, spinning to land in another seat facing his. Within an instant of landing, it sprawled in front of him, utterly relaxed, its great eyes fixed on his with their cross-shaped pupils pulsing.

Connor felt as though ice had entered his blood. Even in their white, featureless suits, the things had been frightening enough. To see one of them almost naked in front of him chilled him with primeval terror.

It sat looking at him for a long time, its deep chest rising and falling in an even rhythm. Connor caught the scent of its breath, hot and unfamiliar. His self-control gave way, and he began to spring to his feet to leap away.

Almost before he had begun to move, a long, cream-furred arm flashed forward, and an inhumanly powerful hand flung him back to his original position. He did not try again.

"All right," he said. "What do you want?"

The wide, salmon-colored lips drew back in quick, complex movement, and the muttering, hissing voice rode out on a gust of fever-hot breath, like a tape-recording played at too high a speed. Without taking its gaze from his face, it reached down beside its seat and produced a device like a small bullhorn, lifting it in front of its face. Connor was momentarily fascinated by its hand. The long, tapering, salmon-tinted fingers had more joints than human fingers, and there were six—no, seven of them, ending in narrow black talons.

The voice came again, softly, and with a slight delay a caricature of human words emerged from the horn.

"Now. We meet. We communicate."

"We communicate." Connor corrected the pronunciation, and at once his words were repeated, almost an echo of his own voice.

"We communicate better." The improvement was staggering. Connor almost forgot his fear of the thing sitting in front of him.

"But how?" he asked. "How so quickly?"

The thing made an impatient, brush-aside gesture. It spoke again. "Decision we must make. We spread across stars. You spread across stars. Meet. Now."

Connor didn't like the way the communication was shaping up. "We come from far away," he said.

"From where?" It came like a shot.

"You would have no name for it."

"Have name now. Earth. Is right? But where?"

Connor felt like a man on the brink of a bottomless precipice. He wanted time to think. This thing was asking him the location of the worlds inhabited by the human race. "I'd need charts," he said.

It lifted its wrist close to its mouth and spoke in its rapid, sibilant tongue into a small instrument on a slender metal bracelet encircling its thick, supple wrist. For perhaps thirty seconds they stared at each other, eye to eye. If the thing felt any of the tension Connor was feeling, it gave no hint of it.

The swift-moving form of another of the aliens flitted past Connor, then was gone again almost before he realized it was there. The one seated in front of him riffled through sheets of dull white, paperlike material which the other had handed to it.

It spread the charts on a low, transparent table. "Ours, yours."

Connor looked down at the spread-out charts. Some were copies of those from his own ship. The others were alien, vastly more detailed. He looked at them for a long time, trying to see where their coordinates were based. Then he became aware that the being was holding something out towards him—a short, triangular bar with a tapering tip.

"You mark Earth." Holding the bar in three of its fingers, it made a vivid orange mark on the margin of one of the charts, then held the pen out to Connor. He made an experimental mark with it; it seemed quite dry at the tip, and marked only the paperlike material.

"Why don't you mark *your* world?" he challenged.

The eyes watched him unwinkingly. Then the being took the pen back from him, moved one of its own charts to the top of the pile, and drew an orange circle around one of the smaller dark dots in the star field. It offered the pen and the chart to Connor.

He took the pen, hesitating. He was damned if he was going to tell this thing the location of the home of the human race. He took one of the copies of his own charts, picked at random an undistinguished star far away from the Solar System, and drew a rough circle around it with a shaking hand.

The being took back the pen and chart, looked at the marked point with a concentrated tension, then laid it aside. Connor studied the chart he had been given, trying to determine how to read it.

The creature in front of him suddenly shook with a rasping, hissing vibration of breath, inward and outward. The triangular ears, which had been flattened like the ears of an angry cat, flickered suddenly erect a few times. Connor suspected the spasm may have corresponded to laughter, but he wasn't sure.

He felt tired, drained. Dully, he watched the salmon-tinted hands spread charts in front of him—the marked ones, his and theirs. The two long forefingers thrust like stilettos to paired points on the different charts, and the voice made subtle, incisive sounds that could have been alien place names.

Connor felt the information coming too fast for his concentration. He was not sure of the exact moment when he slipped into unconsciousness.

He awoke lying flat on his back under open sky, with a figure bending over him.

"He's coming round, Jiro," It was Harn's voice.

Connor sat up, shaking his head. He was back at their own base, and the flier and shuttle were parked nearby. He looked quickly round. "Where are they?"

"Relax," said Harn. "They're gone. Yesterday."

"Yesterday?"

Harn looked at his watch. "You've been sleeping for nearly forty hours. How're you feeling?"

Connor's muscles crackled as he stretched. "Hungry. But where'd they go?"

"Left the planet. Left the system, I think. Heard their takeoff from a distance—saw their contrail. They stripped their buildings, but they left us our shuttle. Jiro's checking it for bugs."

"Did you contact the command ship?" Connor got shakily to his feet.

"Yes. They want to rendezvous in sixty-five hours. That okay?"

"Sure."

While the others prepared the shuttle for liftoff, Connor worked alone at the charts, while he still remembered a little of what the alien had tried to show him. Fragments of unpronounceable names flittered through his mind, and, oddly, mental pictures of places he had never seen. He had fleeting impressions of cast metal cities under strange-tinted skies, of sunlit machines against the night of space. He tried to relax, to let the pictures come without forcing them, but the memories slipped away from him even as he tried to clutch at them.

"What's the matter?" asked Harn, alongside him. Connor hadn't noticed his approach.

"Eh? Something bothers me. He went to a lot of trouble showing me his charts and trying to get me to see how they corresponded with ours. But *why*?"

"You mean—what did *he* get out of it?"

Connor nodded. He shrugged after a few seconds, and turned to the charts. "I think I'm beginning to see how these work. They have different axes of reference from ours. Beta Tauri is one of their key stars, see? Natural enough—it dominates the Hyades. Give me time and I'll figure the others."

Slowly it fell into place. The alien charts were detailed perspective photographs of space from three directions, meant to be used in conjunction. There were fine markings that meant nothing yet, but he located some of the main stars in the field—Aldebaran, Hamal, Beta Aurigae. Then abruptly Connor sat back with a sharp cry that brought the others to him.

"What is it?"

"Look. I can read their charts. That's Vega. Sirius."

"What's the one with the orange circle?"

"That's the Solar System."

They looked at it. "How did you draw such a perfect circle?" asked Kosaka.

"That the point. I didn't. *He* did."

"He *what?*"

"He marked the Solar System. The Earth!"

"But how?"

Connor spread his arms. "Maybe they got it from our charts. Maybe from my mind. The fact is, they *know*."

"What happened?"

"He asked me to mark my home world. I marked the wrong dot on our own chart, and I assumed he'd done the same on his. Now I find he was way ahead of me."

For a long time all three were silent. Then Harn looked up. "The other point is—*why?* Why did he let you know he knew?"

"That's what bothers me," said Connor. "I simply don't see his reasoning."

They looked at each other in silence.

"Banzai!" said Kosaka suddenly.

"What's that?"

"Banzai. A shout ancient warriors made to unnerve the opposition."

2

With the approach radar locked on to the command ship, Connor was at last able to relax. The ship grew slowly in the center of the forward vision screen, a long, spearhead shape against the diamond dust and black velvet of the background. The hot, white sunlight gave it an almost incandescent brilliance.

"Space," said Connor as Harn moved alongside him. "You know, it's never going to be the same for us again."

Harn gestured at the blue and white crescent of the planet filling the rearview screen. "Because of—*them?*"

Connor pressed a couple of keys on the console before him, and read out the range and coordinates of the command ship from the VDT. He grunted, then looked back at the screens.

"It'll never be the same," he repeated. "Before, it was an infinite stage with man as the only leading actor. The future was wide open to us, as far as there were stars. Now, all of a sudden, we have a competitor."

Harn nodded towards the expanding image of the command ship. "Well, it's not our responsibility now. The decisions are up to the top echelon."

Connor spun to face him. "Charl, remember something: I'm the only one who actually *met* these things. You and Jiro were pushed around by their equipment, sure—but you didn't meet them face to face. And neither did anyone on the command ship. I'm going to have a tough job convincing the chief they exist.''

"We've photos and videos of their gear, Con.''

"But not close—'' Connor broke off as the squawk of a buzzer drew their attention to the communication screen. Nordstrom's face looked down at them, his bright, faded eyes alight with barely controlled enthusiasm.

"Historic moment, boys. If it checks out, it's the first contact *ever* with an intelligent alien race.''

"How d'you mean, *if it checks out*, Chief?''

"Routine, Con. Routine.'' Nordstrom's face broadened in a professional smile. "I'd bring you straight to my cabin as soon as you link up—but Marek felt you should spend some time in the White Room. You know—unknown viruses, and so on. I'll see you there—through windows, of course.''

"Of course,'' agreed Connor. He glanced at his two companions. "We feel okay, but you have to be sure. By the way, where did Marek come in to it?''

"I've given him a tentative promotion in view of the contact. He once did a course on theoretical contact with alien intelligence, you know. Part of his military training.''

"Chief, I don't think this thing needs a military approach.''

"Maybe not, Con. We'll cover that in a session later.'' Nordstrom punctuated the statement with a brief, brilliant smile. "When you link with us, come out with your suits on. You'll be sprayed with decontaminant—that may or may not be effective, as we don't know what we're up against. Follow the lights straight into the White Room. Right? The doc will go in with you.''

"Which one?''

"Zella. She volunteered.''

"But we might have picked up something that affects females and not males.''

"That's why she volunteered. Anything dangerous, better we know about it at the start.''

"Okay.'' Connor managed a smile. "See you, Chief.''

"See you, boys.'' The screen was instantly blank.

Harn gave a short laugh. "I like the 'boys' bit.''

Connor shrugged. "I suppose we're all boys to him—after all, he's in his third century.''

Harn shivered. "Damned if I'd like to live like that. Ninety percent of me replaced by metal and plastic and transistors.''

"See how you feel when you're a hundred years old," said Connor. Then they gave all their attention to the viewing screens as the spreading bulk of the command ship began to shut out the background of space.

The White Room, close to the flight lock of the command ship, was in effect a quarantine station, a small suite of rooms with its own air and water supply, sealed from the rest of the ship. All the internal walls, floors, and ceilings were of smooth, white-enameled metal, with no sharp junctions between surfaces and no crevices where microorganisms could hide. Floors curved smoothly into walls, walls into ceilings.

Zella, the younger of the ship's two doctors, gave Connor and his team a thorough examination, using extremely sophisticated equipment which Connor had not known to be on board. Watching her examining Kosaka, he looked at the red-gold curls brushing the smooth, clear skin at the back of her neck, the smooth curve of her hips below the slim, firm waist, and the light swiftness of her unmistakably feminine style of movement. The pulse in his ears was the soft beat of wings. Suddenly it came to him that he had not used the regulation sex suppressants all the time he had been down on the surface of the planet.

Getting to his feet, he walked irritably around the room a couple of times, then pressed the button of the outside intercom.

"Could I have some paper, or a recorder?" he asked. "I want to get my report under way."

"There's a recorder in the locker marked E," came a voice from outside. "And a stack of paper, if you want it."

Connor said, "Thanks," and set to work. First he tried to draw the frontal view of the alien who had examined him. Strangely enough, he found it very hard to remember the actual relationships between eyes and ears and mouth. He made several sketches, but some looked like a cartoonist's impression of a semihuman cheetah, and some like a man in a carnival mask. He tended to make the eyes look like either a man's or a leopard's, yet in fact they had been nothing like either. Above all, he could not capture the impression of appalling *vitality*. In the end he scrapped the sketches altogether.

Nordstrom came to see him through the sealed window at one end of the White Room, and they talked to each other through microphones.

"Con," said Nordstrom, "is there any chance—this is only kicking the idea round, of course—is there any possibility these . . . beings you saw could have been human? In disguise?"

"No chance. The one I was close to was taller than me. Covered in fur. Even a different smell from anything I've known."

Nordstrom nodded, his relaxed smile trying to indicate that he was a broad-minded man who was willing to be convinced. Connor had to make a conscious effort to control his rising anger. "Let's take a look at this from another angle, Con."

Connor shrugged, one eyebrow raised. Nordstrom was wearing a white plastic garment somewhat like an old-fashioned raincoat. He made no secret of being partly cybernetic, and beneath the coat his legs were slim, bright stilts of silver metal, ending in segmented metal feet. Now he slipped off his coat and swung it aside like a mannequin. His head was the only part of him that looked organic. The rest was mostly metal, proportioned like an athletic man, except for the functional legs.

"Could you have been looking at someone like me, Con?" Nordstrom swung one of his metal legs forward. "I could have had these made longer; I could be three meters tall, if I wished. I could wear a fur suit, a mask." He lifted one of the slim metal and plastic hands to touch his face. "Actually, this isn't real skin now. It wears out, you know."

Connor shook his head stubbornly. "I was nearer the thing than I am to you now. *It was not human.* It moved like lightning—and it *thought* like lightning. Wait until I get my full report on record."

Nordstrom hesitated a second, then seemed to brighten. "Looking forward to it, Con," he said, then put on his coat and stalked away. Connor turned to Harn, who had been standing nearby.

"What do you make of him?" he asked. "Does he believe me?"

Harn shrugged. "May be playing devil's advocate."

For the rest of their time in the isolation of the White Room, Connor worked on his report, making it as detailed as possible, and including Harn's report on the vegetation of the planet and Kosaka's on its geology and mineral potential.

From time to time Marek came to interiew them through the glass. He was a thin, wiry man with the prematurely white hair and tanned leather skin that comes from early overexposure to a sunlight too rich in ultraviolet. He had an air of awkward self-importance.

"You're clear to come out of isolation at 900 hours," he announced on one of his visits. "I've scheduled a meeting with the chief at 1100."

"*You've* scheduled it?" said Connor.

"Yes. This contact possibility has changed things. I did a course in Alien Contact Theory back on Denebola 4. Since I'm the only one with the specialized know-how, I've had to step into the slot. Right? See you at the meeting."

They watched him go. "Specialized know-how," echoed Harn. "What the hell does *he* know?"

"About anything," added Kosaka.

"Gentlemen, please!" said Zella. Her voice sounded cold, but when they turned, she was smiling.

The meeting was at the long table in the conference room adjoining Nordstrom's cabin. There were not many there. Nordstrom chaired the meeting, with Marek fussing with papers on his right, the chief biologist, the two doctors—including Zella—Connor and his team, and a team of three from another shuttle.

"We'll get straight to the point," said Nordstrom. "You've all had copies of Con's report. What's the general feeling?"

"It could be the biggest single event that's ever happened to the human race," said the chief biologist.

"Possibly," agreed Nordstrom. "On the other hand, as I've suggested to Con, he and his team could be victims of a trick."

"A trick?" said the chief biologist. "How?"

"Men using cybernetic bodies—like mine. We don't *have* to be built to look like human beings. We do it because it makes us socially acceptable. We *could* look like something else."

"Why?"

"In this case, to keep control of a newly developed planet."

"Chief, could I show you something?" The interruption came from the skipper of the other shuttle.

"Okay," said Nordstrom. As the shuttle man rose to walk around the table, the chief watched him intently. He reached out and took a square piece of some kind of card, sealed in a clear plastic bag. "Looks like a photograph. Where did you get it?"

"Near the base on the plateau."

Nordstrom looked up. "While Con and his men were isolated in the White Room, Alan and his team went down to the planet. They located the base set up by Con."

"Did you find the alien base?" asked Connor.

"No," said Alan. "We didn't know where to look."

Nordstrom handed the card to Marek. "Blow that up with the epidiascope so we can all look at it."

There was silence until the picture appeared on the white wall. "It's a different format from our pictures—I'll have to show you a bit at a time," said Marek.

It was obvious at once that the picture was a reject. It had been taken from beneath a tree, and a bunch of leaves had blown in front of the camera, masking the center of the field with a slanting blur.

"It's a picture of your base," said Alan. "That's the radio room and part of the landing shuttle. But move it across and look at what's standing beside the shuttle."

Marek moved the picture jerkily to one side, and a multivoiced shout shook the room.

"Focus!" snapped Nordstrom.

It was not the being who had questioned Connor. It wore no enclosing suit, and its fur was not white, but dappled with orange and cream. Marek made the image larger on the screen. Except for the blur of the obscuring leaves, the picture was incredibly sharp. The huge, slanting eyes—green in this case—were looking at the camera, and it was possible to see the strange, cross-shaped pupils.

"The hand; look at the hand," shouted the chief biologist.

Its fingers were longer than human fingers, each with at least one extra joint. And there were seven digits, separated to form five fingers and two thumbs. The finger and thumb on each side of the gap were obviously very powerful, the others slender and supple.

"All right," said Nordstrom. "It's over to you, Con."

Connor looked around the table. Their expressions had

changed completely in the last minute. The thing in the picture had stunned them. He gestured to the screen.

"The picture says most of it," he said. "One of *their* pictures, remember. I think you're looking at a more highly evolved life-form than we are."

There was an awkward silence broken at last by Nordstrom.

"You mean—as a chimpanzee is to a man, so a man is to one of these?"

"Not quite. That implies another step along the same evolutionary road. These things have come along a different road. From a different starting point."

"True." Nordstrom pointed suddenly to the picture. "But we have similarities, haven't we? Bipeds, bilaterally symmetrical eyes, hands, and so forth. Therefore they must think somewhat like us. Right?"

Connor shook his head slowly. "I met one of them, remember. I was sitting opposite it, close as this. Now, you can't say that surprise was on its side. A few hours before, neither of us knew the other existed, or anything like it. Yet *it* ran the interview, not me."

Nordstrom glanced slightly away. "Well, Con, after all, you haven't been trained as a diplomat. I think you were just unfortunate enough to be handled by one of their experts."

"Experts at *what?* Listen. That place down there is a future colony, being transformed by vegetative seeding to build a breathable atmosphere. I suppose they thought, like us, that they could expand forever across the galaxy without meeting intelligent opposition. Now that we've had a collision, I can't help feeling they came out of it better than we did."

Marek gave a short, barking laugh. "Or, rather, one of them came out of it better than you did. Eh?"

Connor stared hard into his eyes. "You're suggesting I handled the contact badly—is that it? What would you have done differently?"

"I'd have had to be there to answer that."

"Maybe you'll have a chance later on."

Nordstrom broke in. "We may all have a chance later on." He looked around the table. "In the meantime we'd better sort out everything we've learned about them to date. Any questions?"

"Yes," said Connor. "I believe you tracked their ship leaving the system. What sort of acceleration did it have?"

Nordstrom looked slightly uncomfortable for the first time. "We thought at first we had a fault in our measuring systems. Actually, the acceleration was unbelievable. Thousands of gravities. Nothing could have withstood it, without some inconceivable method of cancelling inertia."

"Did it go towards the Hyades?"

Nordstrom looked across at Marek, who nodded. "Yes— but we lost it in the outer fringe of this system. There's a dense ring of asteroids and meteoric matter."

"So they could be there? Orbiting?" Nordstrom looked thoughtful. "They could be waiting for us to head back home—to follow us."

"Not necessarily," said Marek. "They deliberately used the asteroid belt to hide their course. They knew where we were—I'm sure of that. They got straight into the ecliptic, then headed out through the belt on a curve that matched their *angular* velocity with the orbiting asteroids. Soon we didn't know which blip was their ship and which an asteroid. Then they were through and away."

There was a heavy silence.

"Reinforcements," muttered someone down the table.

Zella spoke for the first time, her voice surprisingly light and clear. "Should we head for home at once? Before they can follow?"

It was Nordstrom who answered. "We have a long way to go, and we've seen their capacity for acceleration. Frankly, I don't think we could outrun them."

"You mean we're trapped here?" said the chief biologist. "Forever?"

Nordstrom spread his hands. "Unless we want to lead an unknown race back to human civilization—perhaps we are."

Half an hour after the meeting had finished, while Connor was lying on the bunk in his tiny cabin, a number of floating ideas seemed to fall together like pieces of a jigsaw set. He sat up, looked at his intercom, and punched the number of Nordstrom's cabin.

The chief's secretary appeared on the screen. Connor said at once: "This is urgent. I have a suggestion I want to make to the chief."

Nordstrom must have been listening himself, for immediately the screen flashed and his face replaced the secretary's. "Come around right away, Con," he said.

Connor went straight to Nordstrom's cabin, which was located immediately behind the main control room. Nordstrom was standing in the middle of the floor as he went in. Behind him the wall was filled with a photomural of some scene on his home planet, with a broad sweep of coastline bordering a violet sea under a striped tangerine sky, and tapering metallic and crystalline buildings rising from vegetation introduced from tropical Earth.

"Chief, I have a possible solution."

Nordstrom looked at him intently for a few seconds, then waved him to sit down.

"I want to follow their ship," said Connor.

"But we don't know where it went."

"I'm gambling these things came from the Hyades cluster. Hundreds of yellow suns, and nobody knows how many planets."

"Needle in a haystack, son."

"No. Their ship was small. Probably not a long-range ship. Doesn't that suggest a base not too far away?"

"Perhaps. So what?"

"There's a yellow star three light-years away, almost directly towards the center of the cluster; if they're expanding this way, they may have a base there."

Nordstrom said nothing for a time. Then he rose and stalked over to the one-meter cube of the chart tank in the corner of his cabin. He activated it, looking at the tiny sparks of fire in the three-dimensional grid within. "I see," he said. "Other stars beyond it, too. A chain leading to the cluster."

"And this system could be their next link in the chain."

Nordstrom turned. "What did you propose to do?"

"Go out in a shuttle. Look for their base. If I find anything, keep beaming information back here until they stop me."

"It would take you years to get there."

"I know. I'd use the freezer and a proximity alarm."

"But we can't freeze the whole ship to wait for you."

Connor shook his head. "Leave a relay pickup here to send my messages on. After I'm on my way, you can head for home—but not directly. Say towards the star clouds in

Sagittarius. That's close to the right direction, and they'll lose you against that background."

Nordstrom's voice was quiet. "You've thought this thing through, haven't you?"

"I have."

"You realize you're probably sacrificing your life?"

"Probably—yes."

Nordstrom walked across to the chart tank again and stood looking at the bright little points of light, altering the scale up and down so that they rushed apart then crowded together with more stars coming in from the periphery. He turned to his computer console and punched out a series of data that Connor was not able to see, bringing out a hard copy and looking at it thoughtfully.

"You can't go alone," he said emphatically. "And you'd better use the big shuttle. Number 1. We'll fit an extra fuel storage, and long-range radar. Just as well the packages are easily assembled."

"But I realize it's a risk," protested Connor. "I don't want to influence anyone else—"

"Could you work with Marek?"

"I don't know. I think his approach is too military for my liking. I think he's a dinosaur."

Nordstrom smiled. "There wouldn't be just the two of you."

"But who else would you send along?"

Nordstrom looked at him steadily for some seconds. "I'm coming myself."

"What?"

"So surprising? This is more important than our whole survey mission. I'll let O'Donnel take the command ship home. Now, let's get to work on converting Number 1."

The conversion of Number 1 Shuttle went faster than Connor had expected. Grudgingly he was forced to admit that some of the ideas picked up by Marek on his Alien Contact course might prove useful. He didn't like the number of laser weapons and neutron-beam projectors Marek was taking along, but at least he favored weapons that did not *look* like weapons.

Only forty hours before their estimated time of departure, Nordstrom called both Connor and Marek to his cabin. When they reached it, Dr. Zella was there.

As usual, Nordstrom got directly to the point. "Con, Marek. Can you work with Zella on your team?"

"What?" Marek's monosyllable was almost a bark.

"But this could be very dangerous," said Connor.

"I know," said Zella quietly.

"And there's the time angle," went on Connor. "The star we're investigating is three light-years away. Even at an average of six-tenths c, the return trip back to *here* would absorb ten years external time. And our trip back from here would be slower than the command ship's. But you know all about time-dislocation without me hammering it in."

To his surprise, she was repressing a smile that showed mainly in her eyes and one corner of her mouth. "There'd be no time-dislocation between us."

"Marek," said Nordstrom, "I want to show you something in here." And he led him through to the control room.

"Zella," said Connor softly. "Are you sure?"

She nodded. "All quite cerebral. But I'm sure. And when this is all over, it'll be nice to taper off our suppressants."

Smiling, Connor put his hands on her shoulders. They were firm and smooth. But just at that moment Nordstrom stalked back into the cabin.

"As I was saying," said Zella in a cool, professional voice, "I'm volunteering here for the same reason I volunteered to examine you in the White Room after your first contact with the aliens. If there's something that affects human females, not males, we should know about it before it has a chance to infect the rest of our race."

"That's real dedication," said Nordstrom. He glanced at Marek, who had come in behind him, then at Connor. "Think we can all work as a team?"

"I'm sure of it," answered Connor emphatically.

The trouble is, he thought, you can never be sure how much Nordstrom knows.

Once they had cleared the star system, they lay in four of the molecular-stabilization "freezers" and activated them. They would remain in a state of completely suspended animation until the mass detectors indicated their nearness to the target system, or until some other unknown mass was detected in or near their path. Connor had set his unit so that he would be awakened before the others, so that if it proved a false alarm—a passing meteor, for example—he could handle the situation alone.

He was awakened with the sound of the proximity alarm ringing. The color of the warning light indicated that there was no urgency, so he allowed his life-support systems to adjust smoothly for a few minutes before opening the canopy.

He stretched, as though he had just awakened from a normal sleep. He activated the vision screens, and saw nothing near. The target star was still a long way off—at least a light-year.

The alarm had been triggered by some mass ahead, and about ten degrees off their course. Connor heated a bulb of coffee while he waited for the forward movement of the ship to give a different parallax, so that he could estimate the distance of the object.

It was a long way off, so far that the change in parallax was very small. It was only after an hour that he was able to make an estimate of distance. It was about five light-hours.

There seemed little point in awakening the others. His radar picked up something long and diffuse. The thing was not one object, but many—probably a swarm of asteroids or a dead star system.

It was only when he checked it for radio frequencies that something made his heart leap. He tuned the receiver carefully, listening.

No normal radio noise, this. It was a signal. A strange, uneven cadence of notes wavering down the scale, repeated over and over. It was always the same signal, repeated at intervals of about 9.3 seconds, and lasting for about a third of that time.

Connor threw the switches that would awaken the others, and while he was waiting for them to emerge, he turned on the internal gravity field to half Earth-normal and heated three bulbs of coffee. Nordstrom was the first to reach him.

"What is it?"

"That." Connor amplified the signal. Nordstrom listened for a time, drinking his coffee. "There are three separate signals, coming from different points."

"How widely separated? All on one planetary surface?"

"No. Well apart. Separation of two or three light-minutes."

"Get an accurate fix on one of the signals, and get the area on visual—highest magnification you can."

On the main screen the background dusting of stars seemed to rush closer as Connor stepped up the magnification. He punched some of the computer keys and a green marker-light winked near the center of the screen.

"That's where it's coming from."

"Cut your marker intermittently, and let's see what we can see in the same place." They both stared at the screen. Stars—an uncountable dusting of pinpoints against blackness.

"Nothing," said Connor. "It's as if the signal's coming out of empty space."

"Could be a relay from a satellite. Try the others."

But the results were the same. The signals came from something too small to be seen from this distance.

"Do we hold our course for the star? Or investigate this?"

"This might be what we're looking for. Better change course now—the angle will be sharper later, and you'll use more power."

The far-off whistle of positioning jets sounded through the hull as Connor began to swing the ship for the deflecting thrust to change course. At this moment Marek and Zella came into the control room.

"Why the change of course?" asked Marek.

"I think we've found something. Listen."

For the next few minutes Connor was busy. First the carefully timed deflection blast that swung the ship into the approach hyperbola, then rotating it tail first to prepare for the deceleration firing.

"Could be some kind of military installation," said Marek.

"Don't think so," replied Nordstrom. "Not with those continuous signals."

"Can we afford the fuel to decelerate?" asked Connor.

Nordstrom gestured at the screen. "This could be our first real insight into their technology. But don't come right down to landing speeds."

The radar traces spread across the screen from side to side as they approached. "I can't pick any central body," said Connor. "You know, I think these things are beacons."

"Beacons?"

"Warning ships to stay away from the area. Notice, they seem to be outside the periphery of all this." He pointed to the swarm of blips on the screen. "This is like a great shower of asteroids—denser than an ordinary asteroid belt."

"They must be orbiting a central body, surely."

"Don't think so. Lot of mass there—comparable to a small planetary system. But no large bodies."

"How large are the biggest of them, would you say?"

"Fifty, a hundred kilometers diameter. Not big enough to hold an atmosphere."

"Metallic?"

"Stony, I think."

"How do you know that?" snapped Marek.

"Experience," said Connor without looking round at him. After a few seconds, more for the benefit of the others than for Marek, he added: "I can tell by the ratio of the mass to the intensity of the radar blips. Metallic, they'd be denser."

"Urm," grunted Marek.

Nordstrom had been standing motionless for a long time, his eyes focused on a distance that he alone saw. Suddenly he turned to Connor.

"Could there be a discontinuity in there? A black hole?"

Connor looked at him uncomfortably. "You mean all this stuff could be the wreckage of a planetary system? Gradually spiraling down into the hole?"

"A three-dimensional whirlpool disappearing forever. Possible, isn't it?"

Connor looked at the radar screens. "Maybe we'd better get the hell out of here before we become part of it."

Nordstrom thought for a few seconds. "Not yet. Those radio beacons—yes, I think now they *are* warning beacons— must be orbiting a safe distance out. Let's try to get close to the nearest one. Close enough to see what powers the thing."

"Probably solar cells," said Marek.

Nordstrom laughed. "Out here? Look at the screens. The nearest sun's only another star."

As they swept on in the vast curve that would bring them close to one of the source points of the signals, the proximity alarm sounded. Connor looked at the screens, switched to visual, muttered.

"What is it?" asked Nordstrom.

"Couldn't see. Rock, I suppose. Not enough light out here to see anything. Could have been the size of a house."

Zella spoke for the first time since they had begun the

approach. "Do we really need to see what their beacon is
like? Surely it wouldn't be much different from one of our
own."

"I want to see its power source," said Nordstrom. "No
sunlight out here—yet the thing throws a signal out to a
tremendous distance. I want to see how." He turned to
Connor. "How far from it now?"

"Little over two light-minutes. Say 600,000 kilometers."

"See anything yet?"

"Nothing."

Again the proximity alarm sounded, lifting its note in two
stages. At the first change, yellow lights flashed on all the
walls. Then, only seconds later, red lights. Then a ringing
sound like the striking of an enormous gong sounded through
the ship.

"We're hit!" shouted Marek.

"Turn her outward," said Nordstrom incisively. "Head for
open space."

Connor made the turn, with the red alarm still flashing.
Then an enormous impact flung him from his chair; the lights
in the control room went out, then came on with diminished
power as a backup system took over.

Connor sprawled for a moment on the floor. At least the
gravity was still operating. But the sound of the drive had
ceased, and from somewhere in the rear of the ship came a
hollow roar like the sound of a geyser. The roar of air
blasting into the outer vacuum.

He scrambled to the end of the control console, where the
internal pressure instruments were grouped. A purple light
indicated dropped pressure in the aft section, and near it an
orange light winked on to show a bulkhead door had closed to
isolate the affected area.

"Bad?" asked Nordstrom quietly.

Connor kept snapping switches and looking at dials. His
face felt suddenly cold, as if all the blood had drained out of
it. "Yes," he said. "Looks as if a big meteor went right
through the hull. I think it's taken out the iso-drive."

"Oh, no!" said Zella in a barely audible gasp.

For a long time nobody spoke. Connor moved back from
the control panels and stood looking at the screens. They
were all dark, except for the irregular dusting of background
stars. The yellow dwarf star towards which they had been

moving lay more than a light-year away, and behind, brighter, was the primary of the system from which they had come.

"How far back?" asked Marek.

"Two light-years," said Connor. He began taking a space-suit from a locker.

"Where are you going?"

"Outside. See if it's possible to fix the iso-drive unit."

"Can we get back there without it?" asked Zella, her eyes strangely wide and dark.

"Theoretically, yes—but it would take us more than a hundred years. The chief might make it."

Nordstrom gave a weary smile. "What you youngsters think of as immortality involves a great complexity of intricate and delicate mechanisms; it needs regular expert servicing and checking. Without that I might not outlive any of you."

"We'd better use our radio. Right now!" said Marek.

"Sure," agreed Connor, "but there's no hurry. The signal will take two years to get to the relay. Let's have a look at the drive first." He began climbing into his spacesuit.

"Wait," broke in Nordstrom. "Have you worked on iso-drive equipment?"

"I'm no expert. Only the usual condensed course."

"I once had a lot to do with iso-drive—fifty, sixty years ago. I'd better make the survey."

Connor hesitated, helmet in his hands. "Perhaps we could both have a look."

"As you wish." Nordstrom turned to Marek and Zella. "While we're outside, watch the radar. Slightest suggestion of meteoric matter—alert us at once. We want to be inside if we have to use the jets to evade."

"Just as well the radar's still okay," said Marek. He pointed. "Something going across there now. More rocks—but a couple of kilometers away."

Outside, Connor was shocked at the immense darkness on all sides. He had been outside ships many times, and he wondered for a moment what was different this time. Then it came to him.

There was no nearby sun. He had been used to being outside a ship only within a stellar system. Sometimes the sun had been blindingly white, sometimes a relaxing yellow or sullen red—but there had always been a light source illuminating one side of every object, leaving the shadowed sides to merge with the blackness, in striking contrast.

Here, though, the only light came from distant stars. The star from which they had come, and the one towards which they had been traveling, had been enhanced by magnification on the screens inside. Out here he could not even pick them out.

The only light along the hull came from their own handlamps. "Let's move back and have a look," came Nordstrom's voice over the suit radio, and he moved surely back along the hull of magnetic feet, Connor carefully following. Nordstrom looked like a gigantic insect in the beam of the lamp. A cybernetic body needed less protection from space than an organic one, and his suit consisted only of a helmet with an attached section that covered the shoulders—the limbs and most of the metal and plastic body where uncovered.

The damage was worse than either of them had anticipated. A massive meteor had traveled completely through the ship and out the other side—by looking into the hole, Connor could see a rough circle of stars the other side of the darkness. They shone both their lamps into the hole.

On its way, the meteor had wrecked the iso-drive generator beyond any possibility of repair. It could have been repaired with the facilities of the command ship, but not out here.

Connor felt as if part of his mind could coldly assess the damage while another part stood aside and tried to make sure that all this was really happening.

"This looks like the end of the road," he said.

"It is," said Nordstrom in an emotionless voice. "The end of a very long road for me. On the law of averages, it *had* to end somewhere. But it's the rest of you I'm sorry for. You and the girl—even Marek. You're all kids to me."

Connor looked round at the vast darkness. "There's nothing we can do out here, is there? Let's go in and patch the two holes in the hull from the inside."

"Eh?" Nordstrom seemed lost in some abyss of his own.

"It'll give us more living space, at least."

Nordstrom seemed to come fully alive again. "You're right, of course. Come on." And he led the way back to the airlock.

• • •

Marek seemed sunk in apathy. Zella retained a normal exterior by busying herself in routine things, such as the preparation of food, though there was little scope for talent there.

When they had finished a meal, Nordstrom said suddenly "Let's take a look at our future plan of action."

There was a disinterested murmur of agreement.

"First," said Connor, "the iso-drive is definitely out. If we head back to civilization on the positioning jets, we'd never live long enough to see it. We *could* use the freezers, but I think we'd run out of power before we made it."

"Anyway," said Zella, "what we call our civilization might be gone by then. Or at least altered, so that we belonged nowhere."

"Right," agreed Connor. "I think the only thing we can do is send a help signal, and wait around here."

Marek and Zella exclaimed simultaneously. "What?" "Stay around this swarm of rocks?"

"Yes. It's not much of a chance of survival, but I think it's our *only* chance. The command ship knew we came this way. Some day something may follow us up. It will pick up the signals of the beacons, as we did, and may investigate. It may come near enough to get a direct signal from us."

"I don't like it," said Marek in a flat voice.

"I don't like it much myself," agreed Connor. "But it's all we have."

"You're right," cut in Nordstrom. "We can use the freezers. Set a proximity alarm to detect a ship. First, though, we'd better move out from the rock swarm."

"That's easily done," said Connor. "We'll take a long orbit, clear of the outermost particles, in a plane perpendicular to the one linking the two stars and the center of the swarm."

"Why?"

"Make us easier to find. If we stayed in the plane of the three points, the center of the swarm could eclipse our signal at the wrong time."

"You've really thought this through, haven't you?" said Nordstrom.

"I've spent a lot of time in space," said Connor. "That's where it pays to do all your thinking before you move."

•　　•　　•

This time they had set the proximity alarm to awaken all four of them simultaneously from the freezers, and Connor was a little irritated that Nordstrom seemed to "warm up" instantly, like any electronic equipment. By the time Connor had lurched, yawning, to the control console, the chief had already pinpointed the object that had triggered the alarm.

"Ship, I think," he said. "Seems to be coming from the general direction of the system where we left the command ship."

"Could it be them?"

"The time seems wrong. We've been out for about six hundred days."

"Still, it's coming the right way."

"More or less. I'm beaming them the help signal on automatic repeat, but I'm not getting any response yet."

"Can you get any identification?" Marek moved alongside, followed by Zella.

"Here," said Nordstrom, "you've had more recent practice than I have, Con. Take it."

Connor studied the radar blip of the moving object. "Fast," he said. "Too small for the command ship, I'd say—but too big for one of our shuttles."

"Anything on visual?"

"No. *Yes*. See that?" Something occulted a star. "Hey!"

"What's the matter?"

"Sudden course change—nearly straight towards us. But I didn't see any rocket blast."

"Could it be one of . . . of *theirs?*" asked Zella.

"Yes, it could," said Connor. "The direction doesn't mean much. It could have been coming the other way, towards the system we left. Picked up some trace of us and turned. It would have overrun us by a long way, and come back."

Marek gave a sudden snarl and went away. He returned, strapping the holster of a compact laser pistol to his belt.

"What the hell are you doing with that thing?" demanded Nordstrom.

"This could be a military emergency," snapped Marek. "If it is, I'll have to assume command."

Something seemed to have gone wrong with the vision screens and radar simultaneously. One second the other ship was many kilometers away. The next, their own ship rocked very slightly, and something stood just alongside it, overflowing the main screen.

It was like no ship Connor had ever seen. It was black, unfamiliar in shape, with steeply swept wings and fins that suggested it could make aircraft-type atmospheric landings. Abruptly a number of blue rings of light encircled its body, glowing in the vacuum—then with a sudden movement they encircled the shuttle as well, drawing it against the black ship.

"This is it," shouted Marek. "If they come aboard, we destroy the ship!"

"Listen!" roared Connor. "I've met some of them. I don't think they're violent. They could have killed me, or dissected me—but they didn't."

"I'm damned if I'm going to finish up in a cage, or on a dissection table. I—" Marek broke off. *"What's that?"*

A sound like the high-speed cutting of metal sounded somewhere in the ship.

"That's it!" said Nordstrom.

Marek whipped out the laser pistol. "No. This is a military emergency. From this moment all of you take your orders from me. Understood?"

Connor, at the control console, slid his hand along to the internal gravity control. The gravity was still at 0.5 g. Unobtrusively he locked a knee under the edge of the console. He waited until Marek was looking at Nordstrom.

"Now!" he shouted.

Marek sprang around to face him, and at the moment of the spring Connor cut the gravity to zero. Marek's arms flailed, and then his head thudded against the metal ceiling. At once Connor switched the gravity to full—somewhat above Earth-normal. Marek fell with his feet striking the end of the console and his right arm across the back of a chair. The laser pistol skittered to the floor. As Connor returned the gravity to 0.5g, Nordstrom kicked the laser pistol across the floor to Connor, who picked it up and thrust it behind the console.

Marek was unconscious. His right arm seemed to have been broken between elbow and wrist.

"I'll give him some heavy sedation," said Zella. "He'll be all right."

"I doubt it," muttered Nordstrom. "But do that. *Very* heavy." He looked at Connor. "I hope he wasn't right."

Connor shook his head, wishing he felt the certainty he was displaying.

"Look at the screen!" said Zella.

The main vision screen was pulsing with blue and yellow diagonal bands that rushed swiftly from corner to corner. Other colors appeared, and the angle changed. Simultaneously a strange sound, like a distorted voice, echoed through the ship.

A fragment of a multicolored picture seemed to melt and surge on the screen, and then, suddenly, it was brilliant and sharp. Nordstrom and Zella gave involuntary cries.

Connor alone remained silent. For him there was no element of surprise. He had sat close to one of them—been touched by it. This one was different from Connor's, and different from the one in the photograph found by Alan. Its fur was neither white nor dappled orange, but a cream tint, darker on the pointed ears and in faint stripes. The eyes were turquoise, with the same upward slant and pulsing, cross-shaped pupils. Its wide, flexible lips moved.

"We communicate," boomed a voice through the ship.

"Con!" cried Zella. "It's like *your* voice."

He nodded. "That's where they learned it. They took recordings." He turned to Nordstrom for a moment. "I was right about the yellow star. The team I met must have gone to a base there, and these were on the way back. The time's about right, isn't it?"

"Quick—but possible."

Connor smiled. "They *are* quick. I've been telling you that."

Something like a huge, metallic insect droned through the air and alighted near the screen, a lens pointing at Connor. He remembered the sound of metal being cut back in the ship.

"We communicate," said the being on the screen once again.

Connor waved his hand, looking at the lens. "Yes, we communicate," he answered.

The strange eyes seemed to flame. "Yes," came the voice. "We communicate better."

The lens swung to point at Nordstrom, then at Zella. Connor stepped forward, pointed to his chest and said, "Connor." He pointed to each of the others—ignoring Marek, who was out of sight—and gave their names. Then he pointed to each again and said "man." Not strictly accurate for Zella, perhaps, but details could follow later.

The being on the screen spread its hand across its chest and spoke a word in its own tongue. The nearest Connor could get to it was "kesri." It gestured, and for just a second the screen showed a line of similar beings, differing somewhat in size and color, perhaps eight or nine, in a long compartment with a curving green wall covered with intricate instruments. They all seemed to be watching him. "Kesrii," said the voice, prolonging the ending of the sound this time, perhaps to indicate plurality.

"I think this is going to be all right," said Connor, without looking away from the screen.

The first being spoke again. "Man—to kesrii—come," it said, and its hands exploded into sudden movement. Somehow the gesture conveyed airlocks opening and closing, ending in a sweep towards the compartment of the kesrii and their instruments. Nordstrom moved forward, but the strange hand lifted as if to bar him.

"Con-nor," said the voice. "To kesrii—come."

Connor looked at Zella. Her face was white. He shrugged, lifting an eyebrow, and whispered to her: "Is there a choice?"

He began climbing into his spacesuit again.

3

Connor took a long time putting on his spacesuit, checking
and rechecking everything with an anxious thoroughness he
had not shown for many years—not since his first days in
space. Nordstrom and Zella, helping him suit up, had the
same air of tense yet unhurried care. He found himself notic-
ing little details about them, as though he were imprinting
them on his memory for the last time.

"Let your camera run from the moment you leave our
airlock," said Nordstrom in a strangely flat voice. "We'll
monitor the picture back here, and tape it all."

"Right." Connor was startled by the dry harshness of his
own voice. Zella, who had been putting on one of his multi-
layered gloves, suddenly squeezed his hand, and her eyes
darkened with a quick dilation of the pupils. She returned his
smile, but the tension in the back of her neck gave her head a
faint, involuntary tremor.

"Be careful, Con. Careful all the time."

"Right," he said again. Strange—with a thousand things
he wanted to say, only one word seemed to come. He looked
up at the screen giving a view along the outside of the
ship—the familiar starlit curve of the metal hull beneath the
million stars dusting the immense darkness—but this time the
view was cut off at one side by the black hull of the alien ship
alongside them. An angular black wing, like the wing of a
monstrous aircraft, slanted over their own ship.

Even as he looked, a diffuse glow of electric blue light leaped between the ships, stabilizing into a translucent tube that seemed to link the two airlocks.

"We could learn a lot from them," said Nordstrom.

"If they ever let us take it back," murmured Zella.

"Well, the command ship's on its way back," said Connor, speaking very loudly to overcome the tightness in his throat. "Now—I think I'm ready."

"Good luck," said Nordstrom.

Connor waved his hand in reply and lifted the inner bubble helmet over his head, then locked the outer helmet over it. He walked slowly into the airlock.

Once the inner door of the lock had closed, he could feel his pulse hammering, and his breath rasped hollowly inside his helmet.

"Ready?" came Nordstrom's voice over his suit radio.

"Okay." He watched the wall-mounted pressure gauge, and as its needle dropped, he checked the pressure of his suit. "Holding okay," he said. The red light came on over the outer door of the lock.

The pressure inside the lock did not drop all the way to zero, but stayed at about one tenth of an atmosphere. He told Nordstrom.

"I know. That tube of blue light between the ships must stop the air from leaking away."

"May as well open up. Switching on my camera. You getting this?"

"Got it. Leave it run."

The light went out in the airlock and the outer door swung open, letting in the lambent blue glow of the tubular field between the ships. Connor moved to the threshold.

"That tube of light's about five meters in diameter," he said. "Be about twelve, thirteen meters across to the other ship. *Hey!* Their lock's opening opposite."

On the dark hull of the alien ship, a bright arc of citron-colored light appeared, widening in a crescent as a circular door swung out and downward. The external microphones of Connor's suit picked up an unexpected sound—the rush of air, or something like air, into his airlock. The needle of the pressure gauge on the wall began to climb, leveling off at nine tenths of an atmosphere.

"Con!" Zella's voice came to him with sharp urgency.

"Don't be tempted to take your helmet off. That's not our air. It's theirs, and it's different. The oxygen's up around forty percent. I think the rest's inert."

"Any microorganisms?"

"Don't know yet. We're checking. Trouble is, we don't know what we're looking for."

The circular airlock of the other ship was now wide open, the lowered door barred with steps. It was set well below the midline of the hull, as if for access in surface landings. Connor could not see the floor of the other lock—he was looking upward at the back wall and part of the ceiling, the whole surface of which glowed with that garish light.

He checked that the pressure in his suit was stable, and when he looked up again, he gave a startled cry.

One of the kesrii was standing within the other airlock, without wearing any protective suit. It towered, with its feet apart, cream-furred, its huge eyes fixed on Connor. It extended one of its strange hands, and made a quick, beckoning movement with its long fingers.

"See that?" Connor kept his voice low. "One of them standing in their lock. I didn't see it come in."

"It didn't," answered Nordstrom. "It just *appeared*, while you were looking at your gauges. I think the thing's a hologram."

"Looks real from here. Anyway, I'm going across."

He waved to the kesri, and got an answering movement. He pointed to his chest, then to the other airlock. At once the tall figure stepped smoothly backward and to one side, making a sweeping movement with one hand towards the interior of its own ship.

"Don't trust that tube of light," said Nordstrom.

"Think I've gone crazy?" Connor took a coiled line from the wall of the lock. One end was shackled to a ring in the wall. The other held a magnet. He activated the magnet, swung it for momentum, then threw it across into the other lock. It went to one side of the standing figure, which did not look at it. The magnet bounced from the rear wall without gripping, but something metallic, too swift to follow, snatched the line around the edge of the doorway, stretching it taut.

Connor gave the line an experimental tug. "Firm enough," he said. "Listen. I'm going across."

Pushing off with his feet, he sailed across towards the other ship, with the line running through his hand. As he neared the other lock, the figure standing within abruptly vanished.

"You were right, Chief. It was a hologram. They don't take many chances, do they?"

"Do you blame them? Say, we're monitoring you. That gas is at point nine of an atmosphere, but thirty-nine percent oxygen. Don't think it'd kill you, but you might finish up drunk. Stick with your own air."

Hand over hand, Connor edged the last couple of meters. The alien lock was quite large. At last he stood on the threshold. The lock was clean and empty, lit without shadows by an even glow of the citron light from the whole of the ceiling.

"There's artificial gravity in here—a bit less than 1g, I think."

"What's around the corner?"

"Just an empty room. Walls like satin-finished metal."

"What's holding the end of your line?"

"Eh? Oh, a thing like a spring clamp on the wall. I can—God, I can see how it works, but I'm not strong enough to open it. Might be easier with their type of hand." He attempted a laugh. "Remind me not to get into a fight with these boys."

"They must have a high metabolic rate," came Zella's voice. "That would seem to go with the high oxygen content."

"See if you can find the inner door of their lock," said Nordstrom. "When you fi—"

His voice chopped off in mid-sentence. Connor said, "Chief! Zella!" into his mike a couple of times, then turned.

The outer door of the airlock had closed, cutting his line as cleanly as an axe.

"Chief!" His heart began to pound, and he stepped up his mike gain to its maximum. "Chief! Do you read me?" His own voice boomed deafeningly in his helmet, and he felt sweat on his forehead. *Chief! Do you read me?*

The only sound now was the uneven rasping of his own breathing. The metal of the alien hull must be impervious to human radio frequencies, he thought. It left him completely out of comunication with his own people. He looked around the bare, metallic, featureless walls, where the only irregularity was the clamp holding the severed line. He swallowed, and the sound was loud in his helmet.

"Con . . . nor."

An outlandish voice sounded in his ears. Something inside the ship was reaching his receiver.

"Con . . . nor. Speak if hear."

He wondered if they could hear the beating of his heart. Certainly they would be able to hear his ragged breathing.

"Con . . . nor. Speak if hear."

"I hear you," he said.

"You not need suit. Take off. Breathe."

"Your air is different. Not sure if I can breathe it."

"Is safe. Others breathe it."

"Others?"

"Other mans."

"What other mans? Men?"

"You will meet. You will know."

A sound from his external mikes, not from his radio, made him look around. It was a sound like the chiming of a bell. To one side of the airlock an open passageway led off into the ship. Connor moved slowly towards its entrance, and as he did so, he heard voices coming from somewhere out of sight along the passageway. Human voices, oddly familiar.

He moved slowly along the passage. Above, the ceiling threw down the same shadowless glare, but about five meters ahead the right wall ended, opening into a wide room lit by a cold, white light. He could now hear the actual words that were being spoken.

"Judging from the picture," one voice was saying, "they're bringing them here. Same way they caught us."

Connor's heart gave a great leap, and the taste in his mouth was like metal. He strode quickly forward to the corner of the white-lit room.

The two men standing in the center of the room were Harn and Kosaka, his old exploration team, who should have been on the command ship, well on the way back to human civilization. Kosaka had his back to him, but his wide stance and sleek black hair were unmistakable. Harn, catching sight of Connor over Kosaka's shoulder, stopped talking in the middle of a word, his blue eyes suddenly wide.

"Con!"

Kosaka whirled, and they both began to move forward as Connor stepped to meet them.

"Charl! Jiro!" He extended his hand, but Harn suddenly

halted, with narrowing eyes. His fierce grip on Kosaka's arm brought him also to a halt.

"Hold it, Jiro. It's not him. It's another of their bloody holograms."

Connor laughed, although they did not laugh with him. "Hologram? Rot! I'm real. Feel this."

He reached for Kosaka's extended hand, but felt no contact. His hand seemed to go through the other man's hand, which dissolved into streaks of multicolored light and shadow across his own gloved hand. He stepped back and stared at the two images in front of him.

"But how? How can we see each other?"

"I don't know," said Harn. "They do it all the time. This is how they talk to each other, the way we'd use our visiphones."

"But where are you?"

"On their ship. Their *big* ship. It's *really* big, Con. They've got our whole command ship inside it."

"*What?* But that's impossible!"

"Impossible to you and me, maybe. Not to the kesrii."

"But . . . did anyone get away to take back a report?"

Harn and Kosaka looked sidelong at each other, then both shook their heads. "They got us all," said Kosaka, spreading his hands. "Ship. Shuttles. All our equipment. The lot."

"But are you sure this is true? How the hell could they have that much room on one ship?"

"They have plenty of room," said Harn. "They were bringing out a whole settlement for the planet we explored. Where we found their base. That's why it was sown with vegetation—they'd used it to modify the atmosphere to get it ready for the settlers."

"How many settlers?"

"Don't know. Thousands."

"Thousands of their people?"

Harn hesitated. "No. Not their own people. Something else again. Something they called drom, I think."

"What are they like?"

"We didn't see any. O'Donnel saw some, and he doesn't like to talk about them."

"But . . . what are they doing transporting something else from one planet to another?"

Harn shrugged. "How do I know? Look, an ancestor of

mine used to drive herds of cattle halfway across a continent. He never told the cattle why.''

"You think they look on these . . . drom as cattle?''

"No. They're intelligent. Older race than the kesrii, I think. Had space flight earlier—but only chemical rockets, something like that. The kesrii think they went wrong somewhere along the line—hit a plateau in their development and didn't keep going on and up.'' He shrugged. "Anyway, that doesn't help us. Except they had a lot of empty accommodation space for us.''

Connor looked from one to the other. "Listen, do you sense a bit of a time lag when we answer each other?''

"Yes.''

Connor lifted his gloved hand. "I'm going to snap my fingers at one-second intervals. I want you to keep in time with me.''

As near as they could determine, the time lag was about half a second, although at the end of their experiment it seemed fractionally less than at the beginning. Allowing a quarter of a second in each direction, that meant a separation of seventy or eighty thousand kilometers.

"Did they throw a lot of bands of blue light around your ship?'' asked Kosaka.

"Yes.''

"Then they're bringing it here. They can throw a field around two ships and use one to tow the other, as it were.''

"Look,'' said Connor. "When we arrive . . .''

He didn't go on. There was no point. The images of Harn and Kosaka had vanished. He was in an empty room.

He spun around towards the passageway, but the opening leading to it had closed. His mouth was dry with the taste of fear.

"Con . . . nor.'' Again the synthetic voice sounded in his radio. "Better you take off your suit. Must take off some time. Better soon.''

"Where are you?'' he shouted into his microphone, and the echo of his own voice seemed to ring within his skull.

"We come,'' said the voice, and that was all. For a minute, several minutes, he waited for something to happen. He prowled slowly around the closed room, sweating.

They were right, of course. He could not go on wearing a

spacesuit indefinitely, and it was obvious now that they were not going to let him return to his own ship.

When they moved, they moved unexpectedly and with a deadly swiftness. As he stood in the middle of the room, a screeching howl sounded in his radio and rings of blue light spun round him, contracting until his arms were pinioned to his sides by the force field of which they were the visible by-product. His legs could barely move. He was held upright and almost motionless.

Two of the kesrii walked around him from behind, noses and mouths hidden by white masks connected to cylinders slung across their shoulders. One was dappled like a leopard, the other striped red and cream like a ginger cat. They made no sound. Long, seven-fingered hands unlocked his helmet and whipped it off more efficiently than his human assistants could have done. He tried to hold his breath. A ringing in his head forced him to let his breath out at last, and he drew in a great gulp of their alien air. It felt fresh and cold, with a strong smell that reminded him of seaweed.

Leopard-Spots made a sharp, lateral gesture with one hand, and the rings of light vanished. With the ease of inhuman strength, the kesrii picked Connor up, spacesuit and all, and swung his feet high in the air, so that he actually slid out of his suit. One held the suit while the other took the weight of his body. All within a second, one of them stood him upright while the other flung the discarded suit across the room.

He was wearing only the light undergarments normally worn under a spacesuit. The kesrii felt these curiously, then stripped them off and threw them over near the suit, leaving Connor completely naked.

A door opened, and they gestured towards it. Connor made a dive towards his underwear, but one of the kesrii simply overpowered him and pushed him towards the door. He was not hurt in any way, but the sleek-furred, long-muscled limbs had such an appalling superiority of strength that he gave up all thought of physical contest—for the moment, at any rate.

He wondered if they realized how vulnerable he felt without his clothing. Probably not. They wore none themselves— their fur made it superfluous, and their generative organs seemed to retract within the body, catlike—so perhaps this assault on him was not deliberate.

They thrust him into a small, square room with mirror-smooth walls that showed compound reflections of his body extending in every direction to a blurred infinity. Jets of lukewarm water blasted him, then fierce blasts of heated air that made him feel his skin was peeling—a drying system designed for the kesrii's velvet fur, rather than for sparsely haired skin. While he was still half stupefied, the door opened and hands whipped a kind of blindfold around his eyes.

He heard the door close, then a deep hum. A smarting, tingling sensation spread upward from his feet through his calves and thighs. He started to tear off the blindfold, caught a fleeting impression of violet light of blinding intensity moving up his body, and crammed the dark bandage hastily back over his eyes as the tingling reached his shoulders and neck and head.

Then it was over. When they took him out of the cabinet, they ran some kind of instrument over the surface of his body, while watching dials on a panel. Then, satisfied, they put it away and took off their white masks and breathing cylinders. The inhuman faces somehow chilled him. They had looked better to him in their masks.

Unexpectedly, Leopard-Spots clapped a hand on Connor's shoulder, squeezing his deltoid with a quick, vibrant pressure. His feline ears flicked momentarily erect as he said something in his own incomprehensible language. Connor gave a careful smile, and the kesri, watching his mouth, widened his own orange-tinted lips.

His, thought Connor. He. I'm thinking of him as *he*, not as *it*.

Perhaps that was a step forward. Or a step back? He wished he had time to think it over calmly.

But they didn't give him time. Leopard-Spots turned and strode along the passageway with the smooth, coordinated energy that came from uncounted generations of deadly hunters, and his red-furred companion took Connor's arm in an unbreakable grip and made him follow. A door opened ahead of them—it didn't seem to swing or slide, but within an instant it was simply not there.

They moved through into a large room of irregular shape, evidently taking up a large part of the ship. At first Connor had the impression of huge, fragile-looking windows right around the walls and over the ceiling. Then he realized they were vision screens giving a view of outside space.

Above, nearly half the stars were shut out by the underside of a gigantic ship, vaster than any construction Connor had ever imagined. Darkly metallic in the dim starlight, it showed two bright-lit caverns where great hatchways had opened.

To one side Connor saw his own shuttle, although for some seconds he did not recognize it. He gave a sudden shout of anger as he saw that the wings and control surfaces had been taken off. They had been placed flat against the sides of the hull, as if the whole shuttle were prepared for packaging.

"Why?" he shouted, gesturing at the shuttle.

His captors did not answer, but pushed him inside a cubicle with transparent walls, one of a row like telephone booths. The red-furred kesri went to a control console that he could operate while facing the cabinets. He touched something on the panel, and multicolored lights glowed on it, throwing a changing glare upward on his body. Lit from below, his face looked demonic.

"What are you doing?" shouted Connor. Suddenly the artificial gravity in the cabinet shut off, and he floated, clutching ineffectively at the glassy walls. For a panic-filled instant he thought they were killing him. Then he realized they could have done that easily at any time since he entered their ship.

The single note of a bell chimed; then something like a massive electric shock seemed to convulse the whole of his body. Then everything simply shut off. . . .

How long he remained unconscious, Connor had no idea, but he was sure it was not just a matter of minutes or hours. A stiffness throughout his muscles, and the slow, slow parting of the clouds of unconsciousness, suggested it was a very long time.

He was lying flat on his back, with brilliant white light flooding down on him—light that forced him to close his eyes at the first glimpse; even then, it shone redly through his closed lids.

He felt a piece of flexible tubing being pushed into his mouth, and water trickled across his dry tongue. He swallowed noisily. The water was oddly tasteless. Distilled water.

Some kind of operating theater. An accident? He forced his

eyelids open very slightly, using his lashes to screen the harsh light.

He could see hands busy with some apparatus above him. Long hands in transparent plastic gloves. Something wrong about them. Seven fingers. An enormous thumb and finger, flanked by another, slender thumb and four more slender, supple fingers. The large thumb and finger formed a powerful clamp, while the slimmer digits moved with swift, inhuman dexterity.

The sight of the kesri hands brought him rudely back to full consciousness. He raised his head, his neck muscles creaking like an unoiled hinge, and looked down the length of his naked body. In some places small pieces of adhesive plaster were stuck to his skin, and from some of these, thin wires led away to some apparatus out of his field of view.

He looked up as the brilliance of the overhead lights was suddenly diminished. He was in a large room, with a generosity of space that did not seem to belong on a spacecraft, even the giant kesri ship. The roof, gabled over metal trusses, did not belong on a spaceship, either. And windows . . .

Connor was suddenly more alert. He was on a planetary surface. Through a high window he could see gray and white sky smeared with cloud, and the branches and leaves of a tree. The leaves were dull green, the branches dappled brown and cream—the tree was some species of eucalypt.

Three kesrii in transparent coveralls were working at movable tables and instrument consoles nearby. Connor raised himself on one elbow, in spite of the stabbing of long-unused muscles.

"Where are we?" he asked.

The kesrii looked at him, and one picked up one of the speaking instruments they used to convert their vocal sounds into human speech. "Home," came the synthetic voice.

Connor was shaken with irrational laughter. "My home or yours?" he asked.

"Your home," said the kesri, and all three looked at him as he slowly got the shaky, senseless laughter under control. Abruptly it stopped, and the chill of horror came to him.

Home. One of the human-settled planets, or possibly Earth itself. That meant the kesrii had come to human civilization. He must have been unconscious for years—perhaps many years. But if the kesrii landed on a human-civilized world, there would be war. Or was the war over already? There was a sick feeling of emptiness within him. With their technology, vast experience, and swift, practiced efficiency—and with utter surprise on their side—he could think of only one outcome.

"What have you done?" He tried to sit up. Two of them came forward as if to help him. He watched the thin, bright hypodermic needle driven into his forearm, although he did not feel it.

For a time he slept—but it was normal sleep, nothing like the complete temporary absence of life during the long period of suspended animation. This time when he regained consciousness, he felt actually refreshed.

He was in a different room, with someone standing looking down at him. A woman with red-gold hair. Dreaming? He blinked and stretched his arms, and she smiled, bringing him fully awake.

"Zella!" He sat up, and she slid down to sit on the edge of the bed beside him.

"Welcome back, Con. Looks as if they've brought us home."

"But where?"

"Not sure, exactly. Carl Harn says the vegetation looks like Earth, maybe part of Australia or California. But we haven't seen any local people yet."

"How long have you been awake?"

"Couple of days. I was one of the first two they brought round. They knew we were doctors, and they thought our knowledge of human physiology might help them."

"Did it?"

She nodded gravely. "I think Marek helped them more."

"Marek? How could he teach them anything?"

Her voice was quiet and level. "He taught them a lot. He tried to attack one of them, and they killed him. Oh, it was self-defense, I suppose. But then they dissected him."

"How do you know?"

"I was there. Doc Chang and I. They explained to us why they'd had to kill Marek. They take pictorial records of everything that goes on, and they ran it back for us. Slow motion in places."

"What the hell happened?"

"Marek found his laser gun again. He aimed it at one of the kesrii, then something hit his arm and he dropped the gun—it was too quick for me to see what they did, there. But they picked up the gun, looked at it, and put it down. Then one of them simply killed him, the way you'd kill a poisonous insect. No malice, no pity, just . . .'' She snapped her fingers and let her hand fall open.

''But how?''

She shivered. ''Just twisted his head around, quickly—all the cervical vertebrae . . .'' She shook her head. ''They can be terribly ruthless, Con.''

''Did they threaten you in any way?''

''Not at all. I think they showed us the picture just to explain why Marek had to be exterminated, as if there had been no other way of handling the situation.''

He put his arms around her. Her body was tense, trembling. ''What's the matter, Zel?''

''They gave us a lot of surgical instruments—asked us to dissect Marek's body. When we looked horrified, they didn't persist. They went ahead themselves, with us in the room, although they didn't force us to watch them. Just now and then they'd ask Chang or me something specific about some organ. I suppose they were quite considerate, really. But there was something horrifying about the way they thought of us as an inferior life-form. It wasn't overt. I could just *sense* it.''

''But you said they were considerate.''

''Yes. But like . . . like a person being kind to animals. You know?''

Momentarily he tightened his hold on her. Her trembling had ceased. As he ran his hand down the length of her spine, rhythmically, he could feel her tension ebbing.

''I feel okay to get up,'' he said. ''Is there anything I can wear?''

''They left all our clothing in a big heap at the end of this room. We've sorted most of it. Come and see if you can pick out yours.''

When he was dressed he said, ''I'm hungry. Anything to eat?''

''Yes. Come outside.''

At the door he stopped in surprise. A street of metal and plastic buildings stretched before him, the end of the street opening out to a view of a lightly timbered valley sloping down to a sweep of sea, dark blue under the heavily overcast sky.

"They're our buildings, aren't they? Our prefabs from the ship!"

"Yes. They put them up for us before they brought us out of suspended animation." She smiled. "They're rather nice in some ways."

"Except when they decide to kill you."

"Well . . . yes."

The cafeteria, assembled from prefabricated sections, was the same as a cafeteria anywhere, with the same bright equipment. Its sea of laminated tables was mostly empty, and Connor and Zella drank coffee and ate synthetic cakes at a table near a window.

"It must be Earth," said Connor. "Look at those eucalypts! Must be a hundred years old!"

"That's what Charl said. He says the other trees are myrtle beeches. Funny, though. Jiro isn't so sure. He was *born* on Earth, so you'd think he should know."

"Why isn't he sure?" Connor poured another coffee.

She shrugged. "Something about the sky. A bit of blue showed through the clouds yesterday. Jiro thought it was the wrong blue."

Connor sat with his cup half raised to his lips. "He should know," he said. Looking out of the window, he stood up to increase his field of vision. "Where did they put our ship?"

"We don't know. They left us all the things out of it, but no ship."

"Then we're stuck here. Wherever it is." Looking down the length of the street, Connor saw a group of men and women walking up the grassy slope from the sea. "Is that Charl and Jiro? Yes."

"Some of them went down to have a look at the beach this morning," said Zella. "They don't look exactly excited, do they?"

They went out to meet the others as they came up the street. Kosaka was among those in the front, and as he saw Connor, he sprang forward.

"No hologram this time," he said as they shook hands.

"What's it like to be home, Jiro?"

Kosaka's teeth flashed in a sudden smile—then his expression seemed to go blank. Controlled emotion? Before

Connor could make up his mind, Harn pushed his way through the others, running a hand across his short blond hair.

"Glad you made it, Con. We're still trying to figure where we are."

"You haven't done that yet?"

"We know it's a westward-facing coast in the southern hemisphere, not too far from the equator. Tell that by the sun."

"So that limits it to Australia, South America, Africa. Which is it?"

"The vegetation's mainly Australian, but those palms down by the sea are not. Asian, I think."

"So they were introduced."

"There's another thing," said Kosaka. "We can't get anything on the radio. Bit of static—solar noise. Once we got a whistle that might have been a meterorite. But nobody talking. Anywhere."

Connor felt a sensation of cold seeping into him. "Could there have been a war? Could the kesrii have wiped everyone out?"

"I don't know," said Harn. "They'd be capable of it—but why should they?"

"Do you think," said Zella, "we might have been under suspended animation much longer than we think? It must have taken them years to fly us here."

Connor looked around. He pointed to the ridge of hills behind the valley. "Anyone been up there yet?"

"No. But look there." Kosaka pointed. At the highest point of the ridge, where the trees had given place to wind-swept grass, something like a post or tripod stood sharply against the gray cloud.

"What is it?"

"Don't know. But it's the only non-natural thing in the landscape, except our buildings."

Connor turned. "Hold on. Where's the place where the kesrii brought me around? The place with the operating theater?"

"That went this morning, while you were asleep," said Zella. "They dismantled it, took it into their shuttle, then took off."

"On antigravity, I think," added Harn. "Quite silently."

Connor waved towards the ridge. "After you've eaten, who'll come with me to look at that thing on the hill?"

The others exchanged glances. "The chief had better be in on that," said Harn. "He suggested that earlier."

Five of them made the climb to the top of the ridge—Nordstrom, Connor, Harn, Kosaka, and Zella. They trudged upward through scattered stands of eucalypts, acacias, and palms, coming out after a couple of kilometers to more steeply sloping grassland.

"How are you standing up to the pressure?" Connor asked Zella, who was walking beside him.

"Much easier than I expected," she said.

"That's how it seems to me," he said uneasily.

"Something bothering you about that?"

"Oh . . . nothing."

Nordstrom stalked up alongside them. "Something bothered me a while back," he said. "Notice anything odd about that vegetation?"

"No. What?"

"Does it remind you of something else? Something you've seen recently?"

Connor looked back at the trees, then his gaze swept right across the valley. "I . . . No, that's crazy."

"What were you going to say?"

"Eh? Just that . . . that there seem to be too few species. It's like that planet the kesrii seeded for the drom."

"But these are all terrestrial trees," broke in Zella.

"Yes," said Nordstrom. "I suppose I'm just getting jittery."

They continued their climb towards the ridge, feeling surprisingly little fatigue. Behind them the dark sea spread over the horizon, unbroken by a single ship. The slope steepened towards the crest of the ridge, and they plodded up the last hundred meters or so without speaking.

Seen closer, the structure on top of the ridge looked very old. It was a tripod of brown, corroded metal, almost eaten through in places, with a drilled bracket welded on top. Its feet were set in dull green cement, and a few meters away a slab of the same material had corroded, boltlike pieces of metal protruding from it. The things were mountings for some long-vanished equipment of unguessable purpose.

"Look!" Harn's sharp cry tightened Connor's muscles like

whipcord. The sweeping wave of Harn's hand took in the whole of the plain beyond the ridge.

A broad river wound across the plain. The area was filled with vegetation, but not the eucalypts or wattles, the myrtle beeches or palms they had left behind. It was like no vegetation they had ever seen.

"Look there," called Zella. "Ruins."

The buildings were of some kind of cement, green and brown and dull yellow. They were nothing like human buildings, nor like anything the kesrii might have built. They were shapeless and non-geometrical, some of them like monstrous mushrooms, some with their walls marked with strange patterns. As they watched, the sun broke through below the clouds in the western sky, touching the ruins and the alien trees with a weird light.

The sun threw long shadows of their figures down the slope in front of them. All the shadows were edged on one side with red.

His heart pounding, Connor stared at the red-edged shadows for a long time before he found the courage to turn around.

The cloud bank was clearing over the dark sea, showing lilac-tinted sky. Below the cloud hung two suns, perhaps five degrees apart, one yellow, one red.

"They don't look like human buildings," said Zella.

"It isn't a human scene," said Connor.

She turned, questioning. Without speaking, he pointed to the two suns. She drew in her breath sharply, the back of her hand over her mouth.

"So we're part of an experiment," said Nordstrom in a flat voice.

"The way people keep rabbits, guinea pigs, and goldfish," murmured Harn.

"But the trees—the Earth trees. They're fully grown," objected Kosaka.

"We had seeds to terraform empty planets, remember? They got them from our ship."

Zella turned. "Then . . . we've been under suspended animation longer than we think."

"Hundred years," said Connor, "maybe more." Suddenly he began to shake with a relaxed, deep-throated laughter, while the others stared at him in amazement. Still laughing, he walked away a few paces, then turned to face them.

"This could turn out better than we ever planned," he said. "We were overcrowded, right? We had to move out, to look for more living space. Well, here we have a whole planet.

"But the kesrii are studying us," said Nordstrom.

"And we can study them." Connor gestured vigorously with his hands. "This may be just what we need—a pace-maker. A competitor just a little ahead of us."

He wondered if the others could detect the whisper of doubt behind his enthusiasm.

The others were silent. Kosaka shook his head. "Any time, they could wipe us out—like *that*." He snapped his fingers.

Connor shook his head. "They've gone to some trouble here. At least a hundred years of it. A fellow who keeps rabbits doesn't let them die off."

He began to move back down the slope towards the settlement.

"Come on. We've got a lot to do. And a lot to learn."

4

As they walked down towards the town, Connor kept glancing about him, looking along the crests of the ridges to either side of the valley. Occasionally he looked up at the sky, where rifts of violet were beginning to show between the rolling clouds.

A short distance ahead of him, Nordstrom, Kosaka, and Harn strode purposefully on. As Connor turned again for a survey of his surroundings, Zella fell into step behind him.

"What is it, Con?"

"Just have the feeling of being watched, that's all."

She gave a restrained chuckle. "Don't tell me this environment's bringing out latent psychic abilities."

"It's not that. It's plain common sense. Look, Zel, whichever way we wrap it up, this place is a zoo! The whole planet, maybe. A huge zoological garden laid out by the kesrii."

"You think those ruins over the other side of the range—"

"The remains of an old experiment, like the one they're carrying out with us."

"Wonder what happened to the people who lived in them, after the kesrii had finished studying them." Zella looked furtively around the skyline, then gave a shaky little laugh. "You've got *me* doing it now. What d'you expect to see? Kesrii up trees watching us with field glasses?"

"Nothing as obvious as that. Remember, these boys are

very bright at electronics, unbelievably good at microminia-
turization. They're probably keeping records of everything we
do. All of us. Think back a minute to what you told me about
the way they played back to you that incident where Marek
was killed.''

"God, don't remind me of that! You're most likely right.''

The sky was growing slowly clearer, with the dense banks of
cloud rolling inland behind them on the wind. Overhead, the
air beyond the cloud rifts showed intensely violet, but west-
ward, near the double sunset, the dominant tint was a lumi-
nescent turquoise.

"The suns don't look much lower to me," said Zella.

"Nor to me. Slow diurnal rotation. I think we're in for
very long days and nights.''

"I haven't timed anything since they brought me out of
stasis. That was yesterday, I think, but it seems a long time
ago. It got cold during the night.''

Ahead, Kosaka had turned and was waiting for them to
catch up. He gestured towards Nordstrom and Harn, who
were striding on down the slope. "The chief walks like a
machine," he said. "I'm not going to compete with him at
that.''

"He *is* a machine,'' whispered Zella so that only Connor
could hear her.

Kosaka gestured towards the setting suns. "How did we
ever think this place was Earth?''

"You were doubtful from the start," said Zella.

"Doubtful, yes. There was still a chance I might have been
wrong. But *that* . . .'' He made a gesture toward the binary
suns. "That slams the last door on us.''

"Listen, Jiro," said Connor. "We have a whole world to
develop here. The very thing we came looking for.''

"But it's not like home.''

"Nothing's ever exactly like home. Anyway, we haven't
all come from the same home world.''

They walked on in silence for a while, until Kosaka noticed
an odd outcropping of rock nearby. He unfolded a magnifier
from his pocket and began examining it. "I'll catch you two
up," he said.

Zella moved unobtrusively closer to Connor as they walked
on. "Con, all the time we've worked together, I've never
asked you where you came from.''

"I was born on a space station near a libration point."

"Where? The old L5 in the Earth-Moon system?"

"No. In the system of Van de Kamp's Planets around Barnard's Star in Ophiuchus. We had a big, rotating station. Centrifugal gravity, Earth-normal. The sunlight's red there, so we used white fluorescents to supplement it."

"How long did you live there?"

"Until I was eighteen standard years old."

She digested that in silence for twenty or thirty paces. "So you grew up in an artificial environment?"

"Well, the station was big—plantations, crops in hydroponics, cattle, lemon trees—we had the lot."

"But why would anyone live in a system like that?"

"We mined Van de Kamp's Planets by remote-controlled equipment. The big ones had too strong a gravity field to work in, and the smaller ones were without atmosphere, so we were mostly confined to the station. Big, slowly rotating drum. We kept extending, building more of it along the axis as we needed more room—airlocks on the axis, elevators to the inside surface of the cylinder, where we lived."

"Wasn't it claustrophobic?"

"Not physically. Plenty of space in it. As kids we often had rides in the small spacecraft they used to service the automatic and remote-controlled mining machines on the asteroids."

"No wonder you joined an expedition looking for real live planets."

They were moving on down through the forest now. "I take it you're from dirtside somewhere?"

Zella flashed him a glance of simulated anger. "That's a typical station-born chauvinist's term, isn't it? I grew up in Eridan. You know it?"

"Eridan?"

"Back along the Orion Arm. Omicron-2 Eridani."

"Isn't that a triple-star system?"

"Yes, but the primary's a yellow star a bit smaller and cooler than the original Earth's sun. The other two are very far out, a red and a white dwarf—at night they're just two bright stars. The red one brightens up intermittently with flares. As kids we were kept indoors for hours to avoid radiation damage."

"What was your planet like?"

"Terraformed. Quite a wide range of vegetation in the settled parts, where the soil machines had disintegrated the regolith. Eridan was the main town for the whole system, originally under domes. We had a huge hospital there—that's where I trained."

"Why did you leave?"

"Same reason as you, I suppose. Lack of opportunities. Too many of us there were too highly qualified." She put her hand on his arm. "At least we were both willing to change."

When they reached the beginning of the town, Nordstrom was far away down the street, just turning in to the headquarters building. "You know," said Connor, "something bothers me about this place. About its layout."

"Why, Con? Logically planned, isn't it?"

"Sure. But it was set up by the kesrii, wasn't it?"

"That's right. Before they brought any of us out of stasis."

"But they've built the place exactly the way a human team would have done."

"That bothered Doc Chang and me for a while. Then we found they'd used one of our sets of plans. There's a copy stuck up on a wall in the HQ building." She smiled. "We'll just have to admit that they're very good at their work."

Connor did not smile in return. "It's unbelievable," he said. "Unbelievable that anything can be *that* good."

A scratching sound came from some point ahead of them that they could not at first locate. Then they realized it was coming from a number of loudspeakers mounted on the corners of some of the buildings. Abruptly Nordstrom's amplified voice thundered the length of the street.

"Nordstrom here. As you all know by now, we've had no say in being brought to this place. As yet, we don't know exactly where we are, but it's vital that we pool all our knowledge as soon as possible. I'm calling a meeting of all personnel at the canteen in thirty minutes. That's the long building midway along the street. Thirty minutes from now. Okay?"

As the echoes of his voice died, Connor turned to Zella. "How many of us have you and Chang brought out of hibernation so far?"

She shook her head. "None. The kesrii brought us out, using some of our equipment and some of their own. Chang and I were the first two they awoke, evidently because they realized we had medical knowledge of our own species. Altogether they reactivated forty-nine of us.''

"Forty-nine? A strange number. I wonder if they lost someone?"

"I don't think it'd be an odd number to them. Did you notice the kesrii hands? Seven digits. Seven sevens—see?"

Well before the thirty minutes all forty-nine inhabitants of the town were assembled in the canteen building. Tables had been discarded, seats arranged in rows, and Nordstrom stood on an improvised stage at one end of the room.

"Now that we're all here, we may as well start," he said. "Our first task is to elect a number of us—let's use the word council—to coordinate our activities. To begin with we need a chairman." He looked down at the four rows of people seated before him.

"You're there," said someone in the back row, and there was a murmur of agreement.

Nordstrom moved forward to the front of the stage. "Is it okay if I act as chairman, everyone?"

There was no audible dissent. Nordstrom called for a show of hands for and against, then said, "Thank you. Now, as to the council, I'd suggest an odd number to avoid deadlocked voting. Say nine. Right?"

Again he paused, but there was no disagreement. It occurred to Connor that there was something authoritarian about the way Nordstrom was going about the election, but it was happening too fast for him to formulate his point of disagreement.

"You know," he whispered to Zella, who was sitting next to him in the back row, "we're all being manipulated by an expert."

"He has a couple of centuries of experience," she murmured.

Nordstrom's tall, robotlike figure—partly organic, partly cybernetic—expressed little in body language, so that only his words and his facial expression gave any indication of his thoughts as he spoke.

"Our ship was carrying a total complement of 205 persons, of whom thirty were members of the crew—now twenty-nine, since the death of our colleague Marek—with nine more making up the three planetary exploration teams. The rest consisted of 166 future settlers, held in stasis until a suitable planetary environment can be found for them.

"The kesrii brought forty-nine of us out of stasis, including all the crew—which means that most of us here know each other—and eleven others. Some of you newcomers to our society, as I might call you, are specialists in various fields. The kesrii selected well, although I have no idea as yet how they made their choice."

Again he paused, but no one spoke. He went on.

"Now, since some of you don't know each other, I propose to select the nine for the council, including myself. One, naturally, will be my second-in-command of the ship, Karl O'Donnel."

O'Donnel rose from the front row, rugged, freckled, with strong teeth that flashed in a smile as he turned to look at the audience.

"Democracy in action," Connor whispered to Zella. She did not respond apart from a slight widening of her eyelids, and he looked back to the stage to find Nordstrom looking straight at him. The chief seemed to hesitate for a fraction of a second, then apparently came to a decision.

"Another automatic selection is the exploration team of three men who first experienced contact with the kesrii—Connor, whom most of us know as Con, geologist Kinjiro Kosaka, and biologist Charl Harn. All in favor?"

There was a slight murmur through the room. Zella leaned towards Connor as Nordstrom confirmed the trio's acceptance on the council. "You've just been silenced by an expert," she whispered.

"Again," said Nordstrom, "we want a medical expert on the council. I'm selecting Zella, who volunteered to accompany the team who contacted the kesrii when they were placed in isolation on their return. A very courageous act, because none of us knew what microorganisms might have been caught from the kesrii."

Zella stood up briefly and gave a formal bow. As she sat again, Connor nudged her covertly, but she showed no response.

"That's six members for our council of nine," said Nordstrom. "For the other three I'm selecting three suitable people just brought out of stasis. First, an electronics expert, Nargis Lal."

A tall, dark woman rose in the front row and turned to the audience, pressing her hands together in a *namaste*.

"Then a theoretical specialist in alien contact, Asgard Price."

Price was young, about twenty-two standard years, slim, lithe, with a smooth oval face, dark eyes, and a jutting nose. Boy-prodigy type. As he smiled at the audience, Connor felt an instinctive mistrust of his professional brightness of manner.

"Lastly, Sven, planetary surface engineer from one of the heavy-gravity worlds, Tau Ceti 2."

An enormously broad, blond giant in the front row stood and turned, the round face surprisingly boyish above a massive body that was not as tall as Connor had expected from a view of the seated figure.

"And now," went on Nordstrom, "we have nothing to report to the rest of you, so I'll declare this meeting closed. Will the people selected for the council please remain behind?"

Connor watched the bulk of the audience file out through the doors. "The chief handled that very smoothly," he said to Zella.

"If you have any complaints about his method, Con, think of this: Could you have done it any better?"

He thought for a moment, then shook his head. "I think he's picked a workable team. Where his experience shows is the way the rest of the people *think* they've elected a council."

"Let's meet the new members," said Zella, but at that moment Nordstrom called all of them together.

They dragged one of the long canteen tables, made to seat ten, into the center of the room and arranged chairs around it, Nordstrom taking his position at the head of it. Connor, Zella, Harn, and Kosaka sat down on the left side, and O'Donnel and the three newcomers opposite.

Nordstrom switched on a recorder and spoke a brief identifying introduction into it. "Now," he said, "there's no need for formality at this stage. The idea is to pool all our observations of the planet we've been placed on. First, does anyone have any ideas about its location?"

"The Alpha Centauri system, I'd say," said Asgard Price. His voice suggested the crisp assurance of a school prefect.

"No," said O'Donnel and Kosaka at the same time. They exchanged glances from opposite corners of the long table, then O'Donnel continued. "Jiro and I both know it. I've lived there. Yellow and red binary, sure, but the components are widely separated, from eighty light-minutes at periastron out to two hundred fifty. From the planets orbiting the yellow sun the red one's just a bright star. This binary's close-coupled."

"Let's wait for night to find our location," suggested Connor. "We might be able to pick out stars—the Hyades should be close, and we could use Beta Tauri to work out our approximate position."

"*If* we're still close to the Hyades," said Nordstrom. "Remember, we've been in stasis for a long time. Look at the size of the trees grown from our own supply of seeds."

"There's another thing," said Zella quietly. "The ruins we saw from the top of the hill. They look as if they'd been abandoned for a century or more. If these . . . people are using the planet as an experimental base, it's probably on their track along the Orion Arm."

There was silence for a while as the rest of the council digested her words.

"That's good thinking, Zella," said O'Donnel. "We know they've come from farther out along the Arm than any region we've settled. While we've been expanding out along the spiral arm towards the Rim, they've started somewhere further out and headed in towards the Hub. So this planet should be located along the Arm, between our spheres of influence."

"But closer to theirs," amended Nordstrom. He looked at Zella. "Chang was searching for dangerous microorganisms. Do you know if he's turned anything up?"

"Everything negative, so far. I think we're safe from that direction."

"Then it boils down to this." Nordstrom paused. "Either we put most of our energy into signaling for human help, or we concentrate on adapting life on this planet. After all, as Con said earlier, we came looking for a planet that would give us more living space. From that angle we've done well—even though it was with the unexpected help of the kesrii. Admittedly we don't know what they want out of the project—but this is quite a satisfactory world, provided our crops grow in this soil."

"Several species of our trees are doing well enough," Harn pointed out.

"True," broke in O'Donnel, "but I wonder if they tried others and failed?"

"We'll have to carry out our own tests, of course," said Nordstrom.

There was a pause, then Asgard Price rose to his feet, although all the others had spoken seated. "As I see it," he said, "our top priority should be directing a radio signal to the nearest human settlement."

"Wherever it is," said O'Donnel in a relaxed tone, looking down at the table. "We could make an attempt to locate it tonight."

"What's the general feeling about that?" asked Nordstrom.

Connor looked around the table, as if expecting some of the others to speak. "I think it would be a ridiculous waste of time and energy, this early in the situation. Our primary aim should be self-sufficiency right here. We must be light-years away from the nearest help. By the time we had a reply to a message, we could be dead. Let's begin with an inventory of what supplies and equipment we have."

"We've made a start on that," said Nordstrom. "Food and vitamin supplements should last us until we're producing our own food here."

"How about equipment?" The question came from Sven, and at the sound of the deep yet smooth voice, Connor looked up sharply. For the first time he realized that Sven was a woman. The short hair, the masculine-sounding name, and the massive physique—adapted to almost 2g gravity—had led him to think of the engineer as a boyish-faced man.

"They left us one of our fliers," said Nordstrom. "One small solar generator. Rechargeable batteries, which we'll have to use carefully. And most of the ship's machine-shop equipment."

"Most?" queried Sven.

"Lathes, a milling machine, drill presses, laser gear. They took our electron microscopes, for some reason, even the big optical microscope. But the rest of the stuff seems to be here."

"Why should they take microscopes?" asked Harn "Don't they have things like that?"

"I couldn't believe that," objected Connor. "More likely they wanted to keep us from finding out something. Something that needed high magnification."

"Well, whatever the reason, they seem to be the only part of our gear missing," said Nordstrom. "Not accidental, certainly. The rest of the stuff's undamaged."

There was a pause, then Kosaka started up the discussion again. "Perhaps we could make a search for deposits of fuel. Coal, oil, or whatever. We'll need it eventually."

"One problem there, Jiro," said O'Donnel. "Coal, lignite, even peat, take millions of years to develop into a usable form. I don't think life has existed on this planet for that order of time. Most of the vegetation we've seen was definitely introduced here from somewhere else—from a geological standpoint, only yesterday. Oil, of course—there's just a possibility, there, because we don't know anything yet about the marine life here. Large-scale solar power's naturally out for the present."

"We still have wood," said Sven.

"Wood?"

"We had a similar problem in the early days of settlement on Tau Ceti 2. We had plenty of iron, so we built ourselves a steam-based economy. Smelted the iron with charcoal at first. Made wood-burning boilers, steam engines, the sort they used on Earth a century or two before space flight. We have plenty of forests hereabouts."

"Sounds primitive," said Price.

"It could be a means to an end. That's how our first settlers used it on Ceti."

"Do we have iron here in any quantity?" persisted Price.

"I think we have," said Kosaka. "The dark rocks along the seashore—you've seen them? The colors are iron ore—not high-grade magnetite or hematite, probably taconite, around thirty percent iron. At least it's there, and we might find better deposits elsewhere."

"One thing bothers me," mused Price. "Do you think the aliens might hinder our development?"

"The kesrii?" Nordstrom glanced along the left-hand side of the table, where Connor's team and Zella were sitting. "Let's see. You four have had actual contact with some of them. What do you feel about them hindering us?"

The four exchanged glances. "Physically, they've got us completely over a barrel," said Connor. "But I don't see any immediate worry. They've gone to a lot of trouble to settle us here, whatever their motives."

"Their motives . . ." murmured Zella. "That's what bothers me. I suppose they're roughly equivalent to what the human race might evolve into in a few thousand years, maybe a million years. But I wouldn't have thought we'd develop in quite that way."

"How do you mean, Zella?" asked Nordstrom.

"They've got a very highly evolved brain, but some of what we'd regard as their animal characteristics have gone on developing at the same time, so you have a physical body that's unbelievably fast and strong. I'm still trying to work out what psychological drives you'd get with a mind-body combination like that. I think they'd be a lot different from ours."

O'Donnel gave a short laugh. "If you think the kesrii are hard to figure, you should see the drom—the things they're moving from planet to planet. They're like nothing you ever . . ." He let his voice trail off, shaking his head.

Nargis Lal spoke for the first time. "I'd like to suggest we deal with one problem at a time."

Nordstrom, who appeared to have forgotten her presence, looked at her in surprise, then at O'Donnel. "That's a point, Karl. The drom aren't here. They're not involved in our scene. Not yet, anyway."

"You're right," agreed O'Donnel. His eyes looked haunted. "We don't have to deal with them—*yet.*"

The silence dragged on. It seemed to Connor that the room had suddenly become colder.

"Anything else?" asked Nordstrom. When there was no response, he stood up. "Then I suggest we have a look at our supplies. They're stored in sheds down at the bottom end of the street."

When they stepped outside, the two suns were closer to the horizon, the yellow one almost touching it, its disc flattened. The red sun was barred by strata of cloud, and across its surface and the yellow primary was a straight, golden streak— the edge-on view of a gas torus circling both components of the binary. The sky was the green of corroded copper.

Connor looked higher, towards the zenith. Suddenly he froze. Across the sky ran a thin condensation trail left by some high-flying aircraft.

5

For a long time after their first shocked exclamations, nobody spoke. They simply stood there, staring up at the darkening sky with the thin, sunlit contrail stretching across it like a ruled line.

"It's still extending!" Nargis Lal lifted a slim arm to point to the western end of the trail, where it seemed to taper to a needle point. Sure enough it was lengthening quite rapidly, over the glare of the sunset.

"Can anyone see the thing that's making it?" asked O'Donnel.

Connor shaded his eyes, and several of the others did the same, but whatever was making the vapor trail was impossible to see at this distance.

"Quite high," said Kosaka. "Twenty thousand meters, d'you think? Twenty-five?"

"No way of knowing," said Connor, "until we've had more experience of this atmosphere. It's well above the cloud masses—you can tell by the color of the sunlight reflected from it."

"So they're still watching us," said Zella.

"But they're staying very high up to do it," objected Price.

"That might mean they have very good instruments," said Nordstrom.

The eastern end of the vapor trail, where it must have first appeared above the cumulonimbus, was already feathering out in a high-level crosswind.

"Well," said Sven abruptly, "no good looking at the damn thing. We'd better get on with checking our equipment while we still have some daylight left." She began walking down the street towards the sheds, heavy arms swinging. Her massive torso was as wide as her height, suggesting a gorilla rather than a human shape. She rocked quickly from side to side on her stocky legs, and although her stride was very short, she moved along at normal walking speed.

"We come in all shapes and sizes," murmured Price. He looked around as if he thought he had made an epigram, but nobody else seemed to think it was funny.

O'Donnel and Connor followed Sven down the street, the three of them arriving at the first of the storage sheds at the same time. The large doors at the end of it stood open, revealing the stark interior of a prefabricated metal-and-plastic building with a translucent roof that still let in the waning daylight. A confused array of miscellaneous equipment from the spaceship had been stacked on the dirt floor and on bolted-together metal shelving.

"Looks as if they put things in without worrying about their purpose," said O'Donnel. "Heavy items on the floor, light ones on the high shelves."

"Our main telescope's not here," said Connor. "But that looks like the smaller one from a shuttle. Can we get it out?"

"Probably still got an hour or so of daylight. Let's shift the stuff in front of it."

They began moving smaller items from in front of the telescope, placing things that might be of immediate use near the door, such as a number of battery-powered lights.

"What a bloody mess!" boomed Sven's deep voice.

"You're right," said Connor as he cleared away the last of the things obstructing access to the telescope. "Right, Karl. If you'll take that end . . ."

He and O'Donnel carefully maneuvered the heavy instrument out towards an open space in the middle of the floor. Sven watched their exertions for a few seconds, then moved forward.

"Here, leave it to a specialist."

As they released their grip on the telescope, she put one thick arm over the barrel and the other under the solid mounting, then lifted the whole mass easily and waddled quickly out of the shed with it.

"Where do you want it?" she asked.

"Over in that clear space, I think," said O'Donnel.

Sven carried the instrument over to the place indicated and set it on the ground. She did not show any signs of effort.

"Thanks," said Connor in amazement.

She turned. "I had an ulterior motive. I want you fellows to give me a hand with my lathes."

The larger lathe was a multipurpose machine that Connor thought would take at least six men to move. Yet the three of them managed it, Sven taking the heavier end while O'Donnel and Connor exerted their full strength at the other end. In a few minutes both lathes and some other machines were in an empty building that Sven had secured as a machine shop.

"Thanks," she said.

"You did most of the work," pointed out Connor.

O'Donnel walked over alongside Sven, looking down at her. Like Connor, he was close to two meters tall, and the woman was a head shorter. "Let's feel your arm," he said.

Sven bent her arm, with the fist clenched, and O'Donnel ran his hands over the immense biceps. He looked across at Connor.

"God, it feels the size of an oil drum!"

"Ours was a heavy-gravity planet," said Sven. "We needed a lot of genetic engineering. Stronger bones, bigger muscles, tougher tendons, redesigned heart." She slipped her arm around O'Donnel's waist, and although he was a big man, she lifted him effortlessly off his feet, twirled around, then set him down and walked back into the shed. For a few seconds both men stared after her in silence.

"Might have some problems with that lady," said O'Donnel.

Connor shrugged. "That's twice I've run into superhuman strength. Her people do it by adding more muscle. The kesrii have a different way, I think. They use muscles more completely—maybe by different chemistry, or by different nerve channels." He shrugged. "Need any help here?"

"Not for a while. This thing has equatorial mounting, but I don't know our latitude yet, or our axial inclination to the ecliptic, or *any* damned thing. But leave me with it."

Connor walked up the street towards the canteen building.

Some of the buildings on either side of the street had lights in them, obviously battery powered, and he wondered what the people using them would do when their batteries died. The yellow sun was below the horizon now, and the red component threw a sullen glare over the whole scene, like a globe of red-hot iron in a sky that was now deep purple.

The canteen was brightly lit, with a dozen or more people in it. Zella hailed him from one of the tables, and after collecting his meal from the automatic dispenser, he joined her.

"Making the most of our batteries while they last?" he said, glancing up at the fluorescent lights.

"Someone found a little generator. They haven't got it working yet, but they're confident. Where are you sleeping?"

"Haven't given it any thought yet."

"Some of us put in claims for these empty buildings. There are more people than buildings, so we'll have to share them for a time, but Doc Chang and I are going to set up our surgery along at the corner, where space has been left for an intersecting street. I've taken the building across the street as a house. Like to share it with me?"

Connor looked at her with part of his meal raised halfway to his mouth. "I—I'd like that."

"We can arrange the inside partitions any way we like, Japanese style. Come and see it when we're finished here."

He ended his meal quickly.

Outside, they looked down the street towards the sea. The red sun was now half below the horizon, its reflection across the water a rivulet of molten metal from a furnace. Connor looked up. The vapor trail was now just a feathery band of cloud catching the red glow, wide and diffuse.

The house Zella had chosen was bare and functional, but she was visualising changes to make it more livable. It was already partitioned to form two separate apartments. He wondered if this had influenced her choice.

"I'll see you a little later, Zel," he said. "I'd better go down and see how Karl's getting on with the telescope. I want to know where we are."

"Of course." At the door she ran her finger across his cheek, the bristles of stubble rasping. "You need a shave," she said.

"I know." He hesitated, rubbing his chin. "Zel, how long does it take sex suppressants to lose their effect?"

Her smile was mischievous. "You'll know. When it happens, come and see me."

"As a doctor?"

She lifted one eyebrow. "That, too. If you like."

He'd been tired when he had walked up towards the canteen, but now, strangely, he felt alive with boundless energy. He found he was whistling as he strode down the now deserted street.

O'Donnel was still working at the telescope, with a couple of the battery lamps they had found in the shed.

"Any progress?" asked Connor as he approached.

"Eh? Yes. Look up there. Just coming out, see? That's the Hyades. And the bright blue one is Beta Tauri. We're still a long way from the Solar System. At least as far as Aldebaran. Something like fifty light-years."

"Where's Aldebaran?"

"Don't know. Fifty percent chance it's below the horizon, so it could be quite close. But I'm working out the rotational speed of the planet right now. Just a matter of seeing how long it takes a star to move a particular number of degrees across the sky."

Soon the reason for the planet's slowness of rotation became evident. As the suns set, two moons appeared, a mottled crescent low down in the west and a smaller half-moon near the zenith. Neither seemed close enough to exert much tidal effect. But now, as the red sun was almost below the horizon, an enormous full moon was rising above the ridge of hills inland, its pockmarked golden disc rimmed along one side by crimson.

"Big," commented O'Donnel, "or close. Or both. That's what's slowing our day and night." He glanced at his watch, then aligned the telescope on El Nath, carefully checking its dials. He grunted, and tapped out some figures on a calculator with a small display. "Took a sighting on Beta Tauri thirty minutes ago. This is going to be approximate, but we can refine the figures later. The angular movement of the star was between four and a half and five degrees. That means it would cover the full circle—the diurnal rotation of the planet—in about thirty-eight hours."

"No wonder the sunset seemed slow. What's that going to do to the weather here?"

"Number of factors come into it. Atmospheric makeup, albedo, wind systems—but I'd say it would give you a big range of diurnal temperature. Very hot in late afternoon, cold early morning."

Connor looked at the cloud masses to the east. "That'd account for the heavy cloud buildup earlier."

O'Donnel looked at him searchingly. "That's right," he said, as if surprised that someone he considered non-expert in his field could have arrived at the same conclusion as himself.

Connor walked back up the street under the pallid golden light of the great, crater-scarred moon. He found Zella standing outside the prefab she had claimed.

"I'm glad we've got a moon," she said as he approached. In the moonlight her eyes looked unexpectedly dark. He stood alongside her, then pointed to a different part of the sky.

"The Hyades. See?"

"I know," she said. "I keep on looking at them. I know it's impossible to see anything but points of light from here. But I can't get it out of my mind that *they* are out there. Somewhere."

He put his arm around her smooth, firm shoulders. "I know what you mean," he said quietly. "The feeling we've lost the initiative. But look, Zel. We have a good, habitable planet here. They may never come back."

"You don't really believe that, do you?"

He left his reply too long. In the end he simply tightened his arm around her while they looked up at the brightening cluster of stars in the darkening sky.

Inside the house they talked for a long time before preparing for sleep, partly because of the long night they knew lay ahead of them—some nineteen hours during which the suns were below the horizon.

"Perhaps not nineteen," amended Connor. "Remember, the two suns are slightly out of phase, as it were. One sets an hour and a half before the other. So, allowing for the slow sunset and sunrise, we'll have about seventeen hours of dark."

"You analyze everything, don't you?" said Zella thoughtfully.

"I've been trained for exploration work. A thing you don't understand can turn out to be the thing that kills you."

"I'm not criticizing you, Con. We're going to need some people who think like that."

"Paranoids?"

She laughed. "Tendency, perhaps. But we're in too new an environment to worry about old labels."

He looked towards the moonlit window. "It's going to be very cold in a few hours, Karl says."

"We have plenty of blankets from the stores. Look, Con, I'm using the big bed in the front room. I may have an emergency call—I've left a map showing where I am on the door of the surgery. But will you join me?"

"Why not?" He hesitated. "Except—"

"I know. Aftereffects of the suppressants. Don't rush things, darling."

"Right," he said. He undressed and sprawled on one side of the bed. "Your skin's very white," he said.

"I know. Usually is with redheads."

"I've never really known a redhead. Our population was small on the station, and I don't think we had any redheads—some blond, some dark."

"Your education has a bad hiatus in it." Suddenly she was beside him, her arms around him, and he seized her in an answering embrace. Then she gave a sharp yelp of pain.

"What?"

"Those whiskers! Like the wires on a file card."

"Sorry. Deal with them tomorrow."

He was wondering how she knew what a file card was when sleep overwhelmed him like an avalanche . . .

How much later it was when they were awakened, he had no idea. He was not wearing his watch, since its measurement of time was irrelevant in this place. The thunderous knocking on the door echoed throughout the building.

"Zella! Zella!" A woman's voice sounded outside.

Zella rolled out of bed, shook her hair back, and almost at once began pulling on her coveralls and boots. Connor got up, yawning, and went into the small kitchen as she answered the door. He began heating water for coffee in the battery-operated heater, then Zella appeared at the doorway.

"Someone ill. She thinks it's pneumonia. Be back soon, I hope."

She was hardly outside the front door when Connor's blood was chilled by the sound of a shrill female scream. It sounded high for Zella's voice, but he raced for the door and out into the moonlit street.

Zella and another woman were cowering against the wall, but he could see no reason for their fear until a dark shadow flashed across the moonlit wall of the adjoining building.

"There are two of them!" called Zella.

"Two what?" Then he saw it. It swept silently through the air a few meters above the rooftops, crossing the street in a smooth curve. It was not a bird, nor was it a gigantic bat. It was more like the pterosaurs of Earth's distant past, things Connor thought had existence only in museums.

"Wait!" he shouted. He sprang through the open door, returning with a section of angled metal, part of an unassembled extra bed that had been stacked against the wall.

"Where do you have to go?" he asked the two women.

The visitor, who had a thick scarf wound around her head, pointed. "Other side, there."

One of the pterosaurs perched on a building on the opposite side of the street. Its eyes looked straight at him like the eyes of an eagle or an owl. Predatory eyes. Connor made a sudden rush towards it, shouting with all the strength of his lungs. He couldn't reach it, but his charge had the effect he wanted— with a harsh cry, the thing took off and wheeled away through the air.

He escorted the women across to the other building, where a light showed inside, and Zella followed her companion in. "I'll wait for you," he said.

The two pterosaurs glided in wheeling circles above the town, with hardly a movement of their long wings. Efficient-looking wings, narrow in the chord, high aspect ratio. A long, complex chain of evolution behind them.

Lights appeared up and down the street, and several men came out, some carrying improvised weapons. He saw Nordstrom's unmistakable figure emerge from the HQ building and stalk up the street towards the scene of the disturbance, glancing up as one of the pterosaurs skimmed by overhead, this time at a more respectful height. Nordstrom strode directly up to Connor.

"I saw it all on closed circuit," he said. "This raises a lot of questions, doesn't it?"

"I know. Like, where did they come from?"

Nordstrom waved a long hand towards the slopes inland. "That's Terran vegetation, but they don't belong with it. What other surprises are waiting for us?"

"I don't think they're as dangerous as they look. They're fragile, and they seemed to scare easily."

"Different story when we have young children around here."

They had one more glimpse of the departing pterosaurs, down towards the sea, where the moonlight against a cloud bank silhouetted the two dark shapes swinging northward along the line of the beach.

"Gone. For now," said Nordstrom, and he strode back down the street to the HQ building.

Connor waited half an hour before Zella reappeared. She looked apprehensively into the air as she stepped out, then he took her arm and walked with her quickly across the street to their house. She didn't speak until they were indoors.

"How was the patient?" he asked.

"Not pneumonia. Just a chill. God, we didn't bargain for those flying things. What were they?"

"Maybe there's indigenous life on the planet, after all. Maybe the kesrii only cleared a few square kilometers for us, and these things flew in from beyond."

She sat down on the edge of the bed—as yet they had no chairs—and he noticed that she was trembling. "We didn't allow for this kind of thing."

He sat alongside her and put his arms around her, and for a long time they stayed like that in silence, their eyes on the window.

The night dragged on interminably, the angle of the yellow-tinged moonlight changing with maddening slowness. Once, Connor was on the point of falling into an exhausted sleep, when a shadow flicked suddenly across the window. He waited for a response from Zella, but her breathing was smooth and even, so he didn't tell her about the shadow. But it kept him watching the window until the sluggishly swinging moonlight left it in darkness.

The dawn was preceded by the slanting golden sword blade of the gas torus that encircled the two orbiting suns. Connor rose, stretching his arms, and went to the window. He would have enjoyed a shower, but as yet the buildings were not connected with a system of running water, apart from the gravity tanks in the ceiling of the canteen. There was a tank of fresh water—distilled, from the taste of it—in the house, with a small hand-operated pump to dispense it. He filled a cooking pan with the water and washed as quietly as possible, so that he did not interrupt Zella's sleep. Lying on her side, knees drawn up, she looked like a child.

He was boiling some water for coffee when a subdued knock sounded on the front door. He opened it to find Nordstrom.

"Con, I didn't want to raise the whole town about this, but I want a few of us together to discuss the implications of what happened tonight. Is Zella here?"

"Sleeping. She needs it."

"I've got Karl, Jiro, and Charl Harn waiting for us. I think that might be enough for the purpose. Come with me—I'll explain as we walk along."

They headed down the street towards the HQ building. On the way Nordstrom said, "We've found they left us the small flier from one of the shuttles. Battery powered, of course. The batteries are rechargeable, but their life isn't infinite. Still, I think we're going to need to use it to find out a bit more about our surroundings."

O'Donnel, Harn, and Kosaka were waiting for them in the HQ building. Kosaka appeared to be the only one who had achieved a reasonable night's rest.

"Now," said Nordstrom as soon as he walked in, "we have some evaluation to do. We'd assumed that the kesrii had terraformed just a small area on an otherwise lifeless planet to enable us to live in our customary way, presumably so they could study us. Now it's obvious there are other life-forms here."

"Those things looked like long-distance fliers to me," said Connor.

"You're right," agreed Harn. "Narrow wings, long span."

"No matter," interrupted Nordstrom. "They found us—on our first night here. So what I propose is a program of exploration of the surrounding area, using the flier from the shuttle and aerial cameras. Our primary goal should be a kind of inventory of all the alien life on the planet."

"That's us," said Connor, smiling.

Nordstrom flared in unexpected irritation. "I know that! I mean indigenous life. Native life."

It occurred to Connor that this was the first time he'd seen the chief rattled by something. He had always seemed unshakable. With his vast experience—more than two centuries of it, first as a vigorous, effective human being, then as a virtually immortal human-cybernetic chimera—he had seemed capable of handling anything. He'd ridden out the shock of the kesrii contact. Yet now he seemed thrown by a couple of flying reptiles like something from an ancient past.

Perhaps the key was that the chief was not on his ship, backed up by its awesome network of onboard computers. Here he had to adjust to the idea that he was no longer in absolute command.

6

During the next day the forty-nine settlers carried out an impressive amount of work, helped by more than twenty hours of daylight, and in spite of a thunderous downpour in the middle of the long afternoon. It looked as if this cycle of hot morning, evaporation, cloud buildup in the middle of the day, then merciless rain, was the norm, a function of the planet's slow axial rotation.

The supplies left to them by the kesrii included several small solar generators, which they set up to supply limited power for lights, cooking, and charging batteries.

One of the larger buildings was set aside as a future machine shop, its layout supervised by O'Donnel and Sven. It was Sven who suggested arranging the lathes, milling machine, and grinders in a couple of parallel lines.

"The individual motors on these things will flatten the batteries as quickly as we can recharge them," she pointed out. "We'll have to do it the way we did it on our planet. Line shafts, with fast and loose pulleys operating each machine, and one large power source at the end of the building running the line shafts."

"By that, you mean steam. Right?" asked Connor.

"Can't see any other way yet, Con. The solar units don't give us enough power."

"There's a lot of stock metal down in the third shed," said O'Donnel. "Steel-bar stock, plates of different thicknesses, some aluminum and copper, even magnesium. We should be able to use these two lathes and the miller to make other, specialized machines.''

"We'll need engine lathes, crank shapers—remember, our first products will have to be things like tractors, plows, steam engines.'' Sven's enthusiasm had suddenly ignited.

"We have two small tractors,'' said O'Donnel.

"Yes, but battery powered! We'd be lucky if those atomic batteries lasted a single season. A steam tractor will last a lifetime.''

"Could the existing tractors be converted to steam if their batteries pack up?''

"Yes, Con.'' Sven turned to face him. "That sounds the most practical suggestion yet.''

"Sounds as if our main problem will be fuel,'' said O'Donnel.

But about the time he said this, the solution had already been found by Jiro Kosaka. He had taken the flier on its first exploratory trip in the vicinity of their base, photographing the surrounding countryside from a standard height so that a photomosaic could be built up.

He'd been given the task of beginning the survey because he was the geologist of the original expedition. But his first major discovery was not in the field of geology. He returned from the flight in less than an hour, landing the flier on the level ground behind the HQ building.

"Our fuel worries are over for a long time,'' he said. "Just ten kilometers south of here there's a dead forest. I think it was artificially planted originally. Trees have been planted in straight rows down near the beach. Not Earth-type trees, but I don't think they were native to this planet. Charl would know better than I would. From the plantation they seem to have spread inland, twenty-five, thirty kilometers, as if they had no natural enemies. Then something killed them.''

"What?'' asked Connor.

Kosaka shrugged. After a brief discussion, Harn decided to fly out with him to see the forest, but his greater botanical knowledge was of little help.

"I don't know the species,'' he said on his return. "They're something like our softwoods, rather like pine, but unrelated. I agree with Jiro—they've been planted down near the beach, then ran wild until they were all killed.''

"What killed them?" asked Connor.

"Could have been anything. Acted quickly and completely. My guess is that it was a disease or pest released by someone who didn't want introduced trees taking over the whole planet."

"Is the wood safe to use?"

"Wouldn't like to build anything with it, unless we ran a lot of tests, but it'd be safe enough to burn as fuel."

O'Donnel, listening to Harn's report in silence, turned to Sven. "That how you raised steam on Ceti?"

"We had oil. But wood could serve in a pinch."

"Good. That's one factor we can forget about. We'll bulldoze a road out to the edge of the forest. Ten kilometers is nothing."

Kosaka's next discovery was more controversial. In the early part of the afternoon a threatening buildup of cloud was already massing over the sea. He didn't want to take the flier too far from the base, in case the storm struck suddenly, so he contented himself with a flight out over the sea to a chain of islands ten or twelve kilometers offshore.

"They're part of a reef," he reported over the radio.

"What kind of reef?" asked Nordstrom.

"Like coral. Not coral, but it seems to serve the same function, fill the same niche, to put it that way. I'll call it coraloid, okay? That's why the sea is placid near our base— it's part of a big lagoon. Sheltered. There are a few breaks in the reef system, and a few rocky islands on the seaward side. Ridges of rock going up thirty, forty meters above the water level. The sea beyond is much rougher. Looks deeper. Hey! There's something on one of the islands, on the side towards the sea."

"What is it?"

"I'm going closer to check. You couldn't see it from the land. It's the other side of a ridge. It's artificial. It looks like a couple of big boxes. Black. One bigger than the other. Hey! I know what it is! It's our nuclear generator. From the ship. D'you read me, Chief? It's our generator!"

"You said it was black."

"I know. I don't get that. Someone's painted the top of it black. Only the top. The sides of it are still green, the color they used to be on the ship."

"Why the hell would anyone paint the damn thing black?"

"Come to that, why'd they dump it out here?"

"How far are you exactly from here?"

"Let's see. Twelve kilometers, near enough."

"You said there were two objects."

"That's right. The other one looks like a stack of drums with a black plastic sheet pegged down over them. As if they wanted to protect them from weather." Kosaka paused, then went on. "It's near the beach. Be easy to float it off on some sort of raft—it's too heavy to lift with this flier, of course."

Nordstrom looked at Connor and Sven, who were both listening with him to Kosaka's broadcast.

"Do we want that thing near our base?" asked Sven.

"Why not?" asked Connor.

"On Ceti we were a bit scared of nuclear reactors close to populated areas. We had most of our centers on small islands—a blowup could have wiped a lot of us out."

Connor turned to Nordstrom. "Could we run a power line from the island?"

"Not with our present resources."

"Then how about using the generator, where it is, to recharge our atomic batteries?"

"A good stopgap, Con, but the batteries aren't everlasting, and we can't build others until we find some scarce materials." Nordstrom began to head for the door.

"It's steam, then," said Sven, "whether we like it or not."

"I agree," said Nordstrom from the doorway. "I don't like it, but I think at the moment it's our safest alternative."

"It's a working proposition, Chief." Sven's blue eyes were bright. "Give us a few months and we'll be on our way."

After Nordstrom had left, Connor looked at Sven for a long time, until she said, "What?"

"You're quite happy to make your permanent home here?"

"God, yes! I wouldn't want to go home again."

"You've never told me about your planet. I know it's a heavy gravity world, that's all."

"It's not the gravity that bothered me—we were all modified for that. But it's the things that went with it." She moved closer to him. "My mother was an engineer. She and my partner and I designed a new town. We had to design our own buildings in that environment—thick, inward-sloping walls to stand the fierce winds—you'd have no conception of what really violent wind can do! But the planetary crust's unstable where you have very strong gravity.''

"What happened?" prompted Connor.

She turned away from him as her eyes suddenly became wet. "Volcanic eruption. Killed my mother and my partner. Would have killed me if I hadn't been away on a buying trip. Wiped our whole town out. Everything."

Connor felt inadequate. "I'm sorry."

"Anyway," she said, her voice forced and shaky. "Never look back, right? We go on from *now*. And I think we have a good starting point for an industry here."

He put his hand on her shoulder, feeling the smooth movement of the massive deltoid.

"Sorry," she muttered.

"For what?"

"For bothering you with my past."

"Hell, Sven, we're all going to be stuck on the one world here, maybe for the rest of our lives. The sooner we get to know each other, the better."

The next general meeting of the settlers took place after ten days—ten long local days, which O'Donnel's later observations had determined to have a length of slightly over thirty-seven hours and fifty-six minutes. An awkward length. Nordstrom decided to make the day officially thirty-eight hours, making an adjustment for the small discrepancy every fifth day.

He opened the meeting by having O'Donnel summarize what he had discovered astronomically.

"You've heard about the thirty-eight-hour day. Now, the year. Can't get a precise figure on that yet because I haven't been able to determine the exact center of gravity of the two suns. When I have that, I can use the parallax against the background stars to give us our 'year.' I know already it's much longer than a standard year, maybe eighty percent longer, or about four hundred or more of the local days."

"How about seasonal variations?" asked Sven.

O'Donnel shrugged. "No way of telling yet. We don't know whether our orbit is circular or highly elliptical. And remember, this is a binary system. The angular separation of the two stars hasn't changed enough since our arrival for me to figure their true distance apart. We could be looking at one almost behind the other. In other words, I don't know yet whether we're orbiting one or the common center of gravity."

"How soon will you know?" persisted Sven.

"Is it urgent?"

"Yes. We want to design buildings. If we're going to swing from a blazing summer to a frozen winter, we want to know before we start to build."

"Right," broke in Nordstrom. "We'd better give that a high priority, Karl. Now, the hibernation . . . Zella?"

"Chang and I haven't brought anyone else out of stasis yet. Part of our original cryptobiosis equipment has been replaced by the kesrii with units of their own. They're compact, and apparently very efficient. But we want to make certain we fully understand what they're doing before we interrupt their cycles, so there's no risk to the subjects."

"They left no instructions?"

"How could they? There are printed characters on some of their units, but they have no relation to any human language. Chang tried to decode them, but had no luck. They're not ideograms, like Japanese. They seem to form a sort of alphabet, but there are eighty or ninety different symbols. The sounds they make in their language might be a lot more varied and complicated than ours."

"So you have no immediate plans to bring anyone else out of stasis?" Nordstrom gestured. "Just as well if we don't. We haven't the accommodation for them yet. They've been in cold storage for a long time. A little longer won't hurt."

"Could I say something on that?" broke in Charl Harn. "We've assumed that we've been in stasis here for a long time, because of the fully grown trees the kesrii apparently planted from our seeds and seedlings."

"Right."

"I think we've made a bad miscalculation. A lot of these trees are eucalypts. In the first year or two of their lives, they have a different type of leaf from the adult leaf. The juvenile leaves are sessile."

"What's sessile?"

"Joined to the branch without a stalk. Rounded. The adult leaf is long, tough, looks like plastic. Your normally find the juvenile leaves just at the bottom of a tree. But I've noticed some of the eucalypts around here with sessile leaves ten meters up in the air.''

For a few seconds no one spoke. "I don't see the implication," said Nordstrom.

"Nor did I, at first," said Harn. "Then it hit me. The kesrii have some way of accelerating plant growth.''

"You mean these forests—which we've assumed were fifty or more standard years old—might have been planted quite recently?''

"I think so. And we mightn't have been in stasis as long as we think.''

Nordstrom seemed to digest this information for a long time. When he spoke again, he looked intently at Harn. "Is there any way you might find out what they did to the trees to accelerate their growth?''

"I can try.''

"We might be able to apply the technique to our grains—the wheat, oats, rice.''

"We'd better not rush into that, Chief. There might be side effects.''

"What's happening about the grains?''

"We're putting in experimental plots. Some under inflated plastic domes, some in the open. Too early yet to see whether anything's taking root.''

"Well, there's no immediate urgency. We have plenty of dry food stores from the ship. I don't mean to stop your research. Just be careful.''

After a pause, Kosaka introduced a new thought. "How about the native marine life? Might some of that be edible?''

"Does any exist?" asked Nordstrom.

"Yes," said Kosaka emphatically. "I saw some from the flier when I went out to investigate the islands. Things that looked like fish.''

"You'd have to be very careful," cautioned Zella. "They could have a different chemical life cycle.''

"Right," said Nordstrom. "Let's remember one thing. This is not our home planet. We could be killed at any time by some microorganism we can't even see—if we're not damn careful.''

Nordstrom's warning of the danger possibly coming from something invisibly small came home to Connor almost as soon as he stepped out of the HQ building. Some small flying thing, smaller than a mosquito, skimmed past his head with a shrill, penetrating buzz almost at the upper limit of audible frequencies. He looked after it, but it flew so swiftly that he lost sight of it within a second or two.

"Con!"

He turned to see who had called his name. A hundred meters up the street Asgard Price was hurrying to overtake him, and Con waited until he came alongside.

"How did you feel the meeting went?" asked Price.

"Good, on the whole. I think we have a good team here. We all seem to know what we're talking about when it comes to our own specialties."

"Yes. A thing to remember, though—we're shaping a whole future civilization. As the twig is bent, the tree will lean."

"Sure. I can't see any sign of us pushing the tree over yet."

Price looked over his shoulder, then edged slightly closer to Connor as they walked, lowering his voice. "Back home I spent quite a bit of time with Truline."

"True what?"

"Truline. Its full title was the Society for Maintenance of the True Line of Humanity."

"How was that again? Maintenance of the True Line of Humanity? Who decides what's the true line? I think we keep evolving to meet our environment, wherever it may lead."

Price ran his fingers over his dark hair, flattening it against his scalp with irritable energy. "Our Society has certain guidelines."

"Such as. . . ?"

"Most of them are self-evident." Price was staring straight ahead of him, his lips compressed in a tight line, bright spots of red on his pallid cheeks. Connor looked at him as they walked along.

"I don't see what this has to do with the meeting, Asgard. Or the council. We all seem to be pulling our weight with the same overall goal—to get ourselves established here."

Price walked on for a few seconds in silence, keeping in precise step with Connor. When he spoke again, his voice was half an octave higher. "Why was this woman Sven put on the council?"

"Well, our complement of settlers includes several other

people from Tau Ceti 2, and she's their representative—apart from being a highly qualified mechanical engineer, which is something we need badly.''

"All the other Tau Ceti people are women, aren't they?''

"Yes. Their whole population is female, artificially inseminated, controlled sex of all their children. They maintain a heavy-gravity environment works better with an all-female population. I thought that was generally understood.''

"That's what I think is wrong. The human race was never intended to develop along those lines.''

"You might as well say the human race was never intended to stop living in trees.''

Price gave a brittle laugh. "Looks as if this discussion is getting us nowhere.''

Connor glanced at him. "Any discussion based on prejudice never does get anywhere, does it?''

"You think I'm prejudiced?''

"Listen, Asgard.'' Connor placed his hand on Price's shoulder. "It's not a vital question. Not the way I see it, anyway. We have to survive here, and that means we have to work smoothly together. Divisions in our team are going to have no survival value whatever. Right?''

"I suppose so.'' After a pause, Price added, "If you say so.''

About to retort, Connor changed his mind and let it go.

Kosaka made another journey in the flier shortly after the meeting, hurrying away to avoid the cloud buildup which would come in the afternoon. This time he was away much longer than on previous occasions, and Connor began to look into the possibility of organizing a search party.

Kosaka had flown south along the coast. He had already thoroughly photographed the land as far down as a craggy point thirty kilometers from the base, so this time it was assumed that he'd flown directly there and begun his survey farther to the south.

Connor had just contacted Nordstrom when the flier appeared, a silver dot in the lilac sky, coming in from due south. Kosaka, with uncharacteristic jubilation, made a circuit of the town, finishing with a low pass down the length of Main Street.

"He's found something,'' said Connor as the flier landed.

Kosaka's enthusiasm was evident in his walk. He waved to Nordstrom and Connor, then gestured towards the canteen building.

"Something to celebrate!" he shouted while he was still some distance away. "Tell you about it over coffee!"

The only people in the canteen, they waited patiently as Kosaka gulped down some of his coffee.

"You found oil?" suggested Nordstrom.

Kosaka shook his head,

"Coal?" asked Connor.

Again, a vigorous shake of the head. "Better than that, I think. I found hematite. Huge deposits of it, easily accessible. Probably around sixty-two percent iron."

"Where?"

"Right on the coast, about eighty kilometers down. We should be able to mine it, run the ore down by gravity, and ship it here."

"Ship it?"

"I know: we haven't any ships. But we should be able to build something that could carry the ore."

"How about smelting?" asked Nordstrom.

"Sven's the expert on that. She suggested using the wood of the dead forest, burning it to charcoal, smelting with that. It was the way they made their iron and steel long ago."

Nordstrom looked up at the sky. "Bit late to run down there this afternoon, isn't it?"

Kosaka shook his head. "We could do it—before the storms hit us."

"Then I suggest both of you go down and photograph the deposits in detail. Take Sven with you. Meanwhile I'll see if I can organize a boat-building project."

Connor and Kosaka sat in the front seats of the flier, Sven behind them. In the close space of the small cabin, Connor realized for the first time the full extent of the genetic engineering and subsequent hormone treatment carried out to produce a being like Sven. Her enormous body seemed to fill the two rear seats, and he could hear her deep, even breathing above the sounds of the machine.

"Base looks small once you're above it," said Kosaka as he banked the flier around towards the south. It was true. Even from a height of a couple of hundred meters, the neat group of buildings looked like an array of toys laid out by some gigantic child. Thinking suddenly of the kesrii, it occurred to Connor that this was practically what the base was. A toy town with toy inhabitants, set up by superior intelligences as a bizarre game.

He shook the idea out of his mind.

"What's our air speed?" asked Sven.

"Hundred eighty," said Kosaka. "We could come faster, but I'm conserving power."

"Should be there in half an hour, then." Sven rested her hands on the backs of the front seats and leaned forward, looking expectantly ahead. Her face, under the short, blond hair, looked like that of an overgrown boy. It was a broad face, with disproportionately large, flared nostrils that seemed to open almost straight forward. Connor could feel the warm gusts of breath.

They passed the rugged point which on clear days was just visible from the base, flying by now at two thousand meters. Southward was a long crescent of reddish beach, then a branching delta of a river estuary, fringed with dark green vegetation.

"Are those mangroves, Jiro?" asked Connor.

"Don't know. Could be something like that. Have to ask Charl."

They passed over another long point, with a string of islands curving away from it across the sea.

"See that ridge, and the islands?" Kosaka pointed. "They look to me like part of the rim of an old impact crater."

"You're right," agreed Connor. "Something very big must have come down ahead of us a very long time ago. Asteroid or something."

"Or a bomb?" suggested Sven. From her voice Connor couldn't tell whether she was serious or not.

"Might have been," said Kosaka. "Anyway, so long ago that it doesn't matter. But look here in front of us."

Ahead, a ridge of dark brown hills stretched along the horizon, ending at the sea in a jutting headland.

"See that ridge? Solid hematite, the lot of it. Nearly two-thirds iron!"

"The whole range?"

"That's right. Now, if you tie that up with what I was saying about the other ridge behind us being part of the rim of an old impact crater, *this* range could be the remains of the thing that made the impact, millions of years ago. It's just about at the center of a circle that runs around through the islands we passed.''

He was reducing the height of the flier all the time, and soon they were less than a hundred meters above the sea, which no longer had the flat, metallic appearance it had shown before.

"Look down there," said Sven suddenly.

"What?" asked Connor, looking at the swell of water.

"Saw things swimming. Gone now."

Kosaka grunted. "I saw some when I was down here this morning. Wonder if they're native to the planet, or if they were introduced like the vegetation?"

"Or like us," added Connor.

"Uh-huh. Like us."

They were flying parallel to the coast, which was dominated here by the line of dark red cliffs. Kosaka pointed down.

"I'd say this was a rising coastline, see? The cliffs, and the flat shore platforms. Dead level for kilometers."

"What causes those?" asked Sven.

"When a coast's rising, more and more rock comes up to the surface of the water. Bits keep breaking off, see? The waves push them backward and forward over the surface for a few million years, and they plane the rock off flat. Handy for us. Gives us plenty of landing places."

He selected a landing point near the base of the cliffs, far enough from the water to avoid any incoming tide. They stepped out of the machine into a stillness punctuated by the slap of waves against rock, and an occasional whisper of wind.

"We'd have to get the ore out by sea," said Kosaka as they walked towards the cliffs. "That river between here and the base is swampy for a long way inland. We'd need a long road to link the two places. I'd say 130 kilometers by the time you went inland far enough to build a bridge."

They stopped near the foot of the scree that had fallen from the cliff face, looking up at the fifty-meter high wall of rock. Sven moved forward. She had put on a heavy leatheroid coat as she left the flier, and pulled on a thick pair of gloves, and now Connor saw why. Reaching the slope, she leaned

forward, using her gloved hands in a four-footed scramble up
the incline. The movement was so apelike that Connor was
momentarily shocked. She examined some loose pieces of
rock, then turned.

"There's an easier way, Jiro. We could build a blast
furnace here and ship out the finished iron or steel."

"How about fuel?" asked Connor.

"Easy," said Kosaka. "Forests inland from here, going
back as far as you can see, killed off like the ones south of
our base. We could burn that to charcoal for smelting."

"Another way," suggested Connor. "That nuclear generator back on the island could give us all the power we needed.
Split sea water, use the hydrogen for smelting."

Sven came part of the way down the slope, standing a little
above the others, braced on massive arms. "The council
might want to keep the generator near the base until we can
make them a steam-powered unit. Anyway, we began with
steam and primitive blast furnaces on my planet, and it
worked. The first settlers were scared of nuclear power, I
think. Understandable, because Ceti is nine-tenths sea and
most of our settlements were on small islands that couldn't
risk a nuclear blowup."

"Remote chance these days, isn't it?"

"Sure. Never heard of one in my time, but this was a
century ago, when things weren't so safe, or so they thought."

Connor walked across the rock platform to the edge of the
sea and stood looking down. "Water's deep—and the reef
shelters it. We might make a landing place here—or farther
that way."

Sven came over to join him, while Kosaka began inspect-
ing pieces of rock that had come down in the scree, putting
some into a plastic bag he had brought with him.

"You get on with people easily, don't you?" said Sven
abruptly, looking at Connor.

"I suppose so."

"No prejudices—I think that's what it is about you. Listen,
Karl O'Donnel and I want to set up an engineering plant. He
has the theoretical design ability, and I have the mechanical
knowledge, but we need someone to coordinate our work.
We'll have to get some of the settlers to work with us, too.
Would you like to be our coordinator?"

"If you give me an outline of your project."

"We've got supplies of bar stock and plate from the ship, but they won't last forever. I think the first step is to get a furnace built to smelt this stuff." She jerked her thumb towards the brown ranges. "Then we start turning out steam engines."

Connor looked up at the cliffs, then turned slowly, looking in each direction along the shore. "If possible, I think we'd better make the whole setup here," he said.

"All of it? Nordstrom and Karl are never going to stand that."

"Can't we think of some technical reason, between us, for locating the furnace and the rest of the plant here?"

"But why?"

"The council would want too much say in running the plant, without knowing what they were doing."

Sven didn't speak for a while, but stood looking at the cliffs. Then she turned and looked out at the sea. At last she said, "Back home we had a fairly strict concept of democracy."

"Sure," said Connor. "But where I came from, a lot of situations came up that weren't covered by the rules."

"So you made your rules up as you went along?" She continued looking at the sea.

"Sometimes, yes. It worked better that way."

She spun around to face him, a slight smile lifting the corners of her wide mouth. "You sound a bit subversive to me—isn't that the word? But interesting. Perhaps we'd better work out a few more details first, then put the case the way we think it's going to work best."

Connor glanced towards the cliffs, where Kosaka was still absorbed in his rocks. Suddenly he put out his hand, and Sven gripped it.

"It's going to be interesting working with you," she said.

7

Connor took a number of photographs of the cliffs of hematite, and some close-ups of the broken rock at the foot of the talus. Then he took several shots of the shore platforms, including the landing site of the flier and the edge of the deep-water channel which promised a potential anchorage for future seacraft. He used the figures of Sven and Kosaka in these to give scale to the background.

The sudden darkening of the landscape brought their attention to the towering masses of cloud that heralded the regular afternoon storm, and the three of them hurried to the flier just as the first large drops of rain began to spatter its windows.

Kosaka took the controls, lifting the machine as soon as the others were on board. He headed north up the coastline, gaining height slowly to achieve the best possible forward speed. Seaward, brilliant flashes of lightning linked cloud and water in an increasingly rapid dance of fire.

"Should have seen the storms we had back home," said Sven, hands gripping the backs of the front seats. "A storm during a volcanic eruption—*that's* an experience that really stays with you."

The rain was already cutting visibility to a few hundred meters, and they were still far from the base, a violent line squall racing in from the sea. Kosaka flew low, following the irregular line of the beaches, the leaden water to the left streaked with angry white. When the buildings of the base finally appeared through the murk, he made no attempt at repeating his former triumphant circling of the town, but dived in a straight, shallow approach to the level area behind the HQ building. As he slowed for a landing, the rain pounded the windows of the flier with redoubled ferocity.

"We'll have to run for it," said Connor.

Sven pulled the hood of her coat over her head and began putting on her heavy gloves. Kosaka landed as near as possible to the HQ, about a hundred meters from its backdoor. Then the three of them sprang out of the flier into the shimmering curtain of rain.

Connor and Kosaka ran for the shelter of the veranda over the back door, side by side. Sven overtook them, leaning forward and fusing the immense power of her arms to combine the movement of her gloved fists and her feet in a kind of quadruped gallop. She reached the veranda well before them, laughing as she turned and stood to face them. Connor wondered what Asgard Price's Society for Maintenance of the True Line of Humanity would have thought of her performance.

"You're fast," said Kosaka as they joined her.

"For a short distance, Jiro," she panted. The air whistled through her flared nostrils as she stripped off her gloves and slapped them against the wall to clean them. Then she threw back her hood and unfastened her coat. "Wait until I get my breath before we see the chief."

At that moment, however, the back door of the HQ building opened. "Come in," said Nordstrom. "What happened? Didn't you know the storm was coming?"

"We've got hematite, as Jiro says," said Connor, leading the others inside. "A whole range of it. With a dead forest behind it we can use for charcoal. We can move into the Iron Age as soon as we can build a furnace there."

"*There?*" Nordstrom looked at him sharply. "Why do you say 'there'?"

"It seems the logical place to build a furnace—near the supply of iron." Connor turned. "Wouldn't you two agree with that?"

"Less handling," said Kosaka promptly. "Finished iron and steel's easier to transport than ore. Less bulky."

"Another thing," added Sven, "it'd keep pollution eighty kilometers away from our base. That's worth considering, isn't it?"

The rain was now thundering down on the metal and fiberglass roof, so that all of them had to raise their voices almost to shouting level. In the midst of the turmoil a knock sounded on the door facing the street. Connor, the nearest to it, walked over and opened it. Zella stood outside in a hooded rain cape that glistened with rivulets of water.

"Come in," he said, stepping quickly aside to give her access. But instead of passing him she flung her arms around him, thrusting them out through slits in the cape and hugging him tightly.

"I was frightened," she said quickly, in a low voice, "when the storm struck and you were still down the coast. How did you find your way back?"

"Just followed the beach. Jiro was flying. Did a great job. Come on in."

As she saw the others standing, looking towards her, she hesitated. "Is this a meeting?"

"Unofficial, Zella," said Nordstrom. "Join us."

She took off the dripping cape and hung it over a chair. "I was worried about these three in the flier."

"So was I, frankly," said Nordstrom. "However, you may as well take part in the discussion. There's a suggestion we should locate a furnace to treat the iron ore down where the deposits are—about eighty kilometers away. Yesterday I would have agreed with the idea, but last night changed things. Up till then we thought we were alone on an otherwise uninhabited planet, except, perhaps, for occasional spying by the kesrii—there's nothing we could do about that. But then we have these flying reptiles coming over our settlement in the middle of the night."

"I don't think they're a major threat," objected Connor.

"In themselves, maybe not. But they're a complicated, highly evolved life-form. As you said yourself, Con, they're long-distance fliers. They don't exist here alone! They're obviously predators, which means they have other life-forms to live on. Somewhere else on this planet there may be a whole menagerie of living things that *could* offer a threat to us. For that reason alone I'd prefer to keep our operations consolidated as far as possible in the one place."

"I'd agree with that," said Zella, shifting her voice into a higher pitch to compete with the roar of the rain. "From a medical point of view we don't want to become dispersed this early in our stay here."

Nordstrom looked from one to another. "I suppose we'd better put the matter to a council vote," he said.

Mentally Connor ran through the other council members. He had a fair idea already which way the vote would go.

"We'll have to have some way of getting the ore here," said Sven. "What can we do in the way of shipping?"

Nordstrom gave a gesture of dismissal. "We can put together a prefabricated scow from our supplies. Two electric outboard motors side by side on the stern."

"The transom," murmured Sven.

Nordstrom looked at her in surprise. "You know about seacraft?"

"We used a lot on Ceti, between islands. Powered catamarans, things like that. Nothing very large. How big's this scow of ours?"

"Never seen it assembled. From the drawings, maybe twenty meters long."

"Won't shift much ore in that."

The discussion stalemated for a time, until Connor said, "How about a compromise on the location of the furnace?" When the others looked at him blankly, he went on. "You know that rocky point about thirty kilometers south of here? The ground's obviously firm there—basalt, wouldn't you say, Jiro?—and the point curves around to make a sheltered harbor. We could use the scow to bring ore that far, past the river estuary and the swamps, then carry the finished materials by land up to here. By the beach at low tide, later by a road."

Nordstrom said nothing for perhaps a quarter of a minute. Then he nodded. "The point's within sight of here in clear weather. But it's far enough away to keep the fumes of a furnace out of the town. Why not?"

"You're learning," Zella whispered to Connor as he was helping her put on her cape.

A minute or two later they were walking up the street towards their house, Zella with her hood over her face and her arms inside her cape. Connor, already soaked through to his skin, ignored the rain as he splashed his way along.

Once inside, Zella said, "Sorry, Con."

"Sorry? For what?"

"I realized later you wanted the furnace down south. I let you down, didn't I?"

"Not at all. Your point was a good one. I don't expect you to agree with me in everything."

"I'm glad." Suddenly they had their arms around each other, holding each other tightly while the rain roared on the metal and plastic roof of the building, shutting out all other external sounds. "God," she whispered, "I'm glad they put you in the expedition."

"And for me, you're the one person who makes this planet a potential paradise."

Suddenly she tilted her head back to look into his face. "That's lovely, darling. But it wasn't exactly what I was thinking about. Look, Con, I'm in trouble."

"Trouble? Aren't we all? We'll handle it."

"No. Chang and I are in special trouble. That's why it's important to me to have someone like you to talk with. Listen, Con, Chang and I are responsible for all the people still in stasis, 155 of them. Plus a number of carefully selected domestic animals. Each person in storage has a dossier attached to his unit, showing who, what training, what abilities, you name it."

"Yes?" he prompted as she paused. "So you can bring them awake as needed?"

"We've reached a deadlock," she said.

"But what's the problem? I know accommodation is the main one, but that can be handled if you bring them out a few at a time. Anyway, that's not your personal problem, is it?"

She shook her head. "It's not that. No, the trouble is that the kesrii have replaced some of our equipment with some of theirs. Did you and the other engineering brains around here ever wonder where the power was coming from?"

"Power?"

"The power that keeps them in stasis. It takes quite a bit. Temperature control, monitoring of dozens of different functions. On the ship we have an adequate power supply to draw on. Down here all those people are sleeping away in their units with no power going into the sheds."

"Hell, I never stopped to think of that! What's keeping them alive?"

"Kesrii technology, not ours. Different little units do all the monitoring, the temperature control, the blood analyses, encephalograms, the lot. They're mass-produced, modular units, beautifully made, far more compact and efficient than ours. And they have their own built-in power source.''

"What?''

"Little motors that run without any outside power being fed into them, as far as we can see. They're nearly driving Chang mad. We can't see how they work, and we're frightened to touch anything in case we kill the person in stasis.''

"What are you going to do? Can you bypass the kesrii equipment with your own?''

"We haven't got our original equipment. Anyhow, it would be useless if we had it, because we haven't a reliable outside source of power yet to run it—and that'd be essential, because a breakdown in the electric supply could kill the lot of them.''

"What happens if these kesrii motors stop working?''

"None of them have, fortunately. How long they'll keep going, Chang and I have no idea.''

"Could I have a look at them tomorrow?''

"Of course. But I don't think it'd do any good. The motors are completely enclosed with shells of hard metal.''

"How about one of the units holding one of the domestic animals you mentioned?''

"We don't want to lose one of those either. We have very few, naturally, and if one died at this stage, we might cut down the gene pool too far for the species to survive.''

Connor said nothing for a long time, just standing there and holding her. Then he tilted his head back to look at her.

"Zel, do you have an X-ray unit in your medical gear?''

"Yes. Why?''

"Have you tried X-raying one of those motors?''

"No. Let's go over and try it. But in the morning!''

The kesrii motors powering the hibernation units and their accessories were varied in size but similar in shape, round-ended cylinders, featureless except for an axial shaft protruding from one end and mounting lugs at the side. Their surface was of hard, mirror-smooth metal of a silver-blue color.

"No instruction books of any kind?'' asked Connor.

Doc Chang pointed to an inscription on one of the pumps. "I've tried to decipher that, but . . . Here, take a look.''

He handed Connor a magnifying lens, continuing to talk as Connor was examining the finely engraved characters.

"As you see, Con, the writing has no relation to any human script. We thought at first it might be ideogramic, like Chinese or Japanese, but we know now it's based on some sort of alphabet. I've looked at dozens of these. They use nearly a hundred different characters, which suggests the kesrii vocal apparatus can make a more complicated range of sounds than ours. Then there are other marks which appear to be numbers—see these?—probably giving voltages, amperages, RPM, things like that. They seem to use fourteen different figures, so what their mathematics is like I'd hate to guess."

He produced an X-ray camera, adjusted it to maximum power, and trained it on one of the motors. A medical unit built for exploring flesh and bone, it had insufficient power to penetrate the dense kesrii metal. The casing of the motor was as opaque as lead, giving no clue to the mechanism within.

"Well, it was an idea," said Connor. "Sorry."

By now most of the people at the base had developed a rhythm of two sleeping periods for each thirty-eight-hour day, one beginning around hour thirty-five and running through midnight to about hour three or four, while the other covered the hot part of the late morning and early afternoon. The storms of late afternoon made sleep impossible.

Many were still experimenting with different sleep periods, their circadian rhythms thoroughly disorganized. Only Nordstrom seemed unaffected—his lights were on in the HQ building throughout the night. No one had ever seen him sleep, but Connor was of the opinion that he was a very light sleeper who dozed during his work, waking easily when he heard anyone approach.

He knew about the problem of reactivating the people in stasis, and after the failure of the X ray to give any information about the interior of the kesrii motor, Connor went along with Zella to the HQ building in the early morning light to tell Nordstrom of the result.

"I wouldn't worry, Zella," said the chief. "We can't accommodate them until we have more buildings erected. By then we should have a reliable generating plant that should enable you to take over the load of the kesrii motors one by one, without interfering with the subjects' stasis. Meanwhile I've been going ahead with the boat project."

"Have we all the parts?" asked Connor.

"Parts for three metal scows, each about twenty meters long, four meters wide. Double walled. And when they're assembled, we can run polyurethane foam between the inner and outer hulls—should make them practically unsinkable."

"How about power?"

"Couple of big electric outboards on each. Not much thrust for rough water, but it's a start. First thing I have to organize is a team of about fifteen to put the sections together down on the beach. There's a hard, level stretch of sand where we can assemble them—I went down there tonight and had a look at it in the moonlight."

Soon after sunrise Nordstrom began getting together his team to assemble one ship, selecting a number of people who were physically strong and practical. He had them carry the sections of the vessel down to the hard stretch of beach and begin its assembly. The ship had been skillfully planned, and with the help of generous diagrams, they were able to get it together in a surprisingly short time. Connor, O'Donnel, and Sven went down to the beach only three hours after the assembly had begun, and found the ship almost complete, resting on rollers while the polyurethane foam was being pumped into all its hollow spaces.

Sven, who had more experience with small seacraft than any of the others, was openly scornful of the design.

"When it's loaded, there won't be enough freeboard. The first violent storm will sink it. And it won't have enough power to head into some of the winds we have here. We'll have to design our own ships."

"What would you suggest?" asked Nordstrom coldly.

"Catamaran. Double hull. Did you say you have two more of these?"

"Two, exactly like it."

"That might be a temporary solution—side by side, with a double deck right across, linking them together. Soon as possible we'd better get a steam engine built, with a wood-fired boiler. Propellers might give us some trouble, but with the two hulls we could fit a stern-mounted paddle wheel between them."

Nordstrom pondered. "Sounds like a museum piece. Archaic."

"But it's a tested design. It wouldn't sink. Especially if we used a lot of the foam in the hulls, making them like big floats, and carried the load on the decks.''

"I'll keep that in mind. Meanwhile we'll go ahead with this one as it is."

Sven looked at it. "Even that would be better with steam power. Stern paddle wheel."

"Later, perhaps," conceded Nordstrom. He didn't seem very happy.

Around hour fourteen—almost halfway through the morning—Connor's team rolled the ship down the beach into the water. The tide had just passed its ebb and was beginning to sweep back up the long, shallow slope of the beach, so that when most of the length of the boat was over water, it began to lift and thump on the rollers.

Connor stood alongside Nordstrom on a low dune. Sven had gone. Nordstrom glanced around.

"She's probably right, you know, Con. The men who designed the damned thing probably never saw a sea. All theoretical. Those motors aren't powerful enough."

"You have some for the other scows," said Connor. "Could you fit a third motor between those two?"

"Might. Still makeshift. In the long run steam engines are probably the best answer." Suddenly his voice recovered some of its customary enthusiasm. "Ah! She's floating!"

The maiden voyage of the scow was hardly impressive—a few hundred meters out across the lagoon, a turn into the long-shore current which drove it slowly backward against the thrust of its propellers, then a slanting run back to the beach, its reinforced bow grating on the sand about three hundred meters down-current from its starting point.

Nordstrom stood like a statue for perhaps half a minute. "That's it for now," he said, and turning, he strode up the street towards the HQ without looking back.

Connor stood watching his receding figure, and decided to leave the chief alone with his thoughts. It came to him that Nordstrom was used to having one hundred percent faith in the technology of his ship. Failure was something he had not been accustomed to experience.

He realized an hour later that he'd underestimated Nordstrom. Connor had gone along to help in the preparatory work O'Donnel and Sven and their half-dozen helpers were carrying out in the engineering shop. Suddenly, as they were busy shifting some pieces of machinery, the chief appeared in the doorway.

"You were right, Sven," he said as soon as he entered the building. "The scow is underpowered. How soon can you go ahead with your program for building a few steam engines?"

"A few?"

"The most vital is the one to run your line shafts here. Another, to generate electricity for the town. Another, for a steam truck to transport fuel from the forest. Two more for the ships and two for the tractors—I make that a total of seven engines. Can you do that?"

Sven looked at O'Donnel. "We have some general-purpose cylinders from stores. We could use battery power to operate the lathes to make one engine, then use that to power the plant here. The rest will follow. When we have our own iron, power will be no further problem. Mak says he can build boilers."

"What type?"

"Mak!" called Sven, and a stocky, sandy-haired man came from the other end of the shop. "About those boilers . . ."

Mak looked at Nordstrom. "We have plenty of boiler tubing, or steel tubing that will serve as boiler tube. Two of our boys say they can make bricks from the clay near here. We can build a water-tube boiler for the plant, and for the tractors and truck—and the boat, I suppose—we can use the lighter fire-tube type."

Nordstrom showed a flash of his old exuberance. "It looks as if we're on our way. I've just learned that our wheat is taking root, both in the open and under domes . . ."

The next ten days were filled with many achievements. The forty-nine people brought out of stasis had been, after all, highly selected for the original expedition. They combined a wide range of skills, adaptability, and energy. As work went ahead with the steam-power project, the need to conserve their battery power became less compelling.

A sawmill was set up on the outskirts of the dead forest, electrically powered but made for easy conversion to steam. While they still awaited the completion of the truck, one of the electric tractors was used with a long, improvised trailer to bring sawed planks of the native timber to the base. It was almost grainless, resembling kauri, as if it were a species someone had selected for building material. Someone, or something.

Always there were little reminders of the alien nature of the planet. An upward glance at the violet sky. The double shadows of the binary suns. The shrill buzz of invisibly small flying insects that no one ever succeeded in identifying. Then, several times, far out over the sea, straggling lines of the flying reptiles skimmed along parallel to the shore. Once, a swarm of them accumulated over a spot three or four kilometers offshore, swirling like scraps of burnt paper above a fire and diving repeatedly into the water. Evidently there was a concentration of marine prey there. Even from that distance their harsh screams carried on the wind.

Most of the settlers were stimulated by the activity, the goals, the hope. But Zella seemed to become more and more tense as the days passed.

"I feel responsible for those people still in stasis," she said one night, when Connor had already gone to bed. She was sitting by the battery light at a small table, making endless calculations.

"What are you doing?"

"I've got enlarged copies of the inscriptions on the kesrii motors and pumps. I'm trying to decode their figures."

"But you have no starting point."

"Yes, we have. The motor speed. We put a strobe on some of the motors. The bigger ones turn at 7518 RPM, and some of the smaller ones at 11,277."

Connor whistled. "Those are high revs for motors that don't get hot. And for motors with no power supply feeding into them."

"Yes, but there's a pattern. One of those speeds is exactly one and a half times the other."

"So? Most of our motors run at standardized speeds. Depends on the number of poles, and the frequency of the alternating current feeding . . ." He let his voice trail off.

"Exactly," she said. "There's no AC going into those motors."

"But look, Zel. All you'll ever get is the figures, and the symbols corresponding to RPM. No, not even that! Revolutions per minute! Per *minute*, Zel. An arbitrary period of time that's ours. The kesrii would use their own parcel of time. Could be anything.''

She put her fingers against her temples. ''You're right,'' she muttered, ''useless . . .''

He put his hands on her shoulders and gave her a gentle shake. ''Forget it for tonight, Zel. Listen, we've tested a couple of our steam engines—fitted the little one into the boat, and we've built a paddle wheel. We're testing it tomorrow. Why not take some time off and come with us for the ride?''

''I can't! Oh, I don't know. We're getting nowhere with these things, and Chang's going in circles over them. It'd do him good to handle the small emergencies that come up—cuts, indigestion, and so on. Yes, damn it! I'll take the time off!''

In bed, with the room dimly lit by a streak of yellow moonlight, he watched her lying beside him, staring up at the ceiling. ''Okay?'' he whispered.

She shook her head, her eyes open. ''No, it's not. They've got seven digits on each hand.''

''*What?*''

''The kesrii. They'd never think in tens and hundreds and thousands, like us. It'd be fourteens, hundred and ninety-sixes, two thousand seven . . .'' Her voice grew blurred with fatigue.

''Two seven forty-four,'' he finished for her after a mental struggle with sleep. But she made no answer. She was already asleep. He put his arm over her, and she rolled towards him. Outside, the scream of a pterosaur rang eerily on the wind, but Zella did not stir.

8

Soon after the primary sun rose above the inland ridge, Connor took Zella down to the engineering shop. Busy with her problem of the people in stasis, she had not seen it for several days, and as they walked down the street she pointed suddenly to the steel smokestack tall behind it, with blue-gray wood smoke rising into the air. Near the stack a thinner pipe was exhausting regular puffs of white vapor.

"They've got our first steam engine running," said Connor with satisfaction.

"Already! How?"

"We had some general-purpose cylinders in our supplies. We had to make the crankshaft, valve gear, and the rest of it here in the shop, using our batteries to run the machines."

Zella breathed deeply. "Smell the sea! I'm glad I came out. Those symbols on the kesrii motors were driving me schizoid."

As they neared the engineering shop, they could hear the pulsating hiss of the engine and the slap of belting on pulleys. The boiler had been built outside of the long shed, and the engine had been set up close to it inside.

"Three cylinders," said Zella, looking at it in surprise.

"It's a double-acting compound engine," said Connor, repeating what O'Donnel had told him. "The steam goes into the high-pressure cylinder first, then comes out with still enough pressure to work the other two."

112

A broad belt of woven nylon transmitted power to an overhead line shaft extending the length of the building, with other belts running down to the lathes and a grinder.

"We had to make the big pulleys out of local wood." Connor had to shout above the sound of the machinery.

"Does it have to be this noisy?"

"As long as we have to work with overhead shafting, yes. People back on Earth put up with this sort of thing for a century or more. At least we know it's a stopgap."

Sven, enormous in a gray, oil-streaked coverall, joined them. "Stopgap? We had this setup back home for a very long time. Might be there still, for all I know. We were always too busy with other things to update it."

"How's the engine for the scow?" asked Connor.

"Already in. With its boiler. Mak's got the furnace going now, but he won't have much steam pressure yet. Go down and take a look at it."

Down at the beach the scow still rested with its bow on the sand. "High tide's around the middle of the day," said Connor. "Opposite the biggest moon. As the water rises, we can float her off."

The scow was unrecognizable from the vessel that had been ignominiously beached on its first voyage. A long metal funnel rose above its boiler, which was of the fire-tube type once used in railroad locomotives. Wood smoke was trickling from the top of it. Four men were building a square wheel-house with overlapping boards of the treated local wood.

Mak, who was on board, saw Connor and waved to him to join him. Connor and Zella walked down the hard sand and mounted a ladder leaning against the side of the ship—Connor realized he was beginning to think of it as a ship now, not the scow it appeared to be on the original expedition's inventory. He was astonished at its transformation. Heavy, treated beams of local timber reinforced it aft of center, supporting boiler and engine, and a raised deck formed a floor for the wheel-house. A sheet of transparent plastic guarded the paddle wheel.

"We'll put in a crane later," said Mak, "and a generator driven from the engine for lights."

As the tide neared its maximum, Mak, with Sven and several helpers aboard, backed the ship out into the lagoon.

They made a short experimental journey across the calm water, driving against the long-shore current which had over-powered the thrust of the electric outboards. After half an hour they brought it back to its starting point.

Sven was happy with its performance. She talked of its speed in some archaic units called knots, then realized no one else knew what she meant, and translated it to ten or twelve kilometers per hour.

"Not much, but we could get more with higher steam pressure."

"I'd like to try her out in rougher water," said Mak. "If she has a weakness, better we find out now."

Kosaka, who had joined the spectators on the beach, said, "I'd like to take her out and have a look at the islands. Especially that one." He pointed.

"That the one with the nuclear reactor on the other side?" Connor asked.

Kosaka nodded.

"I'd be game to take her out," said Mak. "She has a sound hull, and the engine's fine."

There was a lull for a few seconds, then Connor said, "An old saying I heard somewhere: A ship is safe in harbor, but that's not what she was built for."

"Let's go," said Kosaka, looking from Connor to Mak.

"Wait a moment," broke in Zella, who had been standing quietly by. "I'd like to come with you."

Connor turned. "There might be some danger, Zel. I don't think the chief would like one of our two doctors at risk. Neither would I," he added in a lower voice.

Zella looked at the ship, her eyes bright, the red spots on her cheeks the only color in her otherwise pale face. "One of you might have an accident. You need a ship's medical officer."

"Let her come," said Mak. "She'll be as safe as on shore."

Connor looked at Zella for a long time, while she stared back at him. "Okay," he said at last.

As Sven had predicted, the speed of the ship rose slightly as the boiler generated a higher pressure of steam. Some of the technology of the interstellar age had modified the float-

ing anachronism of the steamboat, so that instead of shouted
orders, they had practically every function controlled from the
wheelhouse. The short logs of firewood from the dead forest
were carried into the furnace by a kind of moving grating
Sven called the automatic stoker, geared from the engine, but
with its movement controllable from alongside the steering
wheel. The large hand-painted dial of the pressure gauge was
also visible from the wheelhouse, together with a speedome-
ter contrived to operate from a small outboard paddle wheel
driving through a flexible cable.

If the calibration was correct, they moved out towards the
islands at twelve kilometers per hour, the paddle wheel thrashing at the stern. All four of them remained in the wheelhouse,
Mak steering, Connor scanning the water ahead with binoculars, Kosaka staring fixedly at the island, and Zella leaning
out of one of the openings in the wall intended for windows,
breathing in the salt air with an almost ecstatic smile. The
wind ruffled her red-gold hair, which Connor noticed she had
allowed to grow longer.

After about an hour the ship began to pitch slightly. They
were approaching the break in the reef, feeling the heavy
swell of water coming in from the open ocean beyond. Now,
looking through the gap between the islands, they could see
the different color of the sea beyond the reef line—a dark
indigo blue, flecked near the opening with white.

"It's around to the left," said Kosaka, "on the seaward
side of this island."

"I'll keep well out from the rocks at the end of it," said
Mak.

As they entered the break, it seemed they were not moving
forward at all, only pitching and wallowing as the waves
struck them from an angle. But by taking a line of sight on
the rock formations of the island, they found they were
moving steadily out into the deeper water.

Mak turned left, and they ran along parallel to the island's
outer coast. There were jutting promontories enclosing small
bays, with startlingly white beaches.

"Rocks look like granite," said Kosaka, peering through
binoculars. "Ha! There's our generator!"

"We could get in there, I think," said Connor. "Sheltered,
shallow. Look at the color of the water."

The water within the bay was a clear turquoise, lightened by a white sandy bottom in the shallows. Mak reduced speed, chugging carefully in under the shelter of an outlying islet linked to the beach by a spit of sand. At last the reinforced bottom of the scow grated on the sand.

"I'd better stay aboard, in case the tide floats her off. Hate to be stuck out here without transport."

Connor, Zella, and Kosaka sprang ashore, walking up the beach above the line of flotsam left there by the highest tide. There seemed to be no shells of fish, although there were bands of brown weed somewhat like terrestrial bladder wrack.

The nuclear generator stood well clear of the farthest reach of the waves, with a covered stack of drums near it. The generator was a cube of green-enameled metal with rounded edges, the top of it painted black.

"But why?" muttered Connor.

"Why what?" asked Zella.

"Why'd they paint the top of the thing black? It wasn't to hide it—the black shows up against this sand as well as the green. Not to protect it either. The original finish would stand up to anything."

"Perhaps they just liked the color."

Connor shook his head. "Everything else they've done seems to have had a reason, even though sometimes we've been slow to see what it was."

Kosaka had walked from the generator down to the edge of the water. Now he came back. "We could float it off at high tide," he said. "Maybe rig a crane up and lift it aboard the scow. We could use rollers to get it down to the edge."

Connor walked over to the fuel drums, feeling one corner of the black plastic cover. "Thin, this stuff, but tough," he said, trying to tear it.

"Here," said Kosaka. He produced a vibroknife and switched it on while Connor held the fabric taut. The blade, blurred with ultrasonic vibration, cut slowly through the black fabric. Connor looked at the piece as it came away, then borrowed the knife and cut away a piece of dried paint from the generator. He wrapped it in the piece of fabric and folded it, putting it in his pocket.

"I'll get Nargis Lal to analyze this stuff in the lab she's setting up," he said.

Zella had walked a few meters along the beach. "Wonder what's beyond that next little point."

"Let's find out," said Connor. As they walked along together, she gave a sudden laugh.

"I feel as if I'm sixteen."

"Standard years? Or this planet's years?"

She slapped his arm, and they walked happily along towards the point, where broken rock jutted out towards the ocean. They climbed carefully over the rocks and down onto another crescent of white granite-sand beach, utterly deserted. The fine sand squeaked under their feet.

"Worth remembering this place," said Connor. "In case we need optical sand some time. This is the stuff they use to make lenses."

"I thought the best lenses were done by bending light magnetically now."

"Be a long time before we get around to that here."

Connor was walking on the side next to the sea. Suddenly Zella screamed. The sound seemed to send an electric shock through all his muscles. She was pointing out to sea. Connor spun around, his heart pounding violently.

Hovering above the water, half a kilometer offshore, was a black flying machine, nothing like a human-designed flier. It looked as if it had been molded from a single piece of metal, with a pointed nose and a triangular wing whose tips swept backward and sharply upward to form rudders, or stabilizing fins. It hung motionless about five meters above the tops of the waves. For perhaps two minutes they stood watching it, while it made no movement. How long it had been there, they had no idea.

As they looked at it, it suddenly turned, the needle nose pointing straight towards them. It showed no outward sign of the power that lifted or propelled it. Then Zella shrieked as it skimmed directly towards them at a frightening speed, accelerating like a projectile fired from an invisible gun.

With a shout, Connor flung his arm around Zella and threw both of them prone on the sand. The machine came to a complete halt with its needle-sharp nose only ten meters away from them, motionless in the air despite the blustering wind.

Connor had the feeling he was looking at a picture faked by double printing. The thing seemed to have no connection with its environment. It sank down until its flattened lower surface was only twenty or thirty centimeters above the beach, and now he could see a disturbance in the loose grains of sand immediately below it. It was not the kind of disturbance that would have come from downward-thrusting jets. Instead it gave the effect of the sand being compressed by an unseen weight.

He put his hand on Zella's arm. It felt tense, but was not trembling. "Let's get up," he whispered.

They stood up, dusting the sand grains from themselves. The machine turned very slowly in the air, so that one side of it was partly towards them. It seemed to have no doors or windows, although where windows would normally have been on an aircraft, there were roughly rectangular areas where the texture of the metal surface looked slightly different. It was as though the black metal had been fitted with inserts of black obsidian.

"What do we do now?" asked Zella quietly.

"Wait."

The machine was about twenty meters long, and as he looked at it with some of the panic in him subsiding, Connor noted something wrong with the shape of it. The back-swept wings seemed too small to support it, and their center of lift would have been much too far aft of the thing's center of gravity. At least by the standards of human aeronautical engineering, the object could never have flown—yet he had seen it give a performance that no aircraft made by man could have equaled. As he stood there, he felt a strange sensation of emptiness within him.

Suddenly the side of the craft opened, as if a large door had slid silently aside. He did not see whether it slid sideways or upward. Within an instant a large section of the side of the craft was not there. He remembered the doors that seemed to vanish and reappear in the kesrii laboratory where they had communicated with him through their language machine.

With a smooth, effortless movement, a tall black-and-white figure stepped out on to the sand, facing them. Tall even for a kesri, it wore a close-fitting airtight suit of gleaming black material, with a white helmet, white gloves enclosing its seven-digit hands, and white boots on its three-toed feet. Through the transparent panel in the front of the huge helmet, large, lime-yellow eyes looked at them with the unmistakable cruciform pupils.

It strode unhesitatingly towards them, stopping only an arm's length away. It was more than a head taller than Connor's height of nearly two meters. Then, through a vibrating diaphragm in the front of its helmet, it spoke to them.

"Zel-la. Con-nor. I greet."

It was not using one of the translation machines the kesrii had used before. It seemed to be achieving human speech, or a reasonable imitation of it, by its own vocal apparatus. The voice was deep, reverberating, carefully articulated. With a quick movement it lifted one of the gloved seven-fingered hands and spread it against its chest.

"Kralg," it said.

Connor could only assume that was its individual name.

"Kralg," he repeated. "I greet."

Zella took a short step forward. "Kralg," she said, "I greet." Her voice sounded high and light compared with Connor's, and the kesri's eyes moved quickly as they scanned her body. Perhaps it was the first female human voice it had heard.

Connor whispered from the side of his mouth, "What comes after hello?" He expected the kesri's helmet would not allow the slight sound to reach its ears, but the strange eyes immediately turned to him. From their expression, he had the impression it had not only heard him, but understood him. After this brief glance, it turned its attention back to Zella. Then, with lightning swiftness, it whirled and looked at the rocks at the end of the beach from which Connor and Zella had come.

Following its glance, Connor saw Kosaka's head and shoulders disappearing behind a cleft in the ridge of rock. The kesri made a beckoning movement with both arms, and now its strange voice was a crash of thunder.

"Ji-ro. I greet. Come!"

There was something so compelling in the kesri's movement that Connor was not surprised when Kosaka emerged into full view and began scrambling down the rocks to the beach. He walked along the squeaking sand until he was standing alongside the others, with Zella between him and Connor.

On an impulse Connor waved a hand towards Kosaka, then to the kesri. "Jiro, this is Kralg."

"Kralg," said Kosaka, making a stiff little bow.

Kralg acknowledged his greeting with a hand movement, then turned his attention to Zella.

"You and Chang re-ac-ti-vate—"

"We bring people out of stasis," finished Zella. "Yes. But we have trouble."

The kesri said a word they couldn't identify. Zella went on.

"We don't understand your stasis machines." She spoke very slowly and distinctly. "We cannot reactivate people."

The kesri said something in a rapid, torrential language, and reached one hand behind him towards his aircraft. He did not turn around.

From the door of the machine came an object like a flat box. How it was supported or propelled, Connor was unable to determine, nor did he have any idea who controlled its movements. It moved straight through the air to the kesri's extended hand. He took hold of it without looking at it and held it in front of Zella.

He said some word, unpronounceable to humans, which might have been the name of the device. It resembled a calculator with a display screen. It was obviously built for manipulation by the kesri hand, and he held it with his two large, opposed digits gripping it like an immovable clamp, leaving the five slender, flexible members to dance with lightning speed over the array of tightly congested keys.

A picture appeared on the small screen, showing in excellent color and sharpness one of the kesrii motors of the type used on the stasis units. A touch of more keys showed detailed views of the mechanism and its controls, then three-dimensional diagrams that could be rotated on the screen to show the interior workings of motors, pumps, and regulators.

"The thing's the equivalent of an instruction book," said Connor. "An owner's manual."

"It's marvelous." Zella raised her eyes to the helmeted head of the kesri. "But how . . . how did you know I . . . ?" She didn't finish.

Kralg switched the unit off, then on and off again, making sure she was watching what he did. Then he turned it around and held it out to her.

"You take," he said. "Tell what needed."

Zella took the unit from him. She had a little difficulty holding it. "Hold it for me, Con," she said. "It's made for those two long thumb things to go around here, while his fingers reach the keys."

Connor held the body of the unit. It was somewhat heavier than he expected. The keys were of different colors, although about half of them were black, and they were so closely set together that she had to take a pencil from her pocket to press them. The fingers of the kesri tapered to what were really claws. The keys had different symbols engraved in them, but they were meaningless. Zella touched some experimentally, and an array of images flashed on the screen. She looked up at the kesri.

"Thank you. Thank you very much. But how did you know—"

But the kesri was already turning away. His machine moved a little closer to him. He stepped into it, giving the three humans a gesture of farewell. Then the door in the side of the machine was instantly shut. The windows resembling obsidian shielded all view of the interior. The machine turned and shot away from them over the sea. Air swirled around them as it went, but it was not the drive of a jet. It was simply air rushing in to occupy the space left by the departing machine.

Out over the sea it suddenly pointed its nose vertically upward, and they heard a rising whistle as it climbed with unbelievable speed into the clouds. From far, far above came the sounds of a trans-sonic boom.

"But how? How did he know?" Zella looked at Connor, her red brows pulled together in a frown. "Only Chang and I knew about the trouble we were having with the stasis machines. And you, of course, and the chief. But how did Kralg know?"

"Perhaps their machines were bugged," suggested Kosaka. "The motors, say. You and Chang could have talked about your problems near the machines. Could that be?"

"It's possible."

"But something else bothers me more than that," said Connor. "How the hell did he know how to find you *here*?"

Her eyes were wide. "It's as if they know everything we do. It's almost . . ."

"Almost what?"

"It's almost as if they could read minds."

Connor thought about that idea for a while, a sensation of cold seeping through him. Then he took a long breath.

"No. I don't think so. Otherwise they wouldn't have needed things like their translation machines."

"You're probably right. But God, Con, they're good!"

"Too damn good for us, from the look of it."

"There's another thing that worries me," said Kosaka. "How did he know I was up there on the rocks? He didn't look towards me, I'm sure of that, because I was watching him from the moment he stepped out of his machine."

"When did you first see the machine?"

"I looked out to sea, and it was hovering over the water. Perhaps five hundred meters away. I didn't see it come. I ran along to warn you, but by the time I climbed the rocks, the thing was hovering right on top of you."

"We couldn't see inside it," said Connor. "Perhaps he had a mate inside who was looking out. He might have spotted you, alerted Kralg by helmet radio, something like that."

"There must have been someone else inside," agreed Zella. "Did you see the way something floated this instrument out to him while he stood with his hand behind him to take it?"

"I saw it. I want to forget it."

Zella looked upward towards the cloudy sky. "I wonder if they watch us all the time, from up there?"

"Maybe," said Connor. "But how did they know *you* were going to come out to the island?"

The three of them, as if by unspoken agreement, began walking back to where they had left the scow.

"Point is," said Kosaka as they walked, "what do we do about it?"

"I know what I'm going to do," said Zella emphatically, lifting up the instrument Kralg had given her. "I'm going to learn how to use this thing. Get all I can out of it. Never mind why he gave it to us, or how he found me. Or how he knew it was me who needed it."

Connor had nothing to say until they reached the scow. Mak called to them as they approached, standing on the roof of the wheelhouse with a pair of binoculars.

"What was it?"

"He'll have to know about this," said Connor to the others. "But for now, just the four of us. Okay?"

"See the thing take off?" shouted Mak as they drew nearer. "Reckon he went straight into orbit."

"One of the kesrii," said Connor, climbing aboard the scow. "Checking up on us, I think."

"Because we came looking at the generator?" Mak saw the instrument Zella was carrying. "What's that?"

"Wait a moment," said Connor. He waited until all of them were on the deck, including Mak, who had come down from the roof. "I think we'd better say nothing about this encounter, outside of the four of us and just the chief and one or two of the people we know who are not likely to panic. Obviously we're being watched a lot more closely than we thought. How, I don't know. But for the present it's better if it stays between us. Right?"

Zella shook her head. "You have a medieval streak in you sometimes, Con." She made her voice sound sepulchral. " 'There are some things it is better for man not to know!' Is that it?"

Connor shrugged. "Let's play it by ear. You'll have to tell Chang, of course—but he's level-headed enough to take it."

"Who else should know?" asked Kosaka.

"The chief, of course. Maybe Charl. Fewer the better." Connor looked at the sky. "We'd better start back. How's the pressure, Mak?"

"Ready to go."

The reverse drive of the paddle wheel dragged the scow off the sand, helped by the still rising tide. The craft rolled and pitched as it slanted across the long, incoming swell from the open ocean, but once through the gap in the reef it ran smoothly enough.

Zella was absorbed in the instrument Kralg had given her. "We might be able to decode some of their symbols from this," she said. "But I wonder why so many of the keys are black, when they've used different colors on the others."

"Let's have a look." Connor frowned. "Some of these 'blacks' are slightly off-black. See, that's a very deep violet. Say, I wonder if they see different frequencies from us? Further into the ultraviolet?"

"Possible." Zella suddenly shook her head angrily. "We

know almost nothing about them, medically. But they know quite a lot about us, from their dissection of Marek. Very likely they *do* see other colors from us, but I don't know where that gets us.''

"Nor do I, at the moment. But it's something to keep in mind.''

Connor stared thoughtfully ahead as the ship pounded its way onward.

9

As they neared the beach the whole of the sky was black, with an ominous ceiling of cloud only a couple of hundred meters above. Behind them lightning was already flickering between sky and sea like a giant welding arc.

The temperature had dropped sharply with the shutting out of direct sunlight, and Mak was left shivering alone in the wheelhouse to steer while the others crowded down close to the boiler and the hissing steam cylinders.

"At least they can't spy on us in this," said Kosaka, pointing upward. Connor was about to reply that he had seen vidicons that could penetrate the densest cloud, but he decided that would add nothing to the peace of mind of either of his companions.

The lightning came closer, a blinding double flash lighting up the ship from either side and bringing a surprised yell from Mak. Zella moved a little closer to Connor, and he put his arm around her shoulders.

"No welcoming committee on the beach," said Kosaka. "The storm's taken care of that."

"Just as well," said Connor, indicating the instrument still clutched by Zella. "I wouldn't want to explain *that* to too many people."

Connor and Kosaka moved forward as Mak drove the scow carefully up to the edge of the beach. When its reinforced bow grated on the sand, they jumped overboard with the mooring cables, dragging them up the shallow slope and looping them over the bollards that had been driven into the ground above high-tide level. Mak shut the furnace door, turned off the steam valves, and dropped a ladder over the side. Climbing down, he helped Zella down to the sand while she still held the precious kesrii instrument against her as if it had been a baby.

"Remember," said Connor, as the four of them hurried up the street, "apart from the four of us, only the chief, Karl O'Donnel, Chang, and Charl Harn get to know anything about what happened out there."

"Why not all the council?" asked Zella.

"Who else would that bring in? Nargis—she'd be okay. Sven, okay. Asgard Price—I'm not sure about him."

"But if all the council knew, we could discuss it freely in the meetings," said Zella. "We don't want our society to break into a number of competing dictatorships. Do we?"

"I think she's right, Con," said Mak. Kosaka gave a noncommittal grunt that could have been taken to mean anything.

Connor plodded up the slope in silence for a few paces. "All right. I can see the sense in that. But we must emphasize to the rest of the council that it goes no further. Right?"

The others, after a moment's hesitation, agreed.

"Now," said Connor, "the chief first, eh?"

Again, agreement. They headed for the HQ building.

Nordstrom showed unexpectedly little surprise when they told him about the black kesrii aircraft.

"I expected something like that. This morning I saw an orbiting satellite go over. It was just before dawn, but high enough to catch the sunlight."

"What was it like?"

"Just a bright point of light, like a star. A slight dimming about three times a minute, suggesting it was rotating."

There was silence for a few seconds. "And yet," said Connor thoughtfully, "the kesrii don't seem to have used rotation in their spacecraft, from what we've seen of them. They make their internal gravity with some kind of field."

"True," agreed Nordstrom. "That bothered me, too. But sometimes they might use rotation to save power, especially in a satellite in a long-term orbit."

"Which way was it traveling?"

"Northeast to southwest. Disappeared into the shadow of the planet about halfway across the sky. I think the thing's in a permanent surveillance orbit—we just haven't noticed it pass before." He looked at the instrument Zella was carrying. "Let's have a look at the gizmo he gave you, Zella."

She seemed to clutch the device more tightly against her. "Not yet, Chief, if you don't mind. I want to get all our people safely out of stasis before anyone tries to pull this thing to pieces."

"That makes sense." Nordstrom laughed. "But you'll have to learn to use it first. I think we'd better get Nargis in on this. She has her electronics lab set up now."

"How would that help?" Zella sounded defensive.

"I'd suggest we use a video camera to cover the keyboard and display screen, so we can keep a record of what happens when you touch each of those keys, or any combination of them."

Zella thought for a moment. "I'd go along with that."

At the emergency council meeting called by Nordstrom within the next hour, the thunder of rain on the roof compelled everyone to shout to be heard, a situation hardly conducive to a placid session. Reactions to the news of the visit by the black machine of the kesrii were mixed. The most emotional response came from Asgard Price.

"Then we're only specimens in a zoo!" he burst out.

"We knew that all along," said Connor.

"But this means we have no real privacy!"

"So what do you want to do about it?" asked O'Donnel, deadpan. "Walk up and down the street with protest banners?"

Price looked around the table with eyes that seemed to bulge. "Could someone have tipped them off?"

"What do you mean?" Nordstrom's voice sounded dangerously calm.

"How did they know Zella—the only person who could benefit from that instrument—would be out there on that island?"

Nordstrom's voice hardened. "Are you seriously suggesting someone among us contacted the kesrii? How?"

Price gestured towards the kesrii instrument. "They gave

Zella that piece of equipment. They might have given someone a radio.''

There was an angry murmur around the table. Nordstrom
kept looking at Price, his eyes cold.

''Or,'' he said, ''as Jiro suggested, they might simply have
bugged the machines they left to operate the stasis equipment.
Asgard, I think we'd better all cool it on this one.''

He looked around the table, but no one else spoke.

''Now, listen. We know we're under surveillance, but it's
going to achieve nothing to start everyone in the base looking
over his shoulder for kesrii. We can all agree now that we're
up against a race with superior technology, whether we like it
or not. If they wished, they could at any time have exterminated us like vermin. But they didn't. On the contrary, they've
gone to some trouble to ensure our survival. Apparently at
least one of them has been interested enough to learn some of
our language.''

''This is like the situation of the human researchers who
taught chimpanzees to communicate in sign language,'' said
Nargis Lal.

''Something like that, but not quite. They've gone a bit
further. The researchers you're talking about, as far as I
know, didn't attempt to speak in chimpanzee language.''
Nordstrom looked at Zella. ''How well did this Kralg speak?''

''With an odd accent, but not bad considering he had quite
different mouth formation. Their jaw is more feline, although
their lips seem to be very mobile. He hadn't much idea of our
syntax or idiom, though. Put words together in a different
order.''

''But he tried,'' said Nordstrom. ''That's the point. And
that suggests he expects the experiment to go on a long
time.''

The roar of the rain diminished slowly. The windows were
suddenly incandescent with lightning, and a crash shook the
building only a second or two later.

Price cleared his throat, as his voice seemed to jam for a
moment before he went on. ''It looks as if our first priority
should be to send a message to the nearest human settlement.''

''We've been through that,'' objected Connor.

''Exactly,'' said Nordstrom, looking around the table. ''Anyone with anything positive to contribute?''

There was a pause, and then Nargis Lal's voice sounded on

a level tone, almost a monotone. "I would think the first priority is dealing with the people still in stasis. I think I should set up a camera to record Zella's experiments with the instrument given her by the kesrii. That should take precedence over everything else."

"I agree with that," said Zella emphatically.

"Right," said Nordstrom. "As we carry on with accommodation projects, we can bring small groups out of stasis as needed. We have dossiers on all 155 still in hibernation. "The first priority should be people with food-producing experience. . . ."

As they went into details of the future awakening of their population, most of them forgot, for the time, the overshadowing presence of the kesrii.

But Connor, as he stepped out of the building after the cessation of the rain, was unable to repress a tendency to glance upward at the enigmatic sky.

Nargis Lal and Zella started work on recording the effects of the instrument keyboard on its display screen. The room set aside for an electronics laboratory was already quite well equipped and brightly lit. It had been, with the surgery, one of the first buildings in the center to be connected up to the new steam-driven generator.

Connor watched for a while, but decided it was going to take quite a long time for the two women to master the device. Pressure on one key at a time seemed to achieve nothing, but simultaneous depression of three or more produced bright, sharp images on the screen. One difficulty was the difference between the human hand and the kesrii hand, for which the keyboard had been made. The kesri had been able to grasp the base of the unit in his two opposed thumbs, while the long, supple, clawlike digits curved over the keyboard.

Zella hit the idea of clamping the unit in a frame and making a system of extension rods that had contact with the close-packed keys, but fanned out to let the shorter, blunter human fingers operate them.

"That's going to take a while to set up," said Connor. "I'll call back later."

The regular afternoon storm was over now, and Connor was able to smell wet vegetation as he walked down to the

HQ building. He knocked on Nordstrom's office door and was called in.

"Chief, in view of all the things that have happened, do you think we need to make some weapons?"

"What kind? Lasers? Guns? Bows?"

"I was thinking of the pterosaurs. Some kind of rifle, maybe. Repeating, if they could manage that in our machine shop."

Nordstrom looked at him keenly, and slowly shook his head. "I don't think that's a good idea, Con. It's not the pterosaurs I'm thinking of. It's the kesrii. Remember what they did to Marek."

"Well, he was actually threatening one of them with a gun, wasn't he?"

"The point is that he didn't get far. They reacted very quickly. We have to remember that, Con. Provoked, they're damn fast—and deadly."

"Uh-huh. Just a thought."

"Let's wait until we see how closely they watch us, and for how long." He stood up. "Come and look at this."

He led the way to one of the windows facing away from the street. "There," he said.

At first Connor didn't grasp what he was supposed to be looking at. The flier stood on the level ground behind the HQ, but he could see nothing unusual about it.

"Not there. Farther away. On the slopes."

Connor gave a sudden cry. "That tinge of green!"

"Right! It's wheat! The last rain brought it up, right along the slopes."

"There's someone over that way still plowing."

"I know. Still on batteries. When Karl had a look at one of the tractors with the idea of converting it to steam, he said it'd be better to build a much bigger tractor." He put a hand on Connor's shoulder. "We're on our way, Con. On our way!"

The next ten days saw a considerable advance in the growth of the settlement, without any further intervention from the kesrii. The large steam tractor was completed; ugly, functional, largely improvised from parts that had been brought down from the expedition ship. Fitted with a dozer blade, it rapidly completed the road out to Furnace Point, as the site of the future iron furnace had become known.

The furnace itself was taking shape under the direction of Karl O'Donnel, built up from laser-sawed blocks of nearby stone. Sven, with experience of charcoal smelting from Ceti, supervised the building of a kiln close to the furnace, and loads of dead wood were brought in by tractor-drawn trailer from the former forest.

Connor, Mark, and a crew of three took the scow down the coast to Iron Ridge, anchoring in a sheltered mooring place. They loaded some of the hematite that had slipped down from the cliffs into a sloping talus—"the easiest first," as Mak said—and took it back to the side of the steadily growing furnace.

Going home on the third day, Connor found the house empty. He crossed to the surgery, where he saw Zella and Chang studying the data they had obtained from the device give them by Kralg.

"We know how their machines work now," said Zella triumphantly. She touched a number of the extension rods fitted to the keyboard, and a series of colored pictures and diagrams appeared in swift succession on the screen. She pointed to controls on the motors and pumps of one of the stasis machines, and their position on a diagram. "Temperature control here. This thing's a thermometer, although we can't read it yet."

"Have you brought anyone out?" Connor looked at the line of stasis units that had been brought up from the shed where the kesrii had left them.

"Not yet," said Chang. "There are more than a 150, remember, and each one has a dossier, giving the experience and capacities of the person within. We're making our selection according to who's most urgently needed."

Connor walked along the line of coffinlike units. "There are different shapes."

"Naturally," said Chang. "The expedition included people from a number of worlds. It's only now that Zel and I are looking through the dossiers that we realize what a diversity of human types we have here."

"You see, Con,'" added Zella, "the original purpose of the expedition was to seed planets out along the Orion Arm.

We didn't know what types of planets we'd encounter. So we carried a wide range of potential settlers."

Chang waved a hand towards the units. "Some, like Zella and me, are from Omicron-2 Eridani. Earthlike, but somewhat lighter grav. We tend to be of three types—dark, like me, or blond and red-haired, like Zel, or more frequently now, a blend of the two. At some point in our development we must have narrowed down to two small but highly selected gene pools.

"Then you have people like Sven, all female, from her heavy-grav world of Tau Ceti 2. And then there are the people who originated on synthetic satellites—as you did."

"Those who came from stations that spun to keep up normal gravity, or who used exercise machines were fine," Zella said. "The ones that are going to give us a real headache are the zero-grav people."

"Why did the expedition include them?"

"Never thought we'd be stranded dirtside," said Chang. "These people have always lived in satellites or small asteroids. They operate machines for mining surfaces of planets by remote control. We'd always assumed there'd be plenty of places for people to work in zero g. As to what we do with them here . . ." He shrugged his shoulders.

"One of them's going to be a special problem for me," said Zella. "Their doctor. He worked with me in the hospital at Eridan. Used an exoskeleton, power operated. Weird. No attempt to look human. Six jointed legs that worked in threes, like an ant, and extended manipulators. Things like that. And he's right there." She nodded to the stasis container at the far end of the line. It was no more than half the length of the others. Connor walked along to it.

"You mean there's a being in *that*?"

"That's right. Nothing much except his head and an almost spherical trunk, with hands and vestigial feet. A sphere's an efficient shape in free fall."

Connor shook his head. "Can't help you with this one, Zel."

"Might have to put them in tanks first," said Chang. "In watertight suits. We can adjust them physically to the gravity. But socially, mentally—aiee!" He spread out his hands.

Connor went home. He sat up for a time, looking at copies of Mak's drawings for a suggested crane to be mounted on the scow. He'd wanted Connor to express an opinion on two alternatives. In one the crane was to be steam powered, with a lagged pipe running forward from the boiler. In the other it was electric, drawing current from a generator run from the existing engine. Connor decided the electric form would give less trouble. He made some coffee and was drinking it thoughtfully when Zella came in.

"Hi," she said in a flat voice. "I'm just about out on my feet." She flopped down on the bed, sprawling with her hands over her eyes.

"I'll get you a coffee," he said.

"Thanks." While he was at the heater she said, "We brought two of them out of stasis tonight!"

"How did they come out?"

"Fine. We just did what the kesrii diagrams told us, and both people are fully conscious."

"Who did you bring out?"

"Two of the food-production specialists, as the chief wanted. They're both from Eridan. From our city. We thought we'd have less problems explaining things to them. One's a man, racially my type, and the other's a girl of Chang's group."

"Must be a relief to have them come through okay." By the time Connor returned with the coffee, she was asleep, lying flat on her back with her lips parted, one forearm over her eyes. She did not even wake while he gently eased her boots off and threw a blanket over her. Sitting on the edge of the bed, he slowly drank both coffees, then carefully rolled her onto her side to quiet her breathing. He undressed and climbed in beside her.

As soon as Zella awoke the next morning she dressed quickly and rushed over to the surgery to see how the two newly reactivated people were adjusting. She returned after a few minutes, while Connor was preparing breakfast.

"They're sleeping. But I'll have to get back there soon. Chang's been up all night."

Connor passed her a bowl of synthetic food cakes and poured some warm water on them. "Just think," he said, "in another few months we might be eating real food. Organic. Grown here on our own planet."

"*Is* it our own planet? Never mind."

They ate in silence for a while. "You know," said Connor, "the development of this base is really accelerating. The wheat they sowed is showing up all along the slopes. Kilometers of it. The furnace is nearly finished, and we've brought the first load of hematite up from Iron Ridge."

"Be more changes when we bring out more people."

"Yes. But there's one thing that bothers me, Zel."

"What's that?" She took her bowl over to the tap and rinsed it with the water from the recently installed heating system.

"It's this: What happens when the kesrii's experiment is finished?"

Her eyes looked suddenly dark as she turned to look at him. She opened her mouth twice as if to speak, then apparently changed her mind. Then she looked at the clock.

"I'll have to go, Con," she said, and ran quickly out.

10

By now the engineering shop team had been augmented by several new recruits, probably because it was showing more obvious results than any other branch of the settlement's activities. Admittedly, the sowing of crops was of vital importance, but so far the only noticeable return for the work was the transparent shimmer of green on the slopes.

The two remaining scows from the expedition ship's supplies had been assembled on the hard sand where the first had been built. They had been placed side by side, and when Connor went down to see the project, they were already linked to form a catamaran, by metal girders and heavy sawed beams brought in from the sawmill on the edge of the dead forest.

"We're mounting the boiler and engine between the hulls," said Sven. "The drive goes back to a big paddle wheel mounted between the rear end of the hulls, and we're putting a wooden deck right across the middle."

"You'd never turn it over," said Connor.

"Right. Might have been quicker driving with propellers, but this way we don't have to put holes in the hulls for shafts. Safer, with our standards at their present stage."

"Good. Anything I can do to help?"

Connor met Zella at the canteen for a mid-morning meal at hour fourteen. "We'll have the big catamaran launched today," he said. "Looks as if it's been designed by a badly run

135

committee, but Sven and Mak are both sure it'll be seawor-
thy, and they've both had experience of seacraft. The beauty
of it is—it makes the first boat obsolete because of the
difference in their carrying capacity.''

"I don't follow, Con. What's good about that?''

"It means the other boat will be free for other purposes,
and Jiro and Charl and I have one planned for it.''

"What?''

"Exploration. We want to see what's up the coast to the
north.''

"That's where those flying reptiles come from. Be careful!''

"They're what makes it attractive to me. Predators like
those have to live on something, and what they live on must
have other sources of food. You know, in most ecologies the
predators only make up about three percent of the large
animals. The rest are the herbivorous animals they eat. Could
be anything up there.''

"That's what bothers me. There could be absolutely *anything*
there. You never know what you might stir up.''

Connor shrugged. "The sooner we know about it, the
better. Anyway, how did you get on this morning?''

"The two Eridan people are okay. Still resting, but they're
showing no side effects of the stasis. Chang and I knew them
in Eridan. Their memories seem to be a hundred percent—
that's the thing we always worry about.''

"Nobody told me that when they put me under.''

Her cheek dimpled on one side in a mischievous smile.
"We never do. But nearly everyone comes through fine.''

He made his eyes look blank, and stared around. "Where
. . . where am I?''

"Stop! You'll give us bad publicity.'' She reached over
and slapped his wrist. "Oh, and we brought out Doc Voll this
morning.''

"Isn't he the one in the short unit?''

"That's right. Zero g type. Linked him up to his autojector
and mechanical lung, and he's conscious. Knows me. First
thing he said was, 'Zella! I'm dirtside! What am I doing
dirtside?' I said, 'We're all dirtside, Voll. You'll be all right.
I've beefed up your autojector so you get a better supply of
blood.' He was quiet for a while, then started yelling for an
exoskel.''

"What?''

"Exoskeleton, like the chief uses. He used to walk around in one of those in Eridan."

"Can you get him one?"

"Should be somewhere in stores. Chang and I are too busy to look ourselves, and no one else has much idea what to look for. He'll just have to wait."

They finished their brief meal, talking of the real, organic food that should be available in the near future. Then they went out into the mid-morning sunshine.

"Strange, isn't it?" said Zella. "I'm quite used to the red-edged shadows now. I'm even getting to like them."

Connor headed off down the street towards the beach, and she walked up the other way to the surgery.

Chang was just finishing the process of sedating two of the latest sleepers to be brought out of stasis. Food-producing specialists like the previous pair, they were both from Eridan. Chang, like Zella, felt most at home in the early stages dealing with people who had originated on his home world, because this planet was sufficiently like it in atmosphere, gravity, and temperature range to avoid too traumatic an adjustment.

"How's Doc Voll?" asked Zella.

"Resting. Back room. He insisted on being treated by you."

"That figures. I was the first person he really got to know back home, after he'd just left his own environment."

Chang nodded. His normally brown skin looked a sickly yellow. "These two will sleep for four or five hours. I'll leave the fort to you, Zel. Must get some rest."

When he had gone, Zella checked the temperatures, pulse rates, and other data of the two Eridanian people. One male, one female. Both showed a blend of the two basic races from which the Eridanian people have evolved, with Asian cheekbones and North European coloring.

Zella walked slowly through into the back room. On the table was the pale tan shell of a compact mechanical lung with a combined circulation pump, running on its own long-term batteries. She walked around it. From it protruded a sleeping human head, eyes closed, mouth and nose hidden by an enclosing mask from which tubes ran down inside the shell, while a microphone wire hung free of it.

"Voll," she said quietly. The eyes did not open. She reached open and tapped her fingers lightly on the shell, and the brown, lashless eyes flew open.

"Zel!" The breathy voice came from a speaker standing on the far end of the table. "I thought you'd left me. You didn't tell me: What are we doing dirtside?"

Zella smiled. "When you joined the expedition, Voll, you knew we were looking for planets."

"But planetary settlement involves orbiting stations. That's where I belong. Not on the surface. This damned gravity'll kill me."

"You put up with it in Eridan." She ran her hand lightly over the bald scalp, feeling the smooth forehead. "After a while you used to stride around our hospital in your exoskel as if you owned the place. Want to see if you're better sitting up?"

"I'll try. But stay with me."

"Of course."

She gently rolled him into an upright position. His head seemed to make up almost half his total height of about sixty centimeters, and was set directly into his nearly globular body. A small, stubby hand protruded where the right shoulder would have been, and a single strong-looking finger on the other side. None of the fingers had nails. He moved them suddenly.

"That's better."

"Ready to get into your prosthetic egg?"

"Yes."

"I've had new batteries put in, and supplies of adrenaline, thyroxine, testosterone, the lot. Nice to be in control of your own brain again, won't it?"

She bent down and lifted a yellow plastic egg on to the table by a pair of recessed handles, setting it on the small, sunken wheels in its flattened base. In front of it projected a short, jointed arm with metal manipulating fingers at the end of it. Opening the back of the egg, she lifted Voll carefully into it, easing his round body into the foam lining. His fingers rested on five keys on the right side, and on the left the single long finger could reach any of a triple row of keys.

"Try your manipulator," she said. The pudgy fingers danced on the keys with practiced speed, and the stubby manipulator arm moved, its fingers flexing. She put a pencil down on the table, and the long finger touched keys on the other side. The egg rolled forward, and the manipulator picked up the pencil and held it out to her.

"Good. When you picked that up, you were too close to it to see it, weren't you?"

"When you live in one of these, it's easy. Should try it when you get old, Zella. When your body wears out."

"I'll keep it in mind," she said, but she had to move quickly to disguise a shudder. "Now, your lens." She fitted the zoom lens to its bracket so that its soft eyepiece came in front of his right eye. Then she fitted a close-focusing lens over the left eye, with a mirror directing his vision down to the keyboard operated by the left finger. Finally she fitted the domed, hard plastic top over the open part of the egg. She switched off the external speaker at the far end of the table and took a small device like a hearing aid from beside it, fitting it into her ear.

"Try zooming your lens," she said. Controlled by a micro-switch actuated by a cheek muscle, the lens revolved by a tiny motor, extending and retracting. "What's that chart on the far wall?"

The egg, less than three-quarters of a meter high, rotated smoothly on its tiny wheels, the lens tilting like a small gun barrel.

"It's handwritten," came his voice from the device in her ear. "List of times. Hours. Hours up to thirty-eight. Is that the length of the day on this blasted planet?"

"That's right. You're quick, Voll."

"Take me to the door and let me see out."

Briskly she swung up the carrying handle from the back of the egg and lifted it off the table, striding to the outer door. Opening the door, she stood on the threshold, turning slowly so that he could look up and down the street.

"What a terrible world," his subdued voice whispered in her ear.

"It's not bad. We're adjusting to it."

"It's the space! The endless space! I grew up in a world of rooms and corridors with ceilings one meter high."

"You were okay in Eridan."

"The hospital? That was still a world of rooms and corridors. Big by my standard, but the scene was always bounded. Walls. Floor. Ceiling. This is terrifying. Will you take me inside?"

She went in, closing the door behind her, and put the egg down on the floor in the middle of the surgery. She sat in a chair, looking at it thoughtfully. "What am I going to do with you, Voll? I can't leave you in here all the time."

The egg rotated on its wheels, and the lens tilted up to look at her. "I'll have to adjust, that's all. Perhaps if I could live with you for a while."

She looked at the lens thoughtfully without replying.

"I don't take up much space," he added.

"I live with someone else."

"With Chang?"

"No. With Connor. You wouldn't know him. Leader of one of the exploration teams. Surface exploration."

He widened the angle of the lens to take in the whole of her body as she sat there, from the slim black boots to the red-gold hair. "You used to wear a green coverall on Eridan. Emerald green. Bright."

"I still have it," she said after a pause.

He closed his right eyelid, shutting off the view through the zoom lens and microswitching a light inside the shell. Magnified enormously by the lens in front of his left eye, the mirror gave him a downward view inside the shell, between the pulsing front of his body and the keyboard, where his finger hung like a fat tentacle. He moved it towards the adrenaline key, then changed his mind. One key was marked with a male symbol. Making a sudden decision, he pressed it, twice. He felt the circulation pump speed up, and so did the rhythm of the mechanical lung. She must have heard the changed rhythms, and she had enough medical knowledge to know exactly what he was doing. He zoomed the lens to bring her face close to him. She smiled, and rose to her feet. Then, before he had time to widen the angle, her boots moved towards him, the rest of her out of his field of view. She picked him up by the carrying handle and went through into the back room, the leg of her coverall swishing against his shell as she walked.

"Time for a sleep, Voll," she said.

"I have no intention of sleeping!"

She went into the other room, then returned with a tool like a screwdriver with a special tip.

"No!" he shouted emphatically, and with a slight frown she took the earphone from her ear and laid it down on the table. She opened the panel in the back of his shell and made some adjustments. The rhythm of the lung became slower. She altered something else that seemed to submerge him in a warm flood of euphoria.

"I don't want to sleep!" He had difficulty forming the words.

"You're my patient, Voll. I say sleep."

"This fellow Connor. What's he like?" Then he realized that without the earphone she couldn't hear him. She turned and strode out of the room with a long swing of her black boots. Alone, he felt a sudden chill of horror. His main goal, right now, was to be given the use of an exoskeleton that would enable him to walk, move like a standard human animal, as most of the people here seemed to be. Tall, strong in an exoskel, he might be considered a nuisance to Zella. She might keep him trapped in this seventy-centimeter prossy.

He'd have to play it extremely carefully.

Zella walked down the street to the HQ building. As she stepped inside, she stopped in surprise. A man was erecting a partition of hardboard and local wooden framework, shutting in a section about three meters square, with a doorway opening into the interior. She went through and found Nordstrom sitting at his desk.

"What's this, Chief?"

He smiled. "Progress. I'm putting in a receptionist, with a desk in the foyer, to filter out interruptions."

"Am I an interruption?"

"Yes, but a welcome one. What can I do for you?"

"Advice, primarily. How many zero g people have we on ice?"

"Altogether, twenty, including your colleague Voll. Why?"

"We may have problems with them. How many exoskeletons do we have in storage?"

"May have the electronic parts of a few. The framework we'll have to build, when the engineers have time to get around to it."

"What do we do with the people until then?"

"They'd better stay in stasis, unless we need some special ability. Voll's useful, because he has medical knowledge of light-gravity effects. But the others will have to stay frozen until we can build an orbiting station."

"But that might be years. When do you plan it?"

"No idea yet. Better leave them in stasis."

Zella nodded slowly, frowning.

"How *is* Voll, on the whole?" asked Nordstrom.

"Surviving, physically. But he's frightened to go out of doors."

"Why?"

"He's used to a milieu of narrow corridors and walls that shut in his space. When I took him to the door of the surgery and showed him the outside, with the sky and the sea and the clouds racing along on the wind, he nearly flipped. Had me take him back indoors. I had to sedate him."

"He'll adjust," said Nordstrom confidently. "He's stable. Experienced. Give him time."

"I can't leave him in the surgery forever."

Nordstrom thought for a few seconds. "Look, he knows you. He's worked with you before. Can't you let him stay over at your place?"

She shook her head. "I want privacy with Con."

"I see. Naturally. Well, you have access to the controls of Voll's prossy. You can put him to sleep when necessary."

"That makes him furious!"

"Cut down his adrenaline, then."

"Chief, the man's a doctor! He'd know exactly what I was doing!" Zella thrust out her lower lip, as she did sometimes when thinking. "I wonder if zero g people ever go mad in those prossies?"

"I've no data on that. Maybe Voll has."

"God, I can't ask *him* that." Zella stood up. "Well, I'll try to sort something out. Meanwhile I'd better go back and see how the four farming experts are coming around. Two of them should be ready to go out and start plowing, or whatever they do."

As she was moving towards the new reception room, a knock sounded on the outer door, and a moment later Connor came in, looking curiously at the half-finished partitions.

"Hi, Zel. Hi, Chief."

"I was just going," said Zella.

"Don't go. Nothing secret. Chief, we've just tested the catamaran on the lagoon. Does everything we expected."

"I know, Con. I saw it." Nordstrom gestured to the TV screen on the wall. "That's hooked up to a camera overlooking the beach. Now, I suppose you want to go ahead with your project to explore the northward coast. Who did you say you wanted with you?''

"My old team. Jiro and Charl.''

Nordstrom seemed to be thinking for a while, and Zella broke in. "How long will you be gone?''

"Few days, I think. Limited by the amount of fuel we can carry, unless we find more burnable timber on the way.''

"Your explorations to the south certainly paid off,'' said Nordstrom. "We have the iron and limestone—although Jiro surveyed that area originally from the air, remember.''

"Perhaps we could coordinate an aerial survey with this.''

"I don't think so, Con. Our batteries for the flier don't have indefinite life. Another thing: it might be safer in the boat, just in case there *is* something more intelligent than those pterosaurs living up that way. They could see the flier from a long way off. It travels fast, and it could have you in someone else's territory before you knew what was happening. In the boat you can feel your way, as it were. Play it by ear.''

"Right. All we need is enough firewood and fresh water for power, a supply of food, and we can be on our way tomorrow.'' He shook his head. "Pity none of us was conscious when the kesrii brought us to the planet. We know almost nothing about it, when you think of it. Only what's near enough for us to see.''

"Karl's worked out some data,'' said Nordstrom. "He's got an approximate diameter, from horizon angles on a base line between here and Furnace Point. He thinks the diameter's between 11,500 and 12,000 clicks. Somewhere about a thousand kilometers less than Earth—not a significant difference. So you have a lot of territory to explore.''

"We'll head up the coast until we get to the equator. Does Karl have any idea of our latitude?''

"He thinks about twenty or twenty-five degrees south.''

"Let's see. Circumference about 37,000, right? That's a whisker over a hundred klicks to one degree of latitude. So the equator would be over two thousand north of here.''

"A bit ambitious,'' said Nordstrom.

Connor looked at Zella, who had been standing a little apart, her eyes dark against the pallor of her face. "I remember seeing reproductions of old Earth maps, with legends saying 'Here be dragons.' '' He waved his hand northward. "It's true up there."

"It's not funny," said Zella quietly. "We know the pterosaurs fly there. But what else is there? You've seen books on pre-history. Look at the pictures of the contemporaries of Earth's flying reptiles!"

"That worries me," admitted Nordstrom. "I think we need to explore further. But Con, keep in radio contact every kilometer of the way."

"We'll do that. Listen, I've already spoke to Charl and Jiro about this. Is it okay if we leave tomorrow morning?"

In the moment of Nordstrom's hesitation, Zella cut in. "It isn't okay with me, Con. You have no weapons, no maps, nothing."

"We have radio, remember."

"What's the good of that if something attacks you?"

Connor shrugged. Nordstrom looked from one to the other.

"I leave it up to you," he said. "I feel two ways about this. First, I think we need to know what's to the north of us, and I think Con and his team are the best men to find out. On the other hand, they're among the most valuable members of our community. But I'd like to remind you of a couple of things. You, Zel, volunteered to accompany Con and the others into the White Room when they first came back from the planet seeded by the kesrii, in case they'd brought back something dangerous to women. You didn't play it safe then, did you?"

She didn't answer right away. "And what was the other thing?"

Nordstrom turned to Connor. "Something you said the day we launched the first boat."

"What was that?"

"A ship is safe in harbor—but that's not what she was built for."

For several seconds none of them spoke. Then Zella said, "I suppose you'd better go. But God, be careful!"

11

It was another five days before Nordstrom gave his official permission for the exploration northward to begin.

"He's right, I suppose," said Connor grudgingly as he and Zella lay in bed that night. "He waited until the catamaran brought the first big load up from Iron Ridge."

"Did everything go as planned?"

"Yes. With the engine amidships they were able to load the ore into the bottoms of the scows. Kept the weight well down, made the whole ship very stable. I suppose he was right to wait and see the result."

"Perhaps," mused Zella. "But I think there was another reason for him withholding his okay."

"Just cussedness, you mean?"

"Look at it from his angle, Con. He's been running starships since long before you and I were born. With all his computer backups, he's never known what it was like to be *wrong*, as long as he's been aboard ship. Now, down here on a planet, he must feel . . . insecure."

"The chief? Insecure?"

"Think back. He was wrong a little while ago, wasn't he? Over the launching of the first boat, with motors too small to handle the conditions here. Sven and someone else who knew boats told him, but he knew better. And he was wrong! A great new experience for him."

"I see. I suppose you're right."

"Now he feels he can't afford to be wrong again, or his credibility will start to slip."

"Would you call it anemia of the charisma?"

"If you like. The thing is, he has to play everything safe for a while, so he can make sure everyone goes on following his orders, simply by making all his plans watertight."

"Well, he's given us the green light now. Tomorrow morning we head north."

She rolled towards him and put her arm over him. "Be very, very careful, darling. Be like the chief for once. Play everything safe. Really safe." She stroked her finger against his chin, the edge of her nail rasping lightly against the long day's stubble. "I want you back. Whiskers and all."

He turned towards her, sliding his hand up her smooth arm and across her shoulder. "I'll be back. Maybe with longer whiskers, if I'm too busy keeping a lookout to shave." Reaching over her, he switched out the light.

Early the following morning Connor, Kosaka, and Harn boarded the stern-wheeler. Mak had been aboard for most of the night, firing the furnace and building up steam pressure. They took food supplies aboard, stowed them in a dry place, and added a good supply of fresh water. Probably there would be fresh water available up the coast, but until Charl Harn had analyzed it carefully, they didn't intend to take the chance of drinking it. The planet was still alien to them, and for all they knew, different regions of its surface might contain unknown microorganisms.

Nordstrom, Zella, Sven, and several of the others went down to the beach in the cool, lilac-tinted morning to see them leave. Harn moved the lever that fed steam to the cylinders, and the paddle wheel began to thrash in the shallow water. The bow grated on sand, and then they were afloat, backing slowly out into the lagoon. Nordstrom and the others, except Zella, turned and went back up into the town after a wave of farewell.

Harn swung the bow slowly around towards the north and began the paddle driving ahead. Connor could see the solitary figure of Zella standing on the top of a small dune, a bright splash of color in her emerald-green coverall. He climbed the ladder to the roof of the wheelhouse and waved. She made an answering wave with both arms, continuing the movement with surprising vigor for a long time. She was still there, a bright green dot against the background, when the ship chugged around the headland to the north, wiping the whole of the settlement out of their field of view.

The sunrise was normal for a planet of a G-type star, because the yellow component was leading the red one up into the sky. Connor, getting down from the wheelhouse, walked to Kosaka, who was standing with his feet apart, looking at the rising sun.

"Remind you of home, Jiro?"

Kosaka turned sharply, as if he had been lost in thought. "A little." He waved his hand to take in the sweep of coastline. "But empty. No people. All ours!"

Connor nodded in the direction they were moving. "It could be all ours, up this way."

"You mean it might be possible to start a separate base?"

"Let's not run before we walk. But it's an idea, isn't it? If we could find something that made it viable."

"Like a food source?"

"Well, that's Charl's department."

"What is?" Charl Harn called from the wheelhouse.

The others turned, and Connor gestured ahead. "If we could find big quantities of something edible up north of here, we might be able to set up another base."

Harn looked ahead to make certain there was nothing in the water to avoid. "Opens up possibilities, doesn't it? Too many restrictions on what we do back there." He jerked his thumb back over his shoulder.

"True," said Kosaka, "but like Con just said, better we walk before we run."

"Sure," said Harn, and returned his concentration to his steering.

To the right, as the ship thrashed its way up the long turquoise lagoon, the coastline showed flat and barren, except for occasional smears of yellow grass or moss—from their distance it was impossible to see exactly what they were. On the left the coraloid reef was a dark, unbroken line that stretched from horizon to horizon. Occasional spurts of white spray on the far side of it suggested that the surface of the reef was quite wide, maybe a kilometer across, unless it was a braided chain of reefs. At this stage of their explorations it would have been unwise to investigate too closely.

Connor went down to the lower deck. Mak, wearing a pair of goggles, opened the furnace door. A glare of hot orange light blazed out at him as he lifted one of the sawed logs with long iron tongs and threw it into the fire, using the tongs to slam the door.

"I'll give you a spell if you like," said Connor.

"Great. I could do with it." Mak pulled off the goggles and held them out to Connor. "Put these on when you open the firebox. If you stop the heat hitting you around the eyes, you can stand it easily on the rest of your face."

"Thanks. I didn't realize that."

"Took me a while to find out. Learning all the time, aren't we?"

"All the time. That's the definition of being alive."

Mak jerked his thumb towards the deck around the wheel-house. "What was the big discussion?"

"Oh, just some wild thinking. About finding good country up north and starting a new base."

"Be nice, wouldn't it? Chance to do what we wanted."

"May not happen. But it's something to keep in mind."

"Sure."

Checking the pressure gauge, Connor pulled the goggles over his eyes, opened the firebox door with the tongs, and swung another log into the glowing mass within. The heat struck fiercely for a few seconds at his cheeks and lips and forehead, but the goggles protected the more vulnerable tissues around his eyes. He closed the door again, put down the tongs, hung up the goggles and went back up on deck, checking the second pressure gauge in the wheelhouse. It agreed with the one mounted directly on the boiler.

Kosaka, who had relieved Harn at the wheel, looked over his shoulder. "Could we push the speed up a bit?"

Connor nodded, and Kosaka moved the lever linked to the centrifugal governor. The beat of the engine quickened, and spray was flung higher from the paddles. The bow wave of the ship, reaching out to either side across the mirror-smooth lagoon, grew slightly more pronounced, its angle sharpening.

"Ten klicks," said Harn, looking at the dial showing their speed. "Doesn't feel to me as if we're moving that fast."

"Nor to me," admitted Connor. "Maybe because we're not used to moving across water."

"Any way we can check it?"

Connor called down to Mak. "How long is this boat?"

"Twenty meters, near enough."

"Throw me up a small piece of wood."

Mak found a small broken branch from the firewood and tossed it up to Connor, who went into the wheelhouse and returned with the stopwatch. He handed the piece of wood to Harn.

"Go up to the bow. The front. When I give you the signal, throw that into the sea exactly level with the front of the boat."

Harn walked to the front of the ship. Connor checked the stopwatch, waved, and started the watch running as the piece of wood hit the water. Harn walked back along the deck quickly, just keeping pace with the floating stick. As it passed the stern Connor clicked the watch and read off the time. He looked up for a moment, then said, "We're moving at a shade over ten kilometers an hour."

"How'd you work that out without a calculator?"

"Back on our station they used to teach us kids mental arithmetic. Still stays with you."

Harn shook his head as if unconvinced. He looked at the water with his brow furrowed, then suddenly lifted his eyes to Connor's. "Say, that'd be just about right. I'm going by the speed I had to walk along the deck to keep level with it. You're good!"

Connor shrugged. "By midday we should have traveled about ninety kilometers from the base, if we keep going like this."

Three hours later, however, the situation looked less promising. Ahead, the coastline was becoming more rugged, sweeping out in jagged headlands towards the reef.

"What happens if we can't get out this end of the lagoon?" asked Kosaka.

"Don't know. If we see a break in the reef, we'd better head out through it."

Halfway through the tenth hour the red sun appeared above the horizon, about five degrees away from the point where the primary had risen. The day did not become much brighter, but within a few minutes a rise in temperature became easily perceptible and the sky's color gradually changed. The crane, funnel, and wheelhouse threw double shadows across the quiet water, diverging as they reached out, one of them tinted red.

Connor scanned the coast from time to time with the binoculars, but saw nothing to warrant making a closer approach. Long, pale beaches, now yellow rather than white, were broken by increasingly rough brown headlands of jumbled rocks that looked, from this distance, like a form of sandstone rather than the granite farther south. They were sedimentary, certainly, because at high magnification he could see the strata.

"You know something?" said Harn. "I'm beginning to get the idea the kesrii picked out the best place for us after all."

"Maybe. But *they* picked it. We didn't."

"Think they've got our base under continuous observation?"

"I'm sure of it. I don't know how they do it, but why else would they have gone to all that trouble?"

Harn gave a long sigh, stretching his arms above his head. "Nothing we can do about it right now. It's a nice day. Let's just enjoy it.

Connor nodded. He looked at the pressure gauge, then went down to the furnace, slipped on the goggles, opened the firebox door and threw in another couple of logs. When he returned to the deck, Harn pointed out towards the reef, which now seemed noticeably nearer. "Still no break."

"The only break seems to be the one down near the settlement."

"You know why," said Harn. "This stuff that forms the reef must be like Earth's coral in a lot of ways. That always has breaks in an offshore reef opposite the estuaries of rivers. The coral polyps are saltwater animals, and the fresh-water outflow from a river keeps them from growing. These must be the same."

"Have you examined them?"

"Not as thoroughly as I want to. I will when I have time. They're different from Earth coral, but I think their lifestyle is similar enough."

"Right. Any sign of a river mouth and we'll head out and have a closer look at the reef." Connor tried to sound confident, but the waters of the lagoon ahead were looking more and more landlocked as they went onward.

"Take us an hour or more to get to the end of it," said Harn. "Let's say we eat, and keep our eyes on the shore and the reef as we go."

"Good idea."

Harn began opening some of the food packages, while Mak took four cups down to the boiler room for hot water. As he went he called over his shoulder, "Wonder how much longer we'll have coffee?"

"You'll be drinking tea, of a sort, next year," said Harn, "provided some disease we've never heard of doesn't attack our plantations."

They ate and drank standing on the deck, so that they could keep observing both reef and shore. Suddenly Kosaka pointed straight ahead.

"Look! The end of that headland is a separate island! We might be able to get through!"

The others quickly moved alongside him.

"Be a tight squeeze," said Mak.

"Not necessarily," said Connor after a minute's scrutiny of the headland through the binoculars. "Looks narrow from this viewpoint, but I think there's a channel running through at an angle."

They finished their meal quickly, and as they neared the headland, Connor took the wheel. He cut the speed to about five kilometers per hour, approaching the channel carefully. The reef came close to shore, the water clear enough to show a sandy bottom strewn with broken fragments of the coral-like rock from the reef.

"Mak, take the wheel. I'll guide you from up top."

Relinquishing the wheel, Connor climbed to the roof of the wheelhouse, standing with his feet apart. The extra height above waterline didn't help much, but at least it confirmed his hunch that it would be fatal to try to go seaward of the isolated island and squeeze between it and the reef.

"Right," he shouted. "Swing her to the right, Mak. Now! We're right in line with the channel!"

They moved slowly forward, still more than a kilometer from the beginning of the channel. Flying things whirled in the air above its cliffs, like fragments of ash above a fire.

They looked like slightly smaller versions of the pterosaurs that had flown over the settlement at night.

"What's that thing on the high point of the island?" asked Kosaka.

Connor steadied the binoculars against the side of the wheelhouse. "Dead tree, I think. No, wait! It's a metal post! Rusty iron, perhaps. Some sort of a bracket on it."

"Probably carried a warning light. Someone's used these waters before."

"Right. But a long time ago."

As they drew closer to the channel, some of the pterosaurs flew towards them, wheeling above the ship, uttering harsh cries. They were about the size of pelicans, but somehow more fragile looking. One suddenly dived from about ten meters into the water, disappeared beneath the surface for a few seconds, then emerged with a fish of some kind in its toothed jaws, shedding a glistening shower from its rubbery wings as it flew back to the cliffs.

"Something odd about this gorge," said Kosaka, pointing ahead along the channel. "It's dead straight, like a cutting."

"Might have been cut over millions of years as the coastline rose," suggested Connor.

"No." Kosaka was emphatic. "It's not a rising coastline. Be impossible with those reefs offshore. They only happen when a coast's sinking."

They were abruptly distracted. Some of the pterosaurs had been skimming low over the ship, screeching as though trying to frighten away this slow-moving thing that was invading their fishing grounds. But now there was a twang like the sound of a harp string as one of them collided with one of the thin steel guy wires supporting the crane. It fell fluttering to the deck, then lay motionless. Connor and Harn walked over and stood looking down at it.

"Dead," said Harn. "Neck's broken against the wire."

"Probably something like a pterodactyl might have looked, millions of years ago," said Connor. "Funny, though, I'd never visualized that iridescent coloring or the fine scales."

"Fossils wouldn't have shown that. Come to that, no one knows what color a tyrannosaurus was."

Kosaka joined them. "It's beautiful," he said in an awed voice.

It was some time before anyone else spoke. Harn turned the limp body over with his foot. "Yes," he said, "it *is* beautiful. Like something bred for its coloring."

"But these things are wild, obviously," said Kosaka, looking at the others still whirling above them.

"Wild, now. But for how long? I think that coloring would have a negative selection value in an environment like this. Suppose the ancestors of these things were kept by someone as pets?"

"Why postulate that?" asked Connor.

"Because they're far too highly evolved for the rest of the environment. The fish here are primitive, and so are the insects. I think these things were brought here, or their forebears were."

"The way we were brought here," mused Connor.

"Well . . . yes." Harn moved away. "Don't touch it. I'm going to get it into one of our plastic bags."

He returned with a large bag and worked the corpse carefully inside it. "Quite light," he said as he lifted the bag. "Almost no weight at all."

There was a sudden shout from Mak. "Hey! Look at the walls on each side of us. This is artificial, this gap. It's a cutting!"

There was silence as the others inspected the almost vertical walls of rock.

"You're right," said Kosaka. "It's been cut. The surfaces have been vitrified. It's been cut with tremendous heat."

"Like a giant laser," suggested Harn.

The cutting was nearly a kilometer long, and midway along its course its walls rose to a height of fifty or sixty meters, glass smooth, sloping back from each other at an angle of about seven or eight degrees. At the water line the width was some thirty meters. Connor looked up at the walls with a frown of concentration.

"Something wrong with the whole setup," he said. "It's been cut to give access to ships. Like this one. But whoever cut it had the use of a technology that would have made waterborne ships obsolete by a thousand years. So why?"

For a few seconds no one answered. Then an idea occurred to Harn. "It could have been a fun thing. The way highly developed civilizations play around with little sailing boats in their spare time."

"Possible. But where are any traces of the civilization—Hey! Let's take it dead slow. We don't know what's out the other end of the cutting!"

The ship pounded slowly on, the beat of its engine and the splash of the paddles echoing from the walls to either side. Gradually, as they neared the far end of the cut, the view ahead began to open out to reveal another stretch of placid lagoon, sheltered by the reef to the left and with a series of sandy, crescent beaches receding on the landward side.

There was no sign of the culture that had made the cutting. No buildings, nothing except the screeching pterosaurs which apparently nested on the headland and the adjoining island. From here they could not even see the corroded metal post they had spotted from a distance.

They increased speed again, driving northward at ten kilometers an hour. Connor looked back along the cutting. It was obvious now that it was artificial, as though it had been made with a titanic saw. In the otherwise primordial landscape the geometrical perfection and the sheer scale of the thing was unsettling. Ahead, the lagoon stretched all the way to the horizon, widening to several kilometers between beach and reef.

"Looks as if we're having a quiet time for a while," said Connor. "We may as well get a bit of sleep—two at a time. The sun's not far past the meridian yet."

After a simple drawing of lots, Connor and Harn slept first, lying on the wooden deck in the shadow of the wheelhouse, Connor impressing on the others the need to wake them at the first sign of any change. After that he slept for several hours, the angle of the suns considerably changed when Kosaka's voice woke him.

"What is it, Jiro?"

"Nothing urgent. But I'd like you to have a look at the water."

Connor yawned, stretched, and got to his feet. Suddenly he gave a shout. "How long's it been like that?"

The water was lime green. Where they had been able to see the bottom before, it was now opaque.

"Silt," said Kosaka. "Must be outflow from a big river. A *very* big river, because we're almost out of sight of land. The sort of river you only get on a large continent."

Connor looked seaward. "Where's the reef?"

"It finished a few kilometers back, when we first hit this yellow-green water. It looks as if the coral here can't grow in silt or fresh water, the same as Earth coral."

"Better head in towards the river mouth."

Mak swung the ship straight in towards the shore, which appeared as a flat line of deep green, quite different from the shoreline farther south.

"How far have we come?" asked Connor.

"We've been running for over twelve hours at ten klicks, except for that slow run through the cutting," said Mak. "We must be more than a hundred north of Central, say a hundred ten."

As they headed in through the silt-laden water, which now became almost lime yellow, the dark green line of the delta opened out ahead of them, nearer than they expected. Harn climbed to the top of the wheelhouse.

"Looks like a mangrove swamp, or something similar," he said. "Lot of different channels."

"Turn north again," said Connor to Mak. "We'll cruise along the edge of this delta until we come to one of the main channels."

"We'll find it by the silt jetties," said Kosaka.

"What are they?"

"Long banks of silt deposited each side of the channel. Run up between them."

They found a wide channel, nearly a kilometer across, after passing perhaps twenty smaller ones. They turned into it and found their speed reduced by about half as they fought their way against the strong current.

"Keep in the middle of the channel, Mak." Connor climbed to the roof of the wheelhouse, set up a video camera and recorder to face astern, and turned it on.

"Why backwards?" asked Harn.

"So we have a record of the way we came in. We could get lost in a delta like this. Channels everywhere. Coming out we just have to play the tape in reverse and follow it."

The delta spread as far as they could see in every direction, its uniform deep green broken by occasional glimpses of interlacing channels of bright water.

"Tidal," said Harn. "These things *are* like mangroves. They're intertidal. But look over there, in the distance. Higher ground, see? And there's something different growing there. A lighter green.''

"I see it. I don't know if the ground's higher though. It might be that the light green stuff grows taller, whatever it is.''

Connor kept turning and staring intently astern, trying to memorize the way back each time they came to a channel junction. There were no pterosaurs here, but a few things like large yellow butterflies fluttered among the mangrovelike plants.

The winding channels seemed to reach on interminably. Eventually the intertidal plants were replaced by the lighter-green vegetation, which covered innumerable islands in the inland reaches of the delta. They could see now that it was a kind of cane or giant grass, somewhat like bamboo or sugar-cane, with segmented yellow stems and long, light green leaves like lance blades. It grew about three meters tall. From the deck it shut out the view in every direction, and even from the top of the wheelhouse there was nothing visible except endless kilometers of the green leaves in every direction.

"What happens if we're in the middle of this when night comes?" asked Kosaka.

"We simply anchor. I don't want to use our lights to find our way along—they could be seen by anyone from a long way off. But I'm hoping we get through to more solid ground before then.''

The suns were very low in the sky when they came to some higher ground, with banks two or three meters high along each side of the river. Here and there outcrops of reddish rock thrust above the yellow-tinted soil which supplied the color to the water.

With an estimated one hour left before the primary sunset, they at last broke free of the delta into a kilometer-wide reach of open river, which flowed in a curve ahead of them, the outer bank on the curve made up of substantial reddish cliffs. They rose at least ten meters above the water.

"Good place to stop for the night," said Connor, pointing ahead to a small island in the river. At the upstream end of it was an outcropping of red rock which had enabled it to resist the erosion of the passing water.

Connor, who was now steering, brought the ship close to the island, using just enough power to keep it almost stationary against the pressure of the current. Slowly he eased it in towards the island until Mak was able to spring ashore and loop one of the mooring cables around a jutting piece of rock that formed a natural bollard.

Kosaka joined him with the other cable. When Mak returned to the ship, Jiro remained on the island, picking up pieces of rock. Suddenly he gave an excited shout.

"What is it?" called Connor.

Kosaka turned, a lump of red rock in his hands.

"Con! I've found something! *This stuff is bauxite!*"

12

Two of the moons were above the horizon after the suns had set, the large one almost full in the eastern sky, its scarred disc bloodred along the edge where the light from the red sun overlapped the terminator. The four men talked on the brightly moonlit deck for hours into the night, fired by the vision of a future settlement that was already taking a coherent shape in their combined imagination.

"Now we have the main thing that's been holding up our development," said Kosaka. "Aluminum! It's going to take us a lot of work, a lot of power. But all those cliffs are bauxite, as far upstream as you can see."

"What do you need to turn it from aluminum ore to the metal?" asked Connor.

"First, you have to wash the bauxite. No problem there, with this river. Then we'll have to get Central to make us a steam pressure tank so we can dissolve the bauxite in hot caustic soda."

"Where do you get caustic soda?"

"It's sodium hydroxide. Look . . ." Kosaka gestured towards the seacoast, then went on. "You precipitate aluminum hydroxide, calcine it to get alumina, then use the electric furnace—"

"What? An electric furnace? How much power does that need?"

Kosaka's dark eyes were blazing like a fanatic's. "Con!

You know how we get it, damn it. We talked about it before. The nuclear generator out on the island. All we have to do is get it aboard the ship, bring it up here, find a site near this . . ."

Some of his enthusiasm began to infect the others, in spite of the magnitude of the project he envisioned.

"Aluminum," said Connor thoughtfully. "That could give us internal combustion engines, if only we had fuel."

"I think we have fuel," said Harn quietly.

"Where?"

"All around us, back halfway to the sea. All this stuff that looks like a cross between bamboo and sugarcane. You remember I gathered a bit of it a while back?"

"Yes. From the island back there."

"It's very like sugarcane organically, wherever it came from. We can use it to make methanol. Methyl alcohol. Quite a good fuel for internal combustion motors. They used to use it once as a racing fuel."

Connor, who had been sitting on the deck with his back against the wheelhouse, suddenly got to his feet. He paced up and down the deck for a few moments, then stopped.

"This could be it. What we've been looking for. Aluminum, fuel, nuclear power. We could put it all together up here, and to hell with Central and their restrictions! We could have motor vehicles for a start, then aircraft, not battery operated, but capable of flying anywhere on the planet!"

"If the kesrii let us do it," murmured Harn.

Connor stopped. "Yes. There's always that. But they might only be watching the base. Central. They might never notice what we did up here."

Harn gave a wry smile. "As you often say yourself: I wouldn't bet that way."

"Anyway," said Connor, "let's sleep on it now, and find a place for an aluminum plant in the morning. And a generating station."

"Good," yawned Harn. "We'll leave the supermarket for later."

They were wakened during the night several times by strange noises from the swamp, although they slept in turns while one of them kept watch. Once, something heavy thumped against the side of the hull and claws scraped on the metal as it attempted to climb aboard. Mak, who was on watch, shone the light of a hand-held lamp towards it, and it slid hastily down out of sight with an echoing splash that sprayed water high above the deck.

"What was it?" asked Harn.

"Couldn't see much of it. Looked nasty, what I could see. Head a bit like a crocodile, but longer arms, claws. Anyway, it's frightened by the light."

Connor looked up at the large moon. "That's odd, when you think of it. Probably seldom gets really dark here. Mightn't have been the actual light that frightened it—just the direct beam."

"Think something else has hunted here with spotlights?" asked Harn.

"Don't know. But it's a possibility that shakes you a bit, don't you think?"

"Perhaps we'd better stay awake two at a time," said Kosaka. And for the rest of the night they did.

In the morning they raised steam pressure early and began moving upstream between banks that grew slightly higher as they proceeded. On their left were low cliffs of the red rock, and to the right, sloping ground covered with the light green cane. There must have been hundreds and possibly thousands of square kilometers of the stuff—if Harn was right, an inexhaustible source of fuel for vehicles, either landborne or airborne.

As they went on, Harn, who apparently had the best hearing of the four, thought he heard sound ahead. They shut off the engine and then all four of them heard it—a deep, continuous roar.

"Could be a waterfall," said Kosaka.

Connor climbed to the top of the wheelhouse with the binoculars. Far ahead he saw a white cloud like fine smoke rising around a bend in the river. "I think you're right. Let's go up to it. It may give us a supply of fresh water from above."

It was a full hour before they reached the source of the sound. Although their speed indicator showed ten kilometers an hour, this was velocity in relation to the water, which was flowing downstream at fully half that speed.

The sound certainly came from a waterfall, but it was not on the main river. It was on a tributary that came in to their left as they faced upstream, a smaller river running through a shallow gorge. A half kilometer up from the confluence, it fell about twenty meters, not in a single fall, but in a roaring series of foaming rapids where it was cutting its way back into the cliffs of bauxite. Opposite, the meeting of the two streams of water had swirled out a rounded basin that made a good anchorage, but it was the red bank that interested Connor, and he steered a short distance up the smaller river, which had a less violent current than the main stream. About halfway to the rapids they found a wider, relatively still pool where they were able to moor the boat safely and climb the twenty-meter reddish cliff.

The top was a surprise—a huge, red area, perfectly flat, extending in front of them for several kilometers.

"Dry lakebed," said Kosaka. "See? The smaller river's cut back into it and drained the lake."

"Make a good airfield," said Connor. "Wonder if it floods?"

"No. It'd drain this way into the river."

Connor walked out onto the flat, sunbaked surface, stamping his feet on it. "Hard as concrete."

Around the edges of the dry lake grew straggling native trees which looked, from a distance, like thin tamarisks, except that their foliage was dark blue instead of green—a blue form of chlorophyll seemed prevalent here. Harn was of the opinion that the green-leaved plants, like the cane, had been introduced from some other world and had spread unchecked by natural enemies. At one side, low dunes ran along the edge of the lakebed, and Connor pointed to them.

"Good place to build a town, when we need it. Keep the lakebed for an airfield. Water in the river behind us, and level land for farming as we begin to clear areas of the cane."

He walked up to one of the low rises and stood looking out over the surroundings. After a while Harn joined him.

"You look thoughtful all of a sudden. What's wrong?"

"Oh, nothing wrong with this place. I was just wondering if I can persuade Zella to move up here with me."

Harn gave a short laugh. "The perils of coming off suppressants too soon," he said. "Me, I'm waiting until they bring the right sort of girl out of stasis."

"And what's the right sort of girl?"

"I don't know yet. But normal, you know. After I've seen

the pictures in the dossiers of some of the types of people they've got in stasis . . . Urk!''

Connor put his hand on Harn's shoulder and they began to walk back to the ship. "It'll sort itself out, Charl. It always does—in time.''

Most of the day was spent exploring the immediate vicinity of the area chosen for their future center. Kosaka suggested a name for it—Red Lake—after a similar place on Earth, and the others at once accepted the name.

There was plenty of fresh water available in the Upper River, as they called the smaller of the two streams. The other was simply called the Big River.

"We'll want a road up there from Central,'' said Connor. "It shouldn't be much problem until it reaches the far bank of the Big River.''

"We could use a punt to ferry vehicles across,'' said Harn.

"I've seen it done without using power,'' added Mak.

"How?''

"Punt moored by a long cable to a point upstream. They just set the rudder one way or the other and let the flow of the current swing it from one bank to the other and back again.''

The others exchanged glances. "Gets over the bridge problem,'' said Connor. "We'll do it.''

"No big timber about here,'' pointed out Harn.

"Well, we could build the punt down at Central, from the logs in the dead forest. Then we could use the boat to tow it up here.''

And so it went on, a long thrashing out of details. It went on far into the long night and throughout the voyage back to Central. Towards the latter part of the journey, when the projected new base had taken on a vivid reality in their minds, most of the discussion revolved about the approach they would make to Nordstrom, O'Donnel, and the rest of the council.

The suns were already setting when they passed through the cutting, and it became obvious that they would not reach the settlement until midnight or even later.

"Might be as well,'' said Connor. "Give us a night's sleep before we speak to the chief.''

"Okay to run with lights after it's dark?'' asked Mak.

"I think so. In any case, the moonlight's bright here.''

They grated onto the sand at the mooring place at the end

of the first hour of the new day, with more than eight hours remaining before the rising of the primary sun. They shut down the boiler, made the ship secure to the bollards, and headed silently up the street.

They had expected it completely deserted at this hour. But it was not. Striding down to meet them was the tall robotlike figure of Nordstrom, stilt legs flashing in the moonlight.

"Maybe it's true he never sleeps," muttered Harn.

"Good to see you safely back, boys," said Nordstrom genially. "Come into the HQ. You can tell me all about it while you eat."

He stalked ahead of them up the sloping street, tirelessly, smoothly, the metal and plastic body a caricature of an athlete's torso balanced on telescopic metal stilts. Usually he wore some kind of coat to give himself a more normal human appearance, but evidently he didn't consider it necessary on this occasion. He had removed one of the metal and plastic hands—the left one—and replaced it with a specialized tool with which he had been carrying out some intricate work.

None of them spoke until they were inside the silent building. Nordstrom waved them to a semicircular array of chairs grouped in front of his desk, and walked around to face them.

"Now," he said, "what did you find?"

"Two main things," said Connor. "First, hundreds of square kilometers of a type of cane, like sugarcane, that Charl believes can yield methyl alcohol. Something we could use for fuel for internal combustion engines."

"I see," said Nordstrom, his pale eyes bright. He said it again, drawing it out. "I . . . see!" There was a curious intensity in his expression. "Get us out of the Steam Age, eh? This is more like it!" His long-fingered hand moved across to his left arm, snapping releases that enabled him to slide off the special tool. Then he picked his other hand up from the desk and fitted it carefully onto the arm, snapping it home, then flexing its fingers. "And the second main thing?"

"Aluminum. Jiro found huge bauxite deposits up there."

"But you need a lot of power to extract aluminum from bauxite."

"I know. We thought of the nuclear generator out on the island."

"What? Ship the bauxite down there? Or here?"

"No. Shift the reactor up there."

"I see." Nordstrom walked across the room then back again. He came around in front of his desk and took up a position in front of the semicircle of chairs, towering over them. Then he retracted the telescopic legs, sinking smoothly down until he had his eyes just slightly above the level of theirs.

"This could solve a minor problem in another direction," he said. "The generator's no use to us where it is, and some of our people don't want it brought nearer the base. This should satisfy everyone. On the other hand, I think the kesrii know where it is—after all, they put it there—and moving it may arouse their suspicions. Incidentally, you wondered why they painted the top of it black, didn't you?"

"Yes. The one thing they've done that seemed to make absolutely no sense."

"We had Nargis Lal analyze the paint you scraped off it— remember?—and the piece of fabric you cut from the cover over the fuel drums. Both black, weren't they?"

"That's right."

Nordstrom smiled. "You pointed out something about the keys on the instrument one of the kesrii gave to Zella. Of the forty-nine keys on the control boards, twenty-eight were black, and six more were very dark colors—dark violet, dark browns, dark grays. That left fifteen keys with bright colors."

"I didn't count them. But it agrees with my impression."

"Of the fifteen, we had keys that were red, orange, yellow, lime, emerald, turquoise, two different blues, indigo, violet in two shades . . . then there were some in two colors— red and black, yellow and black, and so on. Nargis hooked a spectroscope up to a screen that gave false colors beyond our visible spectrum.

"I think you once suggested to Zella that the kesrii see a different range of colors from us. It appears you were right. Their range is enormous. We see light from around 7,700 angstroms—the red limit—down to a wavelength of 3,800 angstroms. They range from around 8,000 down to less than 2,000 angstroms. A bit further than us into the infrared, and about a full octave beyond us into the ultraviolet. Most of those keys on the device that appeared black or near-black to us, are actually in sharply identifiable colors that we can't see."

No one else spoke as Nordstrom looked from one to the other. He went on.

'Now, that black paint from the top of the generator, and the black fabric over the fuel, is only black to our eyes. But to the kesrii it's a vivid color, halfway up the octave of the UV. What it looks like to them, of course, we have no idea, just as a color-blind person couldn't grasp the idea of green or red. In other words, from a kesrii viewpoint we're partly color-blind, all of us. Now, you see the implication?''

Connor snapped his fingers. "I was on the verge of it before. I see it now. They deliberately painted those things a brilliant color that they knew we can't see—so that they know when and where we move them.'' He thought for a moment. "But how did they know what colors we see?''

"Zella thinks they found out when they dissected Marek. Anyway, that trick may have backfired on them this time. Now *we* can tell when they've marked things with colors they think only *they* can see. Nargis fixed up a vidicon that converts the next octave of colors in the UV into false colors that we can see as reds, greens, blues, and so on.''

"And the nuclear generator is the only thing they've marked?''

"As far as we know. I suppose it's the only thing we have that could be a possible threat to them. So they dumped it on an isolated island, painted it with a color that shows vividly to them but means nothing to us, and probably left something in synch orbit focused on it to alarm them if we move it.''

"Ingenious lot, aren't they? If they'd put a radio alarm on it, we'd have found it. This way they'll know the minute we move the thing.''

"Exactly. Which is why we'd better leave it precisely where it is.''

"Damn!'' Connor got up and walked across to the window, staring out at the moonlit street. Then he whirled around. "Chief! There might be a way!''

"What d'you mean?''

"A way to move the generator without them knowing.''

"How?''

"Suppose we make a box the same size as the generator, same shape. Can the top of the housing of the generator be taken off?''

"It could be taken off, yes.''

"Suppose we build another top for it. Out of sheet metal, say. The outer casing's nothing special, is it?"

"Just a riveted tank, as far as I recall."

"Suppose—some time when the sky's heavily clouded, preferably with a storm raging—suppose we switch an empty box for the generator, and transfer the painted top of the generator to the box? Then we could take the generator up to Red Lake."

"They might find out," mused Nordstrom.

"What would they do?" Connor spread his hands. "I don't think they'd exterminate us, after going to as much trouble as they have. Probably the worst thing they'd do is take the generator away from us."

Nordstrom seemed to withdraw into a complex pattern of thought. "If anything really offers a threat to them, they show a completely ruthless streak that comes to the surface as suddenly as an explosion. Marek threatened them, and they killed him after one glance at the gun they took away from him. No second chance. Finished!"

"Marek was a fool," said Harn.

"I wouldn't exactly say that," said Connor. "He just listened to different music than the rest of us."

"Every fanatic is certain he's right," said Nordstrom. He seemed to come to a decision. "The kesrii only react violently to an immediate threat, I think. They meet violence with violence—and the unpalatable fact to swallow is that they're much better at it than a human being. So the thing to avoid is giving them the idea that we're planning violence against them. I think we'd be taking a terrible risk in moving that generator."

"I still feel we could make the switch during a storm," persisted Connor. "Get the generator way up the coast while the sky's still opaque to their spy satellite, and leave the box with the painted cover where it was."

"Just had an unpleasant thought," murmured Kosaka. "Suppose their spy satellite uses a vidicon that sees through cloud? Like the ones our people use to look through the smoke at forest fires?"

"Possible," admitted Connor after a moment's silence.

"Wait," broke in Nordstrom. "Those vidicons use infrared. This color the kesrii have used, the one we can't see, is way up in the ultraviolet. The higher frequencies of light are not good for penetrating.''

"So you think, in a storm, we might get away with it?''

"It's a terrible risk, Con.''

Connor managed a smile. "So's life, the way we live it.''

Zella took the news of the bauxite and cane-fields discoveries with a bland, immobile expression that she usually reserved for patients who had to be confronted by bad news. The only change in her face was a darkening of her eyes.

"It could move us forward into a different era,'' said Connor.

"Does that mean you want to live up at Red Lake, as you call it?''

"A lot of the time, yes. I think you'd like it up there.''

"My work is here!'' She was emphatic.

"We'll have aircraft before long. That'll put the two centers less than an hour apart.''

"It'll be just an industrial area up there, won't it?''

"In a sense, yes.''

"Fumes. Smoke. Toxic gases. This place here is beautiful.''

"But Red Lake could be ours. Out of reach of the council.''

A buzzer sounded, and she walked over to the table and pressed a switch. "Yes?''

A breathy voice sounded in a small speaker on the table. "I saw your light on. Can't sleep. Would I be in the way over there?''

Zella looked across the room at Connor, her lips compressed so that only the lower one showed. "You would, a little. Con's just arrived home. He's been exploring up north.''

"I'd like to meet him.''

"Some other time, Voll.'' She listened for a few seconds, then said, "Voll?''

There was no response. She called him again a couple of times, then flicked off the switch.

"This is just emotional blackmail,'' she said. While she'd been speaking, Connor had been warming some water for coffee, and she went over and joined him at the little autokitchen.

"You work long hours, Zel.''

"Goes with the sense of responsibility.''

"Can't they do anything for that? When it's overdeveloped?" He put his arm around her.

"Would you rather I wasn't a responsible person?"

"No. I like you as you are. But don't overdo it."

After they had finished their coffee, she stood up and walked across to the front window. "His light's still on," she said. "I fixed a switch down low so he could reach it. I didn't like the way he wouldn't answer me. I suppose I'd better go over."

"It's cold out there. Getting near the coldest part of the morning."

"I know." She put on a long coat which she had recovered from the haphazard mass of human clothing left by the kesrii. It had a cowl collar she could bring over her head, and it reached her ankles. "Don't come across with me. Just wait for me at the front door," she said.

He watched her walk across to the surgery. A minute later she came out, holding in one hand something he thought at first was a large bucket. As she walked back across the street he moved forward to meet her and slipped his hand through the carrying handle.

"Thanks, Con, but he's not heavy."

Inside, he put the yellow prosthetic shell on the floor, and it immediately rolled forward on its little wheels, its lens lifting as it turned around. The name VOLL was printed in black lettering across the front of it.

"Why didn't you answer?" asked Zella.

"I knew you'd come if I didn't answer," came an amplified whisper from the grill in the front of the shell. "And I couldn't have stood it by myself in there for another minute."

Zella threw back the cowl of her coat, but did not take the coat off. She stood with her hands in her pockets, looking down at the shell. "You can stay for a few minutes, Voll. Then I'm going to take you back there and put you to sleep." She indicated Connor. "This is Con. Planetary surface explorer. He's my man."

The lens turned to focus on Connor, spinning to wide angle. "Zella's told me about you. You look an excellent specimen of the classic male. You have a superb woman here. I've worked with her in Eridan Regional Hospital. She has a good understanding of zero g people. She's even been up to our satellite."

"Quite an experience, that," said Zella, looking at Connor. "Claustrophobic, if you're not careful. I've never seen so many people packed into such small spaces."

"We learn to cooperate with each other very thoroughly," said Voll. "When you have a population of almost spherical bodies with vestigial limbs, cooperation becomes vital."

"We located your woman's prossy today," said Zella. "Red with a black manipulator, slightly bigger than yours, right?"

"Can you get her an exoskel?"

"Not yet."

"Then leave her in stasis. I'll wait for her until we can get to a zero g environment."

"You may have a long wait. Voll, I'm going to take you back now."

"Allow me," said Connor. He picked up the shell by its handle, and Zella opened the door for him. Together, without speaking, they crossed the street to the surgery. Zella made an adjustment to something in the back of the shell, and they said good-night.

Back home Connor helped Zella off with her coat. "Do you have many like that in stasis?" he asked.

"A few. Mostly women. Useful in a zero-grav satellite, but I don't know what the hell we're going to do with them if we never get a satellite up."

"And that's a possibility. What was their satellite really like?"

"Horrible. Imagine a room this size, with the ceiling as high as the table, and a hundred people packed into it, all talking. Ventilation ducts everywhere. It gave me nightmares after I went up there. Funny thing is, they're quite bright in their own milieu. Do most of their work by remote control, or in exoskeletons, if they leave their 'hive,' as we used to call it."

"The human race has certainly taken some odd paths, hasn't it?"

"Yes. But here we are, back in an environment like the one we started in. I wonder if the kesrii realize that?"

"They realize it, all right. They're going to watch our civilization re-evolve—at high speed. Like the scientists who breed drosophila fruit flies."

"Con! What a ghastly idea!"

"But it's true, Zel. Except we may be able to give them a few surprises. Develop quicker than they thought."

"We've got a long way to catch up."

"But we've got a pacemaker ahead of us. The kesrii. Where they go, some day we'll go!"

"How?"

"In a short time we'll have usable aircraft. Then spacecraft. Do you realize what the kesrii have done for us? They've shown us glimpses of a technology a long way ahead of us. They've given us something to aim at. They've shown us the future is practically infinite."

"God, you're starting to talk like a politician. Connor for president!"

He threw his arms around her and kissed her. After a minute she leaned back.

"Connor for panjandrum! Never mind. I'd vote for you, darling. I might even come up to Red Lake from time to time and see how your empire is coming along."

13

The year on Terranova, as they now officially called their planet, proved capable of handing out some surprises. The binary suns had been moving farther apart in the sky each day during the early settlement, but later they began swinging closer to each other. As they approached syzygy it was obvious that one was going to eclipse the other, but as yet no one was sure which of them was nearer.

One morning they rose together, the red component beginning to eclipse the brighter yellow primary. Later the settlers referred to the period as the Big Freeze. The red sun took two days to move across the primary, never totally eclipsing it, but cutting its disc down to a thin crescent. Snow began falling—the first many of the settlers had seen—and a chilling winter overtook them in a single ferocious stride.

Fortunately they had already completed one harvest of their rapid-growing wheat, but some of their other outdoor crops were killed by a savage frost.

"We'll know next time," said Harn, looking out bitterly at the blackened ruins of young crops half buried in snow that appeared a pink blanket in the red sunlight, under an angry maroon sky. "We'll need hectares of thin plastic sheeting to cover the vulnerable parts of the plants."

At least they would have time to prepare for the next onslaught of cold. O'Donnel had by now worked out the orbits of all the bodies in the system that mattered to them.

The binary suns circled their common center of gravity, which was closer to the yellow star, every eighty-nine Terranova days, or about 140 Earth days. The planet itself had a year of 415 of its own days, equivalent to an Earth time of 656 days, or more than a year and nine months.

O'Donnel suggested that the revolution of the binaries, with its two eclipses per circuit, was a more important factor then the year of the planet, and he called it the "short year."

Nordstrom, accustomed to planning ahead in the finest detail, was profoundly jolted by the eclipse and its fierce two-day "winter," which rammed home the realization that they were on a planet not of their own choice.

The district around Red Lake did not seem to have suffered much from the explosive winter. After all, its plant species had been used to surviving the violent onslaught of cold every eighty-nine days.

With the promise of fuel and light alloys dangled enticingly before the community, the project to develop Red Lake went ahead rapidly. Nordstrom gave permission for use of the battery-powered flier to build up a mosaic of survey photos all the way from the Central settlement up beyond Big River.

From these the route for an all-weather road was planned, following the coast fairly closely for the first fifty kilometers, then slanting inland across the plains directly to the point on the south bank of Big River, where Connor and his team had chosen the location for the vehicle-carrying punt.

While work went ahead bulldozing the road, using the large steam tractor, a massive punt was built from local timber on the beach at Central. Later, Mak and a few helpers used the sternwheeler to tow it up the coast and up Big River to its chosen site. Instead of using the long cable-and-rudder method, which would have necessitated an enormous length of cable, the punt employed a small steam engine to haul itself along a shorter line stretched directly across the river. Its first load was the tractor, with its bulldozer blade, which went to work on the north bank cutting a sloping road up to the dry lakebed. The total distance by road from Central to Red Lake was measured at 110 kilometers.

After the two days of winter the weather grew steadily warmer for the next forty-four days, as the hot yellow component of the double star came around closer to the planet.

There was another drop in temperature for a couple of days as the red sun went behind the yellow, but in this case the change was hardly perceptible except in the disappearance of the red edges to the shadows.

Slowly the population of Terranova Central learned to adapt to conditions not quite like those of any planet where human settlements had been established.

By the time the short year of the binary pair had covered its full cycle, a further 130 people had been brought out of stasis, bringing the total active population to 179. The twenty-five still in stasis were judged to be physically unfitted for life in Terranova's gravity.

"Who decides who's not suitable for life here?" Connor asked Zella one day.

"Three of us: the chief, Chang, and I. You can see the trouble we had with Voll. Twenty-five more like that and I'd go into stasis myself."

"How's he getting on these days?"

"Oh, the engineering people built him an exoskeleton. He's not happy with it, but at least he can move around. He even walked down to the beach with me and back a couple of times this week."

"Long walk, isn't it?"

She didn't reply at once, and he turned to look at her. She looked back at him with a Mona Lisa smile. "Con—I'm pregnant."

"*What?*"

He moved towards her and put his arms gently around her. She laughed.

"There's no need to be that careful—yet."

"How long?"

"You know, darling. Remember the night I told you I'd vote Connor for panjandrum."

"The night you said I talked like a politician?"

"You must have—what do they call it?—charisma!"

He kissed her gently and for a long time. Then he leaned back, tenderly caressing her smooth shoulders.

"It's about seventy-five local days, isn't it?"

"Seventy-six."

"That'd be the equivalent of about four Earth months, right?"

She nodded.

"You'll have to come up to Red Lake with me. Soon."

"I want to be here when he arrives."

"He?"

"Doc Chang ran some tests. He says 'he.' "

"I've built a sort of shack up at the lake. I can extend it. Not a bad spot. It overlooks the river one way, the airfield the other. And it's near a grove of the blue native trees something like tamarisks."

"Sounds nice. Look, Con, things are getting quieter for me here. I *might* come up there, get the place ready, as long as you could get me back to Chang in plenty of time." She frowned slightly with one side of her forehead, lifting one eyebrow. "What's the road like?"

"Rough in a few places. Takes nearly six hours in the steam tractor. But by the time I have to bring you back, we'll have something better."

"What?"

"We're building a couple of cars up there. Synthetic rubber tires. I'm taking engines and gearboxes and steering gear back with me from the workshops. Actually, that's why I came down this time." He hugged her lightly. "If I'd known . . ."

"Huh?" she murmured, as he was silent for a few seconds.

"I hope to bring one of the cars down in a few days. A sort of demonstration run. Will you come back with me?"

"If you drive carefully. If it's not too rough, I suppose I could always come back on the boat."

He looked at her, smiling. "He might be the first human being born on Terranova."

"He *will* be. I'm in the position to know."

As he walked down the street towards the workshop, Connor found himself whistling.

The engines were simple four-cylinder horizontally-opposed units, copied from an ancient design except for minor details influenced by later improvements. There were two of them, and as they loaded them into the steam truck, Connor walked over to Sven, who was supervising the hoisting.

"How much aluminum have you got, Sven?"

"Not much. We've used more than half the stock we got from the ship."

"Could you make one of these with aluminum block and

cylinders? Cast-iron liners, if you like. Aluminum pistons and heads?''

"What are you aiming at? The Terranova speed record?''

"I hold that already. No, something else.''

"An aircraft? True?''

"Try a small two-cylinder version first, if you like. Twin opposed. We're building an ultralight. None of us has the experience to go straight into building a full-scale aircraft. All we have are old diagrams from encyclopedia tapes, and old photos.''

"When will you be back?''

"Less than ten days. Be using one of these engines to push one of our cars back. Should do it in less than two hours instead of six.''

"We can get the main castings of a light twin machined for you. You'll have to do the details up there.''

"Right. Thanks, Sven.''

"Pleasure to work with someone fully alive," she said.

He walked across to the steam truck and checked the pressure gauge. "By the way . . .''

"What?''

He walked back to her. "Zella's going to have a boy.''

Sven looked up at him in surprise.

"How's she know it's a boy?''

"Chang knows, somehow.''

"Yours?''

He nodded. She extended a large hand smeared with oil, and he gripped it.

"Personally, I'd rather our way," she said, "but congratulations, Con. To both of you." She hesitated. "It makes you really committed to this place, doesn't it?''

He waved his arms to take in the whole scene. "It'll do me.''

There were eight of them living up at Red Lake now—Connor, Kosaka, Harn, Mak, and four other men more recently brought out of stasis. Connor had selected them after perusing a large number of the dossiers kept with the stasis machines. He had picked young men from planetary surfaces similar in gravity to this one, from metal-rich areas where mechanical engineering was an integral part of their culture. Brought out of stasis and transferred almost straight up to Red Lake as soon as they could travel, they knew little about Terranova Central and its growing social undercurrents.

He left early in the morning with the new engines in the steam truck on the long road up the coast, wondering if this might be the last time he would have to keep watching the pressure gauge and stopping at intervals to stoke the furnace. He arrived about hour seventeen—two hours before midday—and after a meal he set to work with Mak and two of the new recruits to fit one of the engines into the more advanced of the partly built car chassis. While he'd been away, Harn had managed to extract a few liters of methyl alcohol from the canelike plants with which he'd been experimenting.

That evening Connor said to Harn, "You know, next time we increase our team, I think I should bring a few women up here."

"Why? We want engineers. Chemists. Mechanics."

"Look through the dossiers some time. Everyone we have in stasis is qualified, usually in several fields, and some of the engineers and mechanics are women."

Harn gave a sudden grin, and delivered a playful punch to Connor's arm. "Told you you shouldn't have come off your suppressants yet. Another few days and you'll be prancing around like a stud bull."

"Apparently I already have. Zella's pregnant."

"Ze—the doctor?" Harn stood with his mouth open. "When does she—"

"In about ninety-six days from now, near as we can work out. Local days."

"Say! That's great, Con. Here!" Harn thrust out his hand and Connor shook it. "Be the first born here, won't it?"

"That's right."

Harn grinned broadly. "You'll be Terranova's first patriarch."

Connor looked thoughtful. "I hadn't followed it up that far. I suppose I will."

Two days later one of the cars was ready. It looked archaic but functional, the state of their technology forcing them back to a copy of vehicles used on Earth in the middle and late twentieth century. Its body was practically non-existent, except for a stone grid and windshield of plastic. The engine was rear-mounted, the fuel tank in the front.

Once started, the engine ran with a clattering roar, vibrating the whole car. "Firing on three," yelled Mak. He held a screwdriver against each of the plugs, producing a little violet spark until he came to the one that was missing. "Stop her," he called. And so they went on throughout most of the morning, making experimental adjustments to the timing, the carburetor.

In the early afternoon Connor, with Mak sitting beside him, drove their creation out onto the flat, hard surface of the dry lake. The gearbox Central's workshop had supplied worked more smoothly than he had expected. He drove out across the lake, increasing speed until the wind whistled in his ears.

"We've done it!" shouted Mak, slapping a hand on his shoulder. "We're on our way, Con! On our way!"

Swung in a series of tightening curves, the machine handled surprisingly well, perhaps because its steering geometry had been copied slavishly from old drawings found on the encyclopedia tapes.

Connor headed back across the lake, astonished at the distance they had traveled from their little workshop. On the way he handed over control of the car to Mak, who had less previous experience of handling wheeled vehicles. Mak proceeded at a more dignified speed.

"You can start getting the other engine into the other chassis," said Connor as they came to a stop outside the workshop. He indicated the second shed a short distance away. "Me—I think I'll have a look at the ultralight aircraft. Did you do any more to the frame?"

"No. We've been concentrating on the cars."

"No matter. I'll see what I can do. Call you fellows if I need help. And vice versa."

He whistled happily as he walked towards the aircraft shed.

Ten days later Connor took one of the cars, with a spare drum of methanol on board, and drove down the 110-kilometer road to Terranova Central. In some of the stretches of road— where it crossed the plains at an angle towards the coast, for instance—he was able to push his speed close to a hundred kilometers per hour, the air-cooled engine putting out a sustained, even roar that sent pterosaurs spiraling up from their rocky eyries in alarm while he was still far away from them. The other flying creatures, like the huge butterflies, paid no attention to him. Apparently they were completely devoid of either hearing or intelligence.

He completed the journey in less than two hours, a vast improvement on the time taken by the clumsy steam truck. The north road they had bulldozed approached the town just above the beach and swung into the lower end of the street. Connor drove noisily up the street, past the HQ—wondering what Nordstrom made of the sound—and on up to the surgery, parking the car just around the corner of the building.

Zella came to the door as he climbed out of the car. "It's like one in our museum back in Eridan," she said, moving down to look at the machine more closely. "Does it have to make all that noise?"

"No. We could have fitted some kind of silencer, but that can come later."

"We had electric cars back home. They were practically silent. Although some of the boys used to race in things like this—well away from populated areas, though."

"Can you come back with me?"

"When are you leaving?"

"Maybe tomorrow. I'm taking an engine back with me for our light aircraft."

"I'd better stay here for a while. You'll be down again in a few days, won't you?" As she spoke she led the way into the surgery, where she seemed to be alone.

"Yes. That might work out better, actually. Working on the cars and the planes, I haven't put any time in on extending our house. It's pretty basic at the moment. One room three meters by four, with a veranda along one side. We've got fresh water in the Upper River, and we've run a pipeline—but never mind the details. I'll have it more presentable by the time you arrive."

"Good. Things are winding down here, now that most of the people are out of stasis. Few minor accidents, but Chang's coping with those as they come, and Voll's a lot of help, mostly in an advisory capacity so far."

"He didn't go mad, then?"

Zella started, and didn't answer.

"Certainly not," came a breathy, amplified whisper. What Connor had taken as a piece of equipment suddenly moved forward from near one wall. Turning, he realized that Voll's prosthetic shell was now supported by an obviously jury-rigged exoskeleton of thin metal rods linked by a cage: six rods—three moving together, then the other three—like the legs of an ant. The lens was level with his face now, and it spun to focus on him. The manipulator gave a spasmodic movement that might have been intended as a wave of welcome.

"Sorry," said Connor. "I didn't recognize you."

"No, I didn't go mad," went on the eerie voice. "Close to it, perhaps. The space outside the building was terrifying at first, but the human mind can adapt, can't it?"

Zella said, "Con's just driven a car 110 kilometers down from Red Lake."

"I can't grasp distances like that. In our satellite, as you know, a hundred meters is a considerable distance."

"I know. Sometimes I dream about it even now, although I was only there a short time, and then only in the guest apartments where the rooms have high ceilings—two meters." She shivered.

The lens turned to focus on her face. "You'll be leaving, then?"

"Yes. In a few days."

"There'll be no one here who knows me!"

Zella stood in front of him. "Listen, Voll. I've got them fixing another exoskel for your woman. I'll bring her out of stasis before I leave."

"She won't be happy with this type of skel," said Voll. "She was a very active woman."

"I know. I've seen her dossier. Assembly of space equipment, setting up of mining gear on asteroids. She's been around a lot."

"Yes, but what you don't realize is that she did all that by remote control."

Zella shrugged. "She'll adjust, Voll. *You* adjusted. And you'll be here to help her."

Voll made no reply. It suddenly came to Connor that this was the main trouble in communicating with these zero-gravity people. You were talking to an outer shell which showed no expression. When Voll said nothing, you didn't know whether he was worried, asleep, or aflame with anger. There was no feedback in the conversation.

"I'd better get down to the workshop," Connor said. "See how they're getting on with my engines."

The idea of building an engine for aircraft seemed to have caught the imagination of Sven and her team. They had used aluminum alloy to cast cylinder blocks like those used in the cars, so that in addition to the small twin-cylinder unit they had promised him for the ultralight, they had a larger, flat four-cylinder. It was complete except for the fitting of its carburetors and other accessories.

Connor had both engines loaded aboard the car. Since no backseats had been fitted yet, and no external body, it was easy to rope both units securely in place for the journey north.

Before leaving, he checked with Nordstrom on the possibility of sending a few more selected people up to Red Lake to work on the projects there, some of them female this time. The chief was in favor of balancing the sex ratio of the population in each region, and gave Connor copies of some of the potential candidates' dossiers to make his final selection.

After that Connor had a meal with Zella, then was on his way. His return trip took him slightly longer than the run down, because of the extra load of the engines and the need to protect them from too much rough riding.

By the following day they had the twin-cylinder unit tested and fitted to the ultralight aircraft. This was a flimsy, batlike affair, with high wings and a single seat; the engine set high, with the propeller behind it.

Connor tipped a little methanol into the carburetor, then sat in the low seat, resting his feet on the rudder pedals. He pulled the safety belt tight.

"Now's as good a time as any," he said. Mak swung the propellor by hand a few times, and after a wheezing cough the engine fired.

Chocks in front of the two larger wheels—the rear pair of the tricycle landing gear—held the craft stationary except for the violent shivering of its fragile wings as the engine misfired a few times. Gradually the engine note smoothed into a steady hum.

"Right," shouted Conner. Mak and one of his helpers pulled away the chocks, and the machine rocked its way foreward. The propellor had no such refinement as variable pitch, and Connor's only method of controlling his speed was by the throttle. He opened it fully, and the aircraft lumbered forward across the dry lakebed. Connor was just about to close the throttle, thinking he had no chance of getting airborne, when the wheels abruptly lifted from the ground. One of the wings drooped, and he hastily moved the simple control stick across to regain balance.

The flying speed of the little machine was unexpectedly low. He eased the stick carefully back, gaining height slowly, listening to the load on the engine. About fifteen meters above the red ground he leveled off, looking down at the double shadow of the craft skimming below him like a gigantic bat. Carefully he lowered one wing and used the rudder gingerly, bringing the plane around in a wide curve.

The whole of the remaining population of Red Lake—all seven—were lined up in front of the shed. As he swept around past them, they were obviously cheering and shouting, although he could not hear them above the uneven drone of the engine and propeller.

Connor flew in a wide circle a couple of times, made a figure eight, then headed back for a landing. He jolted down on the surface, then headed back to the shed across the ground, keeping the engine speed low to avoid any risk of unplanned takeoff.

He cut the power, and the others raced towards him across the dry ground as he climbed out of the machine.

"We're on our way!" shouted Mak. "On our way to the stars!"

14

During the next few days Connor divided his time between working on the aircraft and adding to his house on the ridge overlooking the river. The steam truck and its trailer brought up several loads of timber from the sawmill, stained green with a preservative someone in Central had developed, and Connor took what he needed to build three more rooms on to his one-room shack, working with the part-time assistance of two, sometimes three of the new arrivals. There was a veranda along each of the two long sides, one facing the airfield, the other giving a view over a long reach of Big River and its confluence with the Upper River.

He kept in daily radio contact with Zella, and also with Chang. When Chang assured him it would be safe for Zella to travel up to Red Lake, Connor went down in one of the cars and brought her and a considerable amount of luggage back up the 110-kilometer road to Red Lake.

When he drove the car onto the punt and then started the small steam engine moving, Zella got out of the car and stood looking out over the broad river, watching the cable lift from the yellow-green water as the engine wound its way across. About halfway over, the color of the water changed to brownish red, stained by the inflow from Upper River, which cut through the bauxite deposits on its way to join the main stream.

"There's our place, up on the ridge," said Connor, pointing.

"It must have quite a view," said Zella, who up to this point had seemed lukewarm about Red Lake.

When the punt jolted onto the slope cut in the far bank, Connor shut off the drive.

"Isn't there someone who permanently operates this thing?" asked Zella.

"Can't spare the manpower for that. Whoever needs it uses it. If it's the wrong side of the river, you just pull this lanyard, and that runs steam into the cylinder and gets it moving."

A few minutes later she was standing on the veranda of the house, looking out over the river, her hands resting on the sanded wooden railing. "You've made a good job of this, Con."

"Motivation. That's the secret." He put his arm around her shoulders, pointing down the river. "See that road along the far bank? That runs about nine kilometers down to the site of the aluminum plant. Should keep any pollution well away from us."

"Good. By the way, a few kilometers back along the road we passed between a couple of posts, one on each side. What were they?"

"Electric eye beam. When we broke it, we signaled that something was coming up the road. Someone would have checked the steam pressure on the punt and pulled the lanyard to send it over to our side."

Zella walked through the house. "This could be made to look quite livable. What are these walls that look like dried mud?"

"Adobe. Okay as long as it's shielded from direct, heavy rain. I started with that, then added timber." He touched a switch, and electric light shone. "Power on. How about some coffee?"

"Great. Oh, I brought some of the new tea up. Grown in one of the plastic domes, so far, but it's good."

Connor had to resist an impulse to whistle happily as he made the coffee. Zella seemed to be settling in more smoothly than he had expected.

It was becoming evident that the population of Terranova was splitting into two quite different philosophies. One regarded their stay as temporary, awaiting only the time when they might make contact with some other branch of the human race and bring about what they thought of as rescue. The other faction, like Connor—all the people at Red Lake, and the more energetic at Central—had accepted the fact that Terranova was their home, and that whatever the future held for them would develop from here.

Chang was tied for the time to Central, being that settlement's only fully effective doctor now that Zella's pregnancy was beginning to limit her activities. Twenty days after the explosive winter of the next eclipse of the yellow sun, Connor drove her down to Central and left her in Chang's care, with strict instructions to several people to call him as soon as the birth of the child became imminent.

While in Central he looked at the workshops to check on equipment being built for the projected aluminum plant. A large, barrel-shaped steam-pressure tank had been built for the dissolving of the bauxite in caustic soda, and a number of precipitation tanks and parts of the furnace were completed.

"Might come up with this stuff myself," said Sven. "Like to see how you're getting along at the lake. How are the aircraft?"

"The four-seater's almost ready to fly, and we've started work on a twin-engined plane. Long range."

"Sounds as if Red Lake's where a lot of it's happening."

"The next thing will be to grab the generator from the island."

"How many of you?"

"Three or four. Mak, Jiro, me."

"I wouldn't mind being in on that."

"It'll be rough out there. We'll switch it right on syzygy, when the storms are at their worst."

"I'm used to boats. And I'm quite strong."

"I know that. Well, if you feel you'd like to help, Sure."

"Why'd you pick syzygy?"

"It's when the planet's nearest the yellow sun. You get the densest buildup of cloud during the middle of the day, and really massive downpours of rain late each afternoon. I've got the feeling the kesrii mightn't expect us to make a move like that while the weather's so hostile."

"You might be right. I wouldn't even try to figure how they think. Best of luck, though."

•   •   •

On the day they had chosen, the clouds had built up into dark, purple thunderheads by midday, and lightning flickered over the sea and towards the south.

"This could be the time," said Connor, standing with Zella at the window of the house opposite the surgery.

"Be very careful, Con," Zella said. "Listen, is it really needed? We're going along all right at the moment. Is it worth antagonizing them just to get an easy source of power?"

"It could be a shortcut to cheap aluminum and a whole lot of its alloys. You can do a hell of a lot with aluminum, especially in an economy where you haven't got the range of plastics you have where there are oil deposits."

She was silent, looking at him penetratingly.

"What?" he asked.

She lifted her eyebrow with her sudden, asymmetrical smile. "You never like to stand still, do you? Always onward, onward."

He struck a heroic pose. "Onward and upward into the raging storm."

"I think that's what I like about you, Con. But for all the gods' sakes, be careful!"

"I'm always careful. If you spend your formative years in a space station, you learn to plan before you move."

"It's more complicated than that. Nordstrom plans everything before he moves, but half the time he finishes up not moving. You're more willing to take a chance."

During the morning, Kosaka and Mak had flown down from Red Lake, and by the twenty-second hour, about six and a half hours before sunset, they knocked on the door.

"Ready?" asked Mak.

"Let's go," said Connor. He kissed Zella, holding her for a long moment, and then went out with the others. They walked quickly down the street under a sky that was rapidly becoming more overcast. The rolling purple clouds obscured both suns, throwing an eerie gloom over the town. Mak, the most skilled with handling machines, drove the mobile crane up its ramp to the deck of the sternwheeler.

"We have steam up," he said. "We can cast off any minute now—as soon as we've secured the crane."

"Here's Sven coming," said Kosaka suddenly. Connor turned. Sven's blocky figure waddled down the beach, hands

in the pockets of her enormous brown leatheroid coat, short
blond hair disheveled by the rising wind.

"Need some extra muscle on this, won't you?" she asked
as she stamped up the ramp to the deck.

"Do you know where we're going?" asked Kosaka.

She joined them in the shelter of the wheelhouse. "I agree
with what you're doing. I want to help wherever I can."

The three men exchanged glances. Mak gave a short laugh.
"It's hardly a job for a woman."

Sven moved closer to him, then seized him in her grotes-
quely muscular arms and lifted him as easily as if he were a
baby, holding him high above her head. His arms and legs
thrashed for a moment, then he lay still in her grasp.

"Why not, Mak?" she asked in an exaggeratedly sweet
voice.

"Put him down, Sven," said Connor quietly. "He's had
no experience with heavy-gravity people."

"Of course." She swung Mak to the deck, head downward, so that he landed on his hands and scrambled angrily to
his feet, his face red.

"I'm sorry," he said, with a brief glance at Sven. His eyes
were bright with fury.

"That's enough of that sort of thing, both of you," snapped
Connor. "Look, we're in enough trouble here without quar-
reling among ourselves. We have to work together. Smoothly.
Right?"

"Right," said Sven, and Mak grunted. Connor looked at
him intently.

"Right," he said, when it became obvious that Connor
was waiting for an answer.

"Good," said Connor. "Then let's get with it."

They headed south through the lagoon for ten kilometers
under a steadily darkening sky. A weird band of greenish
light from seaward slanted under the cloud. They had just
reached the break in the reef, opposite the river mouth, when
rain began to fall in a gray curtain, cutting down visibility to
a couple of hundred meters in every direction.

Their radar, though primitive, at least showed them the
outline of the reef and the islands, and they headed through
the gap into water that surged in great, rolling swells. The

deck tilted one way and then the other as they crossed the waves at an angle.

"Cut her revs down!" shouted Connor. Mak moved the lever controlling the centrifugal governor so that the engine's beat slowed to a steady, shuddering thump.

"Why?" asked Kosaka.

"Uneven strain on the paddle wheel. Speeds up when the stern rides over a wave, then takes a lot of sudden load when it drops back deep into the water."

It took a long time to reach the island. Connor gave its northern point a wide clearance, since no soundings had been taken in the vicinity and the tapering end of the island finished in jagged rocks that snarled like fangs in the flurry of white water.

There was a small bay on the seaward side of the island, where they had landed before. Connor drove the sternwheeler very slowly in until it grated on the crescent of white sand. They moored to projections of rock, and Mak used the ship's crane to lift off the mobile crane.

Connor climbed through the driving rain to a high point on the island's central ridge, and from two angles took quick-developing photos of the generator. Then he scrambled down again.

The generator was compact and heavy. After a glance at the low, ebony ceiling of cloud, Connor and Kosaka began removing the top, which fortunately had been secured by bolts, not by rivets or welding.

As they worked, Mak used the cranes to get the box they had brought with them alongside the generator. Working silently, they exchanged the top of the generator with that of the box, then lifted the machine with the crane. It took all its power. Next they removed the stock of fuel from under the black cover.

Within half an hour the generator and fuel were safely on the deck of the boat, and the generator had been replaced by the box they'd brought. Connor didn't doubt that the top and the cover, black to his eyes, would show the kesrii that vivid, unimaginable color in the ultraviolet. They left the cover over an array of hastily gathered rocks forming an outline similar to that of the original stack.

Connor made a second ascent of the high point on the island, stood exactly where he'd been when he took the previous photos, and took fresh ones. Scrambling down again while they developed, he compared the pictures with the first pair he had taken.

"See any difference, Jiro?"

Looking for several seconds at the photos, Kosaka pointed. "The corner of the cover over the stack looks a bit different."

"You're right. Let's fix it."

A few minutes were spent brushing away the wheel marks of the mobile crane, and they were ready to leave.

The whole scene was lit by the white glare of lightning, and a deafening crash of thunder sounded no more than a second afterward. They used the ship's crane to stow the generator in the shallow hold amidships, then lifted the mobile crane in ahead of it. Connor started the paddles turning in reverse, but the ship was held firmly on the sand, weighed down by the added mass of the generator.

"We'd better try and lever her off," said Kosaka.

"Wait," said Connor. "Can we get more weight astern? Shift the generator right against the back of the hold!"

Mak used the mobile crane to crowd the heavy generator as far astern as possible, then moved the crane aft until it straddled it.

Lightened at the bow, the ship grated on the sand, but remained stuck.

"Let's go over and push it," suggested Kosaka.

"Here," said Mak. "We can lever it with these." He picked up a long beam of wood while Kosaka grabbed another. They both leaped overboard into the boiling surf, levering at the bow of the ship. It moved slightly. Connor kept the drive on the paddle wheel in reverse.

"The tide's running out," said Sven, taking off the leatheroid coat. "We'll be stuck here."

"Stay as far astern as possible," said Connor.

"Got a better idea," she answered, and before he could argue with her she waddled quickly forward, her thick body like a gorilla's as the rain plastered her clothing against her skin. She swung over the side and joined Kosaka and Mak in the water, pushing upward on the bow of the ship.

"Together!" shouted Kosaka against the howling wind. "*Now!*"

Connor kept the paddles thrashing, increasing their speed.

Abruptly the ship ground its way sidways over the sand, then backward. Kosaka and Mak scrambled aboard.

"Sven!" shouted Mak, turning. Suddenly he sprang overboard again, holding the gunwale with one hand, extending the other. Connor halted the drive of the paddles, and the long-shore current swept the ship sideways. Kosaka reached over, gripped Mak's arm and threw his weight backward, bracing his feet against the gunwale. Mak came into sight again, and after him, bedraggled, came Sven. She clamped a broad hand on the edge of the gunwale, and a moment later all three of them were on the deck. Connor threw the paddles into full speed reverse, and the ship backed away from the beach.

"That was closer than I liked," muttered Kosaka as he ran into the shelter of the wheelhouse.

Mak and Sven followed him in. Sven flung her gigantic arms around the two of them and hugged them against the wet, steaming barrel of her body. She didn't say anything, but to Connor her face said it all. He grinned at the three of them as he swung the ship back in a curve, then threw the paddles into forward and headed north.

"Good work," he shouted above the wind. "We've got a good team here."

They didn't seem to hear him. He began whistling as the ship pounded its way across the diagonal waves on its long journey northward into the deepening gloom.

Heading north up the center of the long lagoon, Connor used their newly fitted radar to keep his course about equidistant from the reef and the shore, because in the shimmering curtain of rain he could see neither. However, as the primary sun was setting, the rain ended, and with some relief he was able to rely on visual judgment.

The red binary was just clear of the eclipsing primary, and their eyes adjusted to its dimmer light as they sailed on across a black sea with its waves tipped bloodred, under a dark magenta sky in which some of the brighter stars began to show. Connor could pick out Beta Tauri in the northeast, an intense, blue point of light sparkling like a welding arc. Near it, the Hyades were a shower of gold dust.

The regular vibration of the paddle wheel pounded as they drove onward. Connor, in the darkened corner of the wheelhouse, watched the small radar screen for any offshore objects, but all that showed was the straggling line of the coast and occasional high points on the reef.

It was the first time they had made the journey to Red Lake in the dark. The early part of the voyage up the broad lagoon was safe enough, as first one, then two of the planet's pockmarked moons shone down on the water, making two tracks of reflected light that converged at the ship.

Danger would come when they neared the cutting. Under normal conditions Connor would have used their powerful halogen light to flood the narrow gap ahead of them, but this time he was acutely aware that the kesrii or some of their automatic surveillance equipment might be watching from orbit.

"Should still be night when we get there," said Mak. "Want to try dumping the generator off in the dark?"

"No, I don't think so. Should be cloudy again tomorrow afternoon, if the weather runs true to pattern. We can get it to its final position, under cloud cover, and get a roof over it to make it harder to spot. Working at night we'd have to use lights, and that's more likely to arouse their suspicions."

"How long do you think we have before they realize we've switched the generator for a dummy?"

"Anybody's guess. They might have discovered it already, for all I know—might be watching us with an infrared telescope."

Mak looked up at the sky, where more of the stars were now showing through ragged drifts of cloud. "Gives you a nasty feeling, doesn't it? Being watched, I mean. And not even knowing *when* you're watched."

"We can live with it," said Connor. "Life's never exactly the way you'd like it."

By the time they reached the cutting between the headland and the island, one of the moons was close to the meridian, and one wall of the artificial canyon was lit by its orange-tinted light. The other side was as black as space. Mak steered while Connor stood at the back of the wheelhouse, knocking a piece of wood against the doorjamb and listening to the double echo returning from the rocky walls to either side. As long as the sharp echoes coincided, he knew they were near enough to the middle of the channel, even though the wall to his right was invisible in the blackness.

At last they glided out into the open lagoon again, and all of them relaxed. Mak increased the engine speed, and a flurry of water lifted from the paddles.

Connor looked at the modified quartz clock in the wheelhouse. Hour twenty-two. It would still be night when they reached the mouth of Big River. He lay down on the vibrating deck and was almost instantly asleep.

He awoke with the cessation of the noise of the engine and the paddle wheel. The silence was punctuated only by the slapping of small waves against the hull and the occasional far-off screech of some living thing in the darkness.

He sat up, then got to his feet, stretching his arms. Kosaka was just coming out of the wheelhouse.

"Where are we, Jiro?"

"Mouth of Big River. We thought it wouldn't be wise to use lights up the channel, and without them we could run aground in the swamps."

Connor looked at the clock. "Only an hour to sunrise! I must have slept like a rock."

"You did. Do you good. You needed it."

With daybreak they moved ahead again up the river. By now they had marked the channel with poles with their top ends painted green and red. Some day they would use lights, but that could wait until the aluminum plant demanded heavy, regular traffic up and down the river.

They reached the bend in the river nine kilometers from the town, the place where they planned the aluminum plant, about mid-afternoon. In Connor's absence the late-arrival boys, as he thought of his recent assistants, had built the shed to house the generator. It looked suitably makeshift to avert any suspicion from a surveyor from orbit. It looked like a large open carport with a thatched roof, the thatching made from some vegetation culled from the swamp nearby. Whether it was good thatching or not didn't matter, as sandwiched within it was waterproof sheeting of plastic from their dwindling supplies.

They moored quickly on solid ground on the outside bank on the curve, and used the ship's crane to lift off the mobile crane. Then they transferred the generator and moved it as quickly as possible under the thatched roof. Connor was unable to resist glancing at the sky, but of course in daylight it told him nothing about the possibility of alien eyes or instruments scrutinizing their every move.

It was still now, and warm. A few of the large, butterfly-like things fluttered above the swamp vegetation, and a few of the buzzing, fast-flying insects whirred past them, too swiftly to be seen.

One of the cars had been left at the site, and Connor drove it up the road to the punt, leaving the others at the site of the aluminum plant. Crossing over, he went straight to his house, where he made a radio call to Zella.

"I'm fine," she said in answer to his question. "Chang says the baby should arrive about seventeen days after the next syzygy—a bit over a short year from now."

"I'll fly down and pick you up in a day or so. You'd better stay up here until the winter, at least."

He checked up on the four-seater aircraft and found it complete, ready for its test flight. Working with one of Mak's protégés, he got the engine running out on the tarmac, letting it idle with the wheels of the aircraft chocked while he made adjustments to the two carburetors.

He had just finished when he heard the sound of paddles thrashing in the river, and a few minutes later Kosaka, Sven, and Mak came up the sloping road from the mooring place to the airfield.

"Here's where your last engine finished up," Connor called to Sven.

"Thought it might have been something like this." Her eyes gleamed with excitement. "Had it off the deck yet?"

"Only a meter or two. Just taxied it so far. Done more flying in the little ultralight next door. This'll be the first real test I've given this."

Mak helped him push the plane out onto the lakebed with the engine dead. They turned it to face the slight breeze, Mak replaced the chocks under the wheels, and Connor turned over the motor.

"You take off that way?" asked Sven.

"Straight into the wind, what there is of it. No need for a control tower around here yet."

Connor tipped a little methanol from a bottle into each of the two simple carburetors, one of which fed each pair of horizontal cylinders. Then he climbed aboard the machine, sitting behind the controls.

"Short on instruments yet," he called. "Tacho, oil pressure, temp, fuel, and that's it. No compass yet, no altimeter, no artificial horizon—they can come later, if we have time."

"At least you have what you need to keep from blowing your motor up," said Sven.

Connor started the engine again. It ran irregularly for a time, coughing oil smoke. Gradually its sound smoothed out, lifting in pitch as Connor closed the choke and opened the throttle slightly. When the engine was fully warmed up he signaled to Mak to pull away the chocks.

He taxied out across the field, back again, out again, gradually increasing speed until he could feel the machine almost lifting. The wind roared around the somewhat angular cabin. He lifted slightly, felt the wings tilt to one side, adjusted the trim until they were level.

One more run, opening the throttle wide. He pulled the wheel back and the ground dropped away. There was an immense difference between this machine and the ultralight, not only in power, but in stability. He climbed steadily for perhaps a thousand meters, finding his height hard to estimate because he was unsure of the various little clues based on horizon distance and the height of trees sweeping below him—they were a species strange to him and he wasn't sure of their height.

Once, as he roared over a swamp, a flight of leathery-winged reptilian things swirled above the mangrovelike trees. He saw no birds anywhere, only the occasional scaly bat-winged predator cruising effortlessly on uptrends from the sun-heated rocks.

Climbing further, he was soon able to see over the undulating hills along his right-hand horizon. Away beyond—he could not estimate how far off—a line of more majestic mountains blended with the overall color of the sky, except for their upper peaks, which were touched with white. Beyond the nearer hills lay an enormous vista of plains.

He swung back southward. The dry lakebed, a vast brick-red oval, was visible from a great distance. He approached it, losing height, picked out the black-and-yellow wind sock drooping against its mast and went in for a landing. The machine touched down smoothly enough, and he closed the throttle until the moving blades of the propeller flickered into view. His spectators were lined up in front of the larger shed,

Sven easy to pick out from the others, squat and impossibly broad.

He brought the machine to a stop on the rolled-gravel section in front of the sheds—they used the archaic word tarmac, although no one in Red Lake knew its derivation.

"You've got it made!" shouted Sven as he cut the engine. "You could fly around the planet in that thing! To hell with Nordstrom and his rationing of batteries."

Climbing down, Connor pointed to a number of drums under a sun roof next to the sheds. "See that? Methanol. Enough to keep this plane in the air every day for a year. Say, how are you going back to Central?"

"Boat, I suppose."

"How about flying back with me? I want to show this thing off to Nordstrom and O'Donnel. Show them what we're doing here."

She looked at the machine dubiously. "Will it take my weight?"

"Should. We built it for four people." Connor grinned. "You know, I'd love to see the chief's face when we first fly in over Central."

"Don't overdo it," cautioned Sven.

A quick meal and Connor went back out to the aircraft, where Mak had been warming up the engine. "She's gassed up," he said. "Oil okay. Don't over-rev her."

"Right." Connor climbed into the pilot's seat and carefully opened the throttle, watching his gauges. Sven came around the corner of the shed, putting on her brown leatheroid coat. She looked like a mythological giantess shuffling forward on her knees.

"Must be a weird planet where they come from," muttered Mak in a low voice. "Wide as they're high."

Sven came to the side of the aircraft, reached up and put a thick hand around the girder above the inside of the door. "Will that hold me?"

"It should," said Connor. "It's one of the main longerons."

Sven grunted, pulled down on it with her hand. The whole aircraft sank visibly on its undercarriage. With a sudden movement she lifted her massive body into the two backseats, and the landing gear settled farther. She gave a short laugh. "Cargo aboard. What do I do with the seat belt?"

Mak leaned in through the door. "Use one part each from two seats."

Connor took the full length of the lakebed to become airborne. He climbed slowly, then banked gradually around towards the south.

"Haven't been in the air since they dumped us on this planet," said Sven.

"Be good to see Zella again," said Connor.

"You have a nice girl there, Connor," said Sven.

"I know."

"Look after her, or I'll come and give you a Ceti hug."

"What's a Ceti hug?"

"It caves in your rib cage and breaks your back."

He digested the thought for a few seconds. "Fair enough. I think you could do it, too."

"I've done it—once," said Sven.

It sounded to Connor like an invitation to him to act as confessor. He declined the gambit. He looked straight ahead and said nothing.

15

Connor made his approach to Red Lake as dramatic as possible. He came from the land side of the town, flying low over the ruined cement buildings they had seen on that first day when they'd climbed the ridge. He passed the corroded tripod structure left by their unknown predecessors on top of the hill, then descended towards the buildings of Central in a shallow dive, the engine revving higher as the load on it decreased.

He lined up with Main Street as if it had been a runway, and roared the length of it at a height of only fifty meters. All the way along people came out of the buildings to stare at the aircraft, which must have looked to many of them like an anachronism from the distant past.

At the seaward end of town he lifted in a banking sweep to the left, circled the settlement, then touched down on a hard, elevated strip of beach he had noted as a potential landing ground long before. He turned with his wheel brake and taxied to the lower end of the street.

"That woke them up," he said.

"You probably frightened the adrenals out of some of them. Remember, most of them have never seen an aircraft like this. They probably thought it was an alien invasion. Lucky someone didn't shoot at us."

A number of the settlers lined up near the end of the street as Connor and Sven walked towards them.

"Where did you get it?" called one.

"We're building them up at Red Lake," said Connor.

Nordstrom was striding down the center of the street, lifting an arm in greeting. "Impressive flying, Con. I hope you've done some preliminary practice."

"Years of it. Not here, of course."

"And that's all done on methanol power?"

"Yes. I think our transport worries are over. Forget about batteries from the ship."

Nordstrom gestured. "Come up to the office."

He turned and stalked up the street, Connor and Sven following. Once inside he closed the door against a number of curious spectators who had followed the trio up the street.

"Any special reason for this visit, Con? Sven?"

"Several," said Connor, as they took the chairs indicated. "First of all, I came to see Zella. Another thing is this: we want to use one of our aircraft for surveying. Are you doing any aerial surveying right now?"

"None," admitted Nordstrom. "You know the extent we've covered, up and down the coast. We haven't added to it, since our batteries are irreplaceable."

"I see. We're producing plenty of methanol now, so we have no restriction on the use we make of the planes. If you could lend us the aerial cameras and a supply of film, we could go ahead and begin surveying very large areas. Right across the planet, in time. We'd supply copies of our pictures to the Central data bank, of course."

"I don't see why not. Take all the equipment and supplies you need."

"What's been happening down here?"

"Quite a bit. Since you've been up north, Karl has jury-rigged a lot of astronomical equipment, optical and radar. He thinks he's located our original ship, parked in orbit around this planet. The orbit's inclined about forty degrees from the equator, so every few days it passes over us a couple of times with a two-hour interval. But there are other things orbiting, one in a synchronous orbit that keeps it right on our meridian, above the equator. Others, smaller, are lower down, one on a high-inclination orbit passing every ninety-four minutes."

Connor shrugged. "They could have been put up centuries ago. By anyone. Might have nothing to do with us."

"Not the one in synch orbit, right on this meridian."

"I suppose not. That *is* pretty definite, isn't it?"

"But there's something else. A number of times our people have noticed things flying past through the air. Things like fast-flying insects, they thought—until someone took a photo of one."

"What did it show?"

"That's the point. Nothing."

"Hard to focus on a thing like that."

"But this was photographed with distant trees in the background. Over a small, circular area, there's a blur. You can't see anything in it, and *you can't see the foliage in the background*!"

"Fault in the film?" suggested Sven uncertainly.

"No. We have no idea how it's done, but the thing seems to be some kind of flying surveillance machine that generates a field that bends light waves around it. Against a clear sky you see only the background sky color. It's only when we got this thing against a complex background—a multitude of small leaves—that bending the light didn't hide it."

There was silence for a time. Then Connor said, "I thought it took an intense gravitational field to bend light."

"Or a system of lenses? But apparently the kesrii have something else that produces a similar effect to a gravity field within a very small space."

"How small?"

"The sphere of the blur wouldn't be more than fifteen or twenty centimeters in diameter. The thing at the heart of it would be much smaller."

Connor sat very still for a few seconds. "Some of those—insects, we thought—were buzzing around up at Red Lake. So they watch us all the time, the way we might watch things in a zoo." He flung his arms wide. "Let's forget about it and go on with making our economy work."

"I haven't told you all of it," said Nordstrom. "After we took the photo, Karl rigged up an insect trap of a type he'd seen described in some article. Mesh of fine net, on the flat roof of a building, with powerful springs and elastic cables that could swing it over like a door. He picked a place where these things often flew, near windows of Nargis Lal's laboratory. A couple of his boys took it in turns to wait, with a radio switch that enabled them to fire the net from a distance."

"What happened?"

"One of the 'insects' flew along, and they fired the net

over it. As the net made contact there was a sharp explosion, like a rifle shot, and a brilliant spark of blue light where the 'insect' had been. They rushed over, noticed a smell like burning insulation. A big hole had been blasted out of the net, and all they could find of the 'insect' was this."

Nordstrom went over to a table and returned with a tray of tiny objects, together with a magnifying glass. "Notice these blades," he said. "Blue metal we can't identify. Thin, less than a micron thick, yet you can't break them with pliers. Six blades, three made to rotate in each direction on coaxial shafts. At the bottom, wide-angle lens. Nearly everything in between was completely destroyed by the explosion—apparently the motor and power source blew up like a bomb—the other pieces are fragments of directional fins that guided the thing, and what looked like tiny aerials."

Connor looked at the minute scraps of metal and crystal through the magnifying glass. "We have further to go than I thought," he said.

"Further to go. . . ?"

"To catch up. Looks as if it may take generations." He looked from Sven to Nordstrom. "But we'll get there. Some day we'll get there!"

Connor didn't tell Zella about the insectlike surveillance machines until a few days after they had returned to Red Lake. During these days he'd seen no sign of the tiny machines, and a radio call to Central established that they were no longer being sighted there. Apparently once one of them had been discovered, the kesrii believed it was useless to persist with the same system. Zella was relieved when he told her this, but Connor, who always tried to look at all sides of a situation, was unable to help wondering why the kesrii had dropped their method after one reverse. It suggested that they had other ways of spying on their human zoo. Perhaps many ways.

He had brought back a couple of good survey cameras—the best the expedition had possessed—and a generous supply of quick-developing film. He did not install the cameras in the four-seater machine, because the twin-engined craft was already almost completed, and Sven had promised to send two more engines up within a few days on the steam truck.

By the time the engines arrived, the new machine had

already been converted for survey flying, with the large camera fitted into a floor aperture. A viewfinder, mounted beside the pilot's seat, was adjusted to cover the camera's field, pointing vertically downward when the aircraft was in level flight. Other modifications included the installation of long-range fuel tanks and the fitting of a compass and an altimeter.

After he had given the machine a thorough test flight, Connor loaded the large camera and made a number of experimental passes over the Red Lake area at a precise height, on a carefully held compass bearing, taking pictures at regular intervals. Landing, he spread the developed prints on a table, with Mak and Harn at his side.

"You could operate slightly higher," said Harn. "You have a fair amount of overlap there."

"I was at six hundred meters. Say a thousand?"

"A thousand should do it."

After a few more tests Connor had the technique evolved to his satisfaction. "I'll start working northward up the coast, and as far in as the ranges," he said. "May as well start now. We'll fill the auxiliary tanks, and I'll get away."

It was an odd sensation, flying over a planet where there were no other aircraft in the air. In fact, there seemed to be nothing in the air except occasional flights of pterosaurs above the coastal swamps, and the large, butterflylike things, some yellow, some white, some blue. But none of these rose near his altitude.

During the next ten days Connor mapped an area of many thousands of square kilometers. The coast extended northward from Red Lake for five hundred kilometers, bringing it within an estimated ten degrees of the equator. Then it swung northeast, and the fringing, coraloid reefs deserted it. A hundred kilometers farther on, it turned almost due east.

Connor flew eastward along this equatorial coast, recording it section by section on his camera. He didn't fly far inland, because as yet their main means of long-distance heavy transport consisted of the two ships, and any future expansion of their embryo empire would be dictated by access to the sea.

Each day, when he returned to Red Lake, he carefully marked suggested place names on the maps compiled from the previous day's photographs. Zella showed an unexpected talent for producing accurate, readable maps from the photos.

By the tenth day Connor reached what appeared to be the most northerly point of their continent, a jutting, eroded headland reaching within a few degrees of the equator. He named it Sandstone Point, after the stratified yellow-brown rock that outcropped along that part of the coast. Beyond, the coast swung southward again as far as he could see, and he decided to go no farther for the time being. In addition, at Sandstone Point there was a level stretch of ground just behind the actual headland, which would make an excellent emergency landing field.

He was on the point of turning back, feeling he had explored far enough northward and eastward for the present purpose, when he noticed something far away across the equatorial ocean.

Against the skyline was a ragged line of slightly deeper violet, touched at the top with white. It took him a short time to realize what he was looking at. Some vast mountain range rose from far beyond the horizon, its crests hoary with what must be permanent snow, despite the fact that they must lie almost on the planet's equator.

A glance at his fuel gauge showed him that the mountains were out of his range across the unknown width of sea. He flew upward until he could feel in his ears the lessening atmospheric pressure, but still he caught no sight of the opposite coast. The distant mountains seemed higher from this altitude, and somehow even farther away than he had thought at first, probably between two hundred and three hundred kilometers away.

He swung the aircraft around and returned to Red Lake, conserving fuel by cutting inland across the corner of the continent. There was no chance of getting lost—the position of the suns gave him direction, and the mountains in this part of the continent were well inland.

Back at Red Lake he showed the photographs to Zella, Harn, and Kosaka, and told them about the remote mountain range to the north—he had no record of this, since his camera had been installed to photograph straight downward.

"Mountain ranges," said Kosaka thoughtfully. "How long?"

"They ran along the horizon for at least ten or twelve

degrees, the peaks I could see. The whole range must be longer.''

''Sounds as if there's another whole continent up there.''

''I'll check it out later. I'll get Mak to install another tank in the plane. We have plenty of room, with everything else cleared out of it.''

Conner set off alone early in the morning two days later, heading straight across the corner of the continent to Sandstone Point. He had adjusted his radio to communicate with Red Lake, using a frequency different from that employed by Central.

He opened the channel as soon as he reached Sandstone Point. ''I'm in sight of the ranges now. I'm flying over the area marked on the map as Sandstone Point. Heading out across the Equatorial Sea, north-northeast, towards the peaks that look to be nearest.''

He increased his altitude to about four thousand meters. Without a pressurized cabin, he could feel the thinning of the air, and the interior of the aircraft seemed much colder. He selected the highest point of the range ahead of him and flew directly towards it.

The mountains were higher and more distant than he had thought, and the ocean wider. He was still over water an hour later, and the continent he had left was out of sight. He was almost tempted to turn back, when he saw a coastline ahead of him. It was flat, fringed by coraloid reefs like the ones offshore from Central, but a few kilometers inland the ground began to slope upward gradually to the foothills of the towering ranges that formed a hazy white-and-violet backdrop to the whole scene. The slopes, misty with distance, were dappled with yellow and bluish vegetation, the yellow areas looking like grasslands.

Far away to his right the slopes had a curious artificial-looking pattern, almost a checkerboard coloring in which a number of rectangular areas seemed to be defined by dark straight lines.

He headed east, parallel to the coast, reducing his height. A few more kilometers and the reason for the pattern was inescapable. He was looking down on plowed fields separated by windbreaks. He seized his microphone and called Red Lake.

"I've found something. Came nor-nor'east across the water from Sandstone Point. Came to the northern continent after about two hundred kilometers. Eastward of the point of landfall I've come to an area of what appear to be plowed fields. Lots of them. Hundreds of square kilometers of them extending eastward, right out of sight over the horizon. Some of the fields are yellow, like wild grass—maybe they're lying fallow. Others are a uniform orange color that suggests crops of some kind. The lines between are dark blue. Trees like the ones around Red Lake. I can't see any people about, but the whole setup is obviously man-made, or kesri-made, or whatever."

Jiro Kosaka's voice came to him over the radio. "Be careful, Con. Make sure they don't see you. They probably don't realize we're capable of flying over their territory in an aircraft."

"I can't see any people, or kesrii, at this height. Think I might try going lower."

"I'll patch you through to Karl O'Donnel. Hold a minute, Con."

Connor reduced height rapidly, then leveled off at about three hundred meters, still flying parallel to the coast about half a kilometer out. The rectangular orange areas were indeed plowed fields of some kind of grain. The windbreaks between them consisted of strange-looking trees with drooping, dark blue foliage. Here and there were round buildings of what looked like mud brick, with conical roofs, possibly some kind of silo.

Connor adjusted his second camera for lateral shooting and set it to record the scene, taking shot after shot automatically in rapid succession without worrying about the degree of overlap between pictures.

Unexpectedly the coast swung out in a flat headland, and he found land directly below him. A straight, narrow road ran between some of the fields, and ahead he could see what might have been a small town. The buildings didn't look at all like kesrii buildings. They were neat and ordered, but with a somewhat primitive look about them, apparently made of some kind of brick, but with dark, smooth roofs of some substance he couldn't identify. A number of figures suddenly appeared from the buildings, standing and looking up at the aircraft. They didn't look human. Yet they didn't look kesrii either.

O'Donnel's voice came sharply over the radio. "Con, Jiro tells me you've found some sort of artifact out there. Don't approach it! Repeat, Con, don't approach it! At this stage we don't want them to know we can get as far as their base."

"But I've seen some of them, Karl. Matter of fact, I can see some now. And you know something? They're not kesrii. Repeat, not kesrii. Not human either."

"Then what the hell are they like?"

"Too far away for detail. But gray. All gray. And all the same, as far as I can see. Some bit of color about them, as if they're wearing something. I'm swinging seaward now. Going out over the beach. Their town, if you can call it that, is about a kilometer inland. Some of them saw the plane, but they wouldn't have got a good look at it."

"How many?"

"Ten. Fifteen. Anyway, I got some pictures of them. Kept the camera shooting on automatic as I banked around towards the sea."

"Come away from there, Con. Come straight back."

"Right. I'm heading straight across to Sandstone Point, then on to Red Lake. Take me several hours."

As he headed out to sea, Connor gained height. Looking farther eastward, he thought he could see a dark area along the coast that might have been a city. It might even have been a very large city. But he had no intention of flying any closer to it now.

Even with the additional tanks his fuel was quite low when he finally came within sight of Red Lake. The four-seater aircraft was standing out on the tarmac, as if it had just landed. Without circling, Connor flew straight in, landing into the slight breeze from the south, and taxied over to the sheds.

He took the automatically developed photos from the cameras, and as he stepped down from the plane, Karl O'Donnel strode to meet him across the hard red ground. He must have had himself flown up from Central.

Connor handed him the photos, and he riffled through them. When he came to the pictures showing the alien figures, he took a powerful magnifier from his pocket and scrutinized them intently.

"They're obviously not human," said Connor, "and neither are they kesrii."

"I know what they are," said O'Donnel. "These are the things the kesrii were moving from one planet to another." He put the magnifier back in his pocket and looked at Connor. *"These are the drom!"*

They were able to hold a council meeting with their television screens via the land line that had been run between Central and Red Lake, with Nordstrom, Sven, Nargis Lal, and Asgard Price in the HQ at Central, and O'Donnel, Connor, Zella, Kosaka, and Harn at Red Lake.

Nordstrom got straight to the heart of the problem without wasting time on preliminaries. "You've heard Karl outline the situation," he said. "Con, in the course of his aerial surveys, has flown across the ocean to the north of Terranova to explore the coast of another continent, which we'll refer to simply as the North Continent. He found what looks like irrigated and farmed land, and what appears to be quite a large city of non-human origin. The question is: Do we make any attempt to contact the inhabitants of the city, or not?"

"Did Con fly over their city?" asked Price.

"No," said O'Donnel, "but he flew over a small settlement a few kilometers away from the city, so they know of his existence by now. Right, Con?"

"They know, all right," said Connor. "They don't know how many of us there are, but they saw my plane, and they must have realized it hadn't come from space. Also, it was so different from any machines we've seen the kesrii use that they must have seen it as utterly foreign."

"I think we should contact them," said Price. "Extend the hand of friendship, as it were."

"I'd be careful about that," said Connor. "They looked nothing like a human being."

"I'd agree with that," said O'Donnel. "From Con's photos, which I think you've all seen, these things are the drom, the race the kesrii were moving from one planet to another— for what reason, I have no idea."

"That's the answer, then," said Price, his prominent eyes

gleaming. "We're both being victimized by the kesrii. We should join forces against a common enemy."

"But we know nothing about the drom," objected Connor. "We know a little about the kesrii, and in many ways they seem quite like us. Both bipeds, a roughly similar type of skeleton, somewhat similar sense organs. But the drom, if that's what these things are, looked utterly different from any life-form I've ever seen."

"I'd go along with that," said O'Donnel. "The kesrii showed me a few of them while they were holding them in suspended animation. I haven't seen them in movement, so perhaps Con has a better idea of them than I have." He turned to Connor. "Could you describe what you saw?"

"Well, I think the photo blowups show most of what I could tell you. They're silver gray, the coloring of some kinds of mollusk. Hairless. White underneath, like the underside of a shark. They seemed to move on four flexible legs, with four other things like tentacles. With the kesrii we can at least communicate, in a way—although I admit they've taken most of the initiative in communicating so far—but with these things, I don't know where you'd start."

"It sounds as if they have a farming economy," said Price. "They must have an intelligence comparable with our own, wouldn't you say? So let's not be put off by their appearance. Listen, I've been trained in extraterrestrial contact."

"Where?" asked Nordstrom.

"At the Futurity Institute on Denebola 4."

"Wasn't that where Marek had his training?"

"Marek? Yes."

"Didn't do him much good, did it?" broke in Connor. "In his contact with the kesrii, I mean. He finished up dead."

Price smoothed his hair, forcing a professional smile. "But Marek was trained primarily for a military approach. I think we can agree that our numbers preclude that. Our disciplines were aimed at peaceful contact."

"But it was all very theoretical, wasn't it?" Nordstrom's voice was noncommittal. "There have been courses in the theory of dealing with intelligent aliens as long as I can remember—I've even participated in one, long ago—but our contact with the kesrii was our first with an alien intelligence at least comparable with our own. In fact, all the evidence seems to point to the fact that their intelligence is superior to ours."

"We don't know that for sure," protested O'Donnel, although his voice held little conviction. "For instance, we don't know the state of their computer intelligence."

"I don't think we can rely on that," said Nordstrom. "Comparing man to kesri, animal to animal, they seem to have the edge. Probably a much larger brain, better physical coordination, faster reflexes, better sensory equipment. I think all that teaches us something. It teaches us we're not necessarily the apex of evolutionary development in the galaxy."

There was silence for several seconds as everyone digested the unpalatable thought. Then Price began speaking in a high, almost hysterical key.

"Then it seems obvious that the best course is for us to explore the possibility of uniting with the drom against a more powerful enemy."

"Enemy?" Nordstrom's eyes were cold. "That's a word Marek was fond of using."

"I know," said Price. "I know. And he's dead! I know! But I still think we should look at the possibility of communicating with these people."

"Could I break in there?" asked Connor. "I'd certainly like to have a closer look at these things, and their city. I didn't see anything that looked like aircraft there, so I think we might try flying past them again, taking more photos. I could get closer to their actual city. That might give us a better idea of them. I'd like to take Charl Harn with me—as a biologist, he might see things I'd miss."

"That's a good point," said Nordstrom. "I agree it's a good idea to have a more detailed look at their culture. But I'd stress that you play it very carefully. Are you absolutely certain they have no aircraft, for instance?"

"I saw none. They had some kind of wheeled vehicles."

"Wheeled? Or ground-effect machines?"

"Wheeled. You can see one in my photos. Like a flat tray truck, four wheels. Some kind of engine driving it. I don't know whether it's electric, internal combustion, or wound-up springs, but the thing was moving, with one of the drom sitting on it, not pushing it."

"Tells us very little," said O'Donnel. "This was only the

fringe of their settled area, wasn't it, Con? Farmers use simple machines like that in all sorts of cultures.''

"You're sure your aircraft is completely reliable?'' asked Nordstrom.

Connor nodded. "The twin-engined machine, yes.''

"Don't fly over the land this time. Keep just offshore. Can you adjust the big camera to shoot laterally?''

"No problem there. I can run along parallel to the beach, as you see in some of my photos, and keep shooting the foreshore. That should take in the major buildings in their city.''

"Could I go along as a qualified observer?'' asked Price.

Connor answered before anyone else had a chance. "I think the most qualified observer would be Charl Harn.''

"True,'' said Nordstrom. "With your extra load of fuel, could you carry three people? Two plus yourself?''

Connor hesitated. "I could take three. I'd prefer the third to be Jiro Kosaka.''

"A geologist? Surely there's time for that later?''

"We work well as a team, that's all.''

"I see.'' Nordstrom gestured. "But remember, this is only in the nature of a preliminary survey. I'd suggest you, Charl Harn, and Asgard Price.''

"As you wish.'' Connor bowed slightly. "I'd like to get away early tomorrow morning.''

16

Late that afternoon Asgard Price flew up to Red Lake with Mak in the single-engined aircraft. He had apparently not flown in small machines before, and the turbulence bothered him. When Mak showed him the twin-engined plane, he seemed relieved at its size and apparent stability.

The following morning Connor, Harn, and Price boarded the long-range machine. Connor used the full length of the dry lake to get airborne, owing to the weight in the extra fuel tanks. Price was silent for the first hour of the journey. He had wanted to sit in the co-pilot's seat next to Connor, but Connor had vetoed that, explaining that Harn would occupy that seat so he could act as emergency pilot. Price sat behind, staring moodily down from the window at the passing panorama.

Connor cut inland towards the northeast to save fuel. He reached Sandstone Point and gave his position by radio to Red Lake. Then he headed out north-northeast across the sea.

"How far across the water?" asked Price.

"Hundred kilometers, if you went straight across. A little longer this way. We should make a landfall about eighty klicks west of their city."

As they neared the coast of the North Continent, Connor cut the throttles back, reducing engine speed and height at the same time. Price stared at the approaching coastline.

"I can see the areas of what look like farming," he said. "You were right."

"I'll go lower." Connor dropped to about a hundred fifty
meters above the sea and flew parallel to a white beach
backed by windblown dunes on which scrubby blue vegetation grew. Inland were the level or slightly sloping fields of
yellow and orange, but this time he didn't fly over them.
Keeping low to the water, he assumed he was probably
hidden from the inhabitants of the area by the line of dunes,
although they must have heard the sound of his engines. Sure
enough, a few kilometers farther east a number of moving
gray figures appeared on one of the higher dunes.

"There," he said, pointing.

"They look the color of steel," said Harn. "Robots?"

"No. Organic. Wait until you're nearer."

Harn crowded close to the window, shading his eyes with
his hand. "I've never seen anything like them," he muttered,
as if talking to himself, then added aloud, "I see what you
meant. Compared with these, the kesrii look practically
human."

"Some of them seem to have some kind of clothing," said
Price.

"You're right," agreed Harn. "Pale tones of gray, beige.
All dull colors."

"Perhaps they have a dull lifestyle," suggested Connor.

They swept onward, leaving the gray-skinned figures far
behind. Occasionally some large structure of unknown purpose loomed beyond the dunes. Then, on the horizon ahead,
they saw the city.

The nearer they approached, the more alien it looked. From
a distance it seemed like a human-built city, with buildings
climaxing towards the center in towers eighty or a hundred
meters tall. But an odd characteristic appeared as they drew
closer. The walls of the high buildings all seemed to slope
inward, like the walls of structures built by the ancient Egyp-
tians on Earth thousands of years ago. These towers, however, were not of stone. Their main structural material looked
like glass, some of it partly opaque, much of it tinted in
delicate colors.

The inward slope of the walls seemed strangely standardized, about five or six degrees from the vertical. As the
forward movement of the aircraft brought different buildings
into alignment with each other, the angle of the sloping edges
always matched exactly, regardless of the height of the structure.

"Somehow the whole place looks old," said Harn, "old and run down. See? Some of those towers have been damaged at some time. Big areas of glass broken, not repaired."

Here and there, where the glassy walls had been shattered, the supporting skeletons of the damaged towers sagged as if warped by heat. The skeletons didn't look like steel, or any other metal. They might have been made from some form of extruded plastic.

"No aircraft I can see," said Connor.

"I've been looking for a place to land," said Price, "but I haven't sighted one yet."

"We won't be landing this time," Connor replied, "but if you see a place where we could set a plane down, note it for future reference. Even a place where you could land Central's flier. I think Nordstrom would supply batteries for this."

"What interests me is the number of damaged buildings," said Harn thoughtfully. "Some of the damage looks years old, yet there doesn't seem to have been any attempt to carry out repairs."

"Some of the buildings have got people in them," said Price.

"If you can call the drom people," amended Harn.

"Anyway," said Connor, "whatever you call them, we have an audience of thousands this time."

Ahead, along the coast, a number of flimsy-looking structures stood in the water, a hundred meters or so from the beach. They seemed to consist of four thin poles slanting seaward, spaced in a square and supporting a large net. Harn gave a cry of recognition.

"They're like Chinese fishing nets."

"Don't tell me the Chinese have been here," said Connor.

"Of course not. It's an independent invention of the same thing. The poles are pulled upright from the shore—see the windlasses? The nets come out of the water, and those small boats are used to get the fish from them. Then they're lowered again. The Chinese have been doing this in some of their rivers for thousands of years."

"Those small boats seem to be the only craft in the water," mused Connor. "Why build a city on the seacoast if they don't use sea transport? There are no piers, wharves, docks."

"Don't know," said Harn, "unless they used the sea in the past."

"Or—wait a minute." Connor snapped his fingers. "The kesrii erected our buildings for us while we were still in suspended animation, and they set them up near the sea. Perhaps *they* built this city for the drom. As to putting it near the sea, that's probably where they put their own centers of population, wherever they are, and they simply chose a site that seemed natural to them."

"Wonder if the kesrii have a settlement on this planet?" said Price.

"If they have," said Harn, "Con will come to it if he keeps on mapping the planet at the same rate."

Connor thought for a while. "I don't think so," he said at length. "Remember, after they'd brought the first few of us out of hibernation, they took off in a thing like a space shuttle. I didn't see it, but everyone who did described it that way. I think they were operating from a space station, or an orbiting ship."

"Maybe," said Harn. "Or maybe that's just what they wanted us to think."

"Could be. Look, we're past the city now. Probably nothing but more farmland out this way. I'll head back. Okay?"

Neither of his companions objected, so Connor swung the aircraft seaward, gaining height for the long haul home. His fuel was still above the halfway mark on the gauge. He waited until he was well out over the sea before he radioed Red Lake. There was no reason to believe that the drom were listening on his frequency, indeed no reason to believe they had radios, but he never took an unnecessary chance.

On the way back across the Equatorial Sea, nobody spoke for a considerable time. The view of the alien civilization of the drom had a curious effect on all of them. The contact with the kesrii had been disturbing enough, but the kesrii had seized the initiative from the humans at the outset and kept a move or two ahead all the time. But the drom were an unknown factor. Their civilization, judging from their city, appeared complex and decadent. It was so different from human settlement that it gave all three occupants of the plane plenty to think about, yet little they could immediately put into words.

"I'd like to make contact with them," said Price suddenly.

"You're crazy!" snapped Harn. "We know next to nothing about them."

"We managed to communicate with the kesrii."

"Hold it," broke in Connor. "The kesrii communicated with *us*, remember? And they must have had previous experience of alien contacts. Look at their language-translation machines. There was a lot of research and development behind those things. Here, we not only have no idea of the drom language, we don't even know how they communicate with each other. They might believe in killing on sight anything they don't understand! Or they might be jumping with disease germs we have no resistance to."

"We didn't pick up anything from the kesrii," said Price.

"No, but *they* were damned careful. The first one to contact me wore an airtight suit with his own breathing apparatus—not just an antiseptic mask, but a thing like a lightweight spacesuit."

"I could do the same," persisted Price. "Wear a spacesuit, I mean."

"Hell of a friendly way to make contact with a strange race."

"The kesrii did the same to you."

"Yes, but that was inside what amounted to a laboratory."

The argument went on in desultory circles all the way back to Red Lake.

Nordstrom listened to all aspects of the problem before coming to a decision. He, with all the members of the council at Central, were linked to the Red Lake contingent by their wide-screen TV setup.

"I think it might be possible for Asgard to make contact with the drom," he said. "It's going to need extreme care, as this will be the contact that will slant their whole future opinion of us. I think it would be unwise to simply ignore them. Since they've seen Con's aircraft, twice, they know we exist. They know less about us than we know about them, little as that is. They might assume we're spying out their city prior to an attack. Con, is there anywhere you can land near their city?"

Connor hesitated before replying. "Actually, there is. A flat stretch of beach where the sand appears hard. Might be a better place on the inland side of the city, of course—I didn't investigate there.''

"The beach," mused Nordstrom. "Let's see. The moons are rising close to the suns around the next few days—that means ebb tide will be an hour or two after sunrise. Not good, is it? Make your landing late afternoon. Suppose you landed on the beach and waited while Asgard made his contact. Are you sure your engines would start when needed?''

"Yes, they're reliable enough. But I don't like the idea of him going in alone to contact a race of beings we know nothing about.''

"I don't like it either. But their sighting of your plane has forced us into acting quickly. We lost the initiative with the kesrii. We don't want to lose it with the drom.''

"They have a big city there. Not overcrowded, as far as I could determine, but there could still be thousands of them. Aren't we taking a chance?''

Nordstrom smiled. "I've seen you take a lot of chances, Con.''

"Yes, but they were calculated chances. This is a leap in the dark.''

"Look," said Price, "if we don't make some attempt to contact them, they're going to come looking for us. That's obvious, isn't it?''

"Not really," said Nordstrom. "From the descriptions, they have a fair-sized city there, with enough arable land to support them. But in the time it's taken them to build a city like that, you'd expect them to have spread all over the planet. They haven't, which suggests they're not colonizers.''

"Well," said Price, "they don't have aircraft, or ships. That would restrict their explorations, wouldn't it?''

"We've learned a bit about them," said Harn. "They cooperate with each other, they eat fish and grain products of some kind, and possibly fruit. But do we know enough to let Asgard go ahead and make his contact?''

"I'd be inclined to wait," said Connor.

"If we're doing it, I think it ought to be now," said Harn.

"I think it's essential we do it now." Price's eyes shone with excitement.

"Looks as if you're outvoted, Con," said Nordstrom.

"Okay. I'll fly him there. Tomorrow, if he's ready.''

"I'll be ready," said Price emphatically.

• • •

They timed their departure to arrive at the drom city during the ebb tide, leaving late in the morning. Price wore a lightweight, airtight suit with its own air supply, although for the journey to the North Continent he did not wear the helmet. He seemed excited by the importance of the coming contact, but with an undercurrent of fear that showed in the way he kept sustaining his spirits with philosophical clichés spoken with emphatic yet hollow fervor.

"Now that we're making a definite contact," said Connor as they headed out across the sea from Sandstone Point, "we'd better begin by taking a more thorough look at their city. Right?"

"Okay," agreed Price.

"We'll take a closer look at the high buildings in the center of the place. Fly around and try to figure what sort of activity they carry out in the various areas."

"We'll be really committed then," said Price, as if talking to himself. "The whole population will know about us—it won't depend on the evidence of just a few of them."

"That okay with you? After all, you'll be making the contact."

"I guess so."

The mountains of the North Continent formed a rampart along the horizon ahead of them, their peaks white in the mid-afternoon sunlight. Connor flew farther to the east than on their previous visit, so that he would come straight in on the alien city from the sea. Before long the glistening towers sparkled along the coast ahead of them, and Price picked up his helmet and checked his air cylinders.

Approaching the city at right angles to the beach, Connor noticed a broad avenue running directly inland, flanked by some of the highest buildings on either side.

"Here we go," he said. "I'll make a straight run right up their main avenue."

He nosed the aircraft down, throttling back the engines until he was only a hundred meters off the water. Leveling off, he lined up for a pass up the avenue and opened the throttles again. This time he'd mounted the large camera well forward, with a wide-angle lens that gave a field of about eighty degrees, from straight ahead to almost directly below.

Some of the Chinese-type fishing nets were in use, with a

few of the drom working them from adjoining platforms in
the water and flat-bottomed punts propelled in the shallow
water by poles. The drom went on with their activities as the
plane approached, apparently unaware of it until it was within
a few hundred meters of them. When they saw it, the effect on
them was electric. They pointed with flexible-looking upper
limbs, and stood perfectly still, as if they hoped by their
immobility to escape notice.

Then the aircraft was over the beach, with its white sand that
looked like broken-down granite. They flew over a broad
esplanade that seemed to have been impressively planned,
yet not maintained, with a broken row of ragged trees. Some
of the gray beings moving about below froze when they
became aware of the roaring thing in the air, like those on the
beach and the fishing platforms.

"You know," said Harn, "I get the feeling they're slow
on the uptake."

"Bit early to make a judgment like that," said Connor.

They roared up the center of the broad avenue, above a
median strip that had once had formal gardens, although now
it was a strip of desolate wilderness. Here and there were
scrubby, untended trees, some with branches broken off and
lying beneath them. To either side rose buildings, some of
them higher than the plane, their sloping walls throwing back
an echo of the engines, which seemed to reverberate along the
avenue like thunder. Drom appeared in doorways far ahead,
then either became motionless or slipped back out of sight.

"What are they, Charl? Reptilian?"

"Wouldn't say reptilian. Not even sure they're vertebrates.
The eight limbs make me think of an octopus, but they're
obviously stiffer than tentacles. See, they walk on four of
them. They seem to bend all the way along their length, so
there's no skeleton in the sense we know. Perhaps a sort of
tough cartilage."

"Certainly inhuman," muttered Price.

"Having second thoughts, Asgard?" asked Connor.

"No!" Price's reply came back like the crack of a whip.
Connor wondered how much thought had gone into it.

The broad avenue ran inland for two or three kilometers,
then ended in a level area covered with blue moss.

"What's this, do you think?" asked Price. "Sports ground?
Parade ground? Airfield?"

"Hardly an airfield," said Connor. "Although we might be able to use it as one. Be safer than the beach."

"Don't see it as a sports ground," added Harn. "No grandstands. They don't look like a fun-loving crowd to me. No race courses, no amusement parks, anything like that."

"Maybe all their amusements are indoors," suggested Connor. He pulled the aircraft into a climb, banking around to the left. "Wait a minute! What's that?"

"What?"

"That building. Different style. Big one. White stone, or what looks like it. It's like a temple of some kind."

"I see it. There, Asgard—dome of what looks like blue metal."

"I'll swing back for a closer look. Do you get the feeling their older buildings are more impressive than their new ones? Look at those little places along the edge of the open ground. They look as if they're built of dried mud, and not very well-built at that."

"I think we were right the first time," said Harn. "A race on the way down."

"Maybe we can rescue them," mused Price.

"What the hell are you, Asgard? A reincarnation of a religious fanatic?"

"Not a fanatic, Con. I just have a reverence for life, if you like." When Connor didn't reply, Price raised his voice. "Look, we came here for me to make contact with these people, and I'm going to do it! I have the necessary training to make the best possible approach to them."

"The best theoretical training, maybe," conceded Connor. "But in practice, what do we know about them? Charl's a biologist, and looking at them from the air, he isn't sure whether they're vertebrates or something else. As to their motives, the way they think, the way they communicate, their attitude to strangers—why rush in?"

He was circling the building with the blue dome. Seeing it at a different angle to the sunlight, they realized the dome was not metal, but some translucent material resembling glass, and covered with a film of dust that had evidently accumulated for a long time undisturbed. The dome was more opaque at the top, less so at the sides, where the steepening angle of the glass had allowed the rain to wash off some of the dust.

"Should be a good job opening here for a maintenance engineer," said Harn.

"Good, if he could figure how to get paid for it. Anyway, let's have a closer look at the ground. I want to see if I can land on it. I'll cut the speed down as low as possible and get right down within a whisker of the deck. See what you can make of the surface. Watch for anything that looks like moisture."

Connor flew back across the level area, and suddenly Harn gave a shout. "I think it's okay. Down there, where the moss is thin, I can see the tracks of some vehicle."

"Aircraft?"

"No. Something slow. Tracks cross each other, curve around."

"Here we go, then. I'll come back into the wind."

"How do you know which way's the wind?" asked Price.

"That feathery grass. See it?"

Connor took his time selecting the actual landing place, making several low passes over the level area. Finally he made his approach run, long and shallow, touching the wheels tentatively a few times on the ground before trusting the weight of the aircraft to them. The surface was hard, not exactly smooth, but acceptable enough as a landing field.

"Now," he said, leaving the engines idling, "better put on your helmet and check your air, Asgard."

Price put on the helmet, Harn helping him lock it into position and connect the air hoses. Price withdrew his arm within the loose-fitting suit and wiped sweat from his forehead with a piece of cloth attached to a string inside the suit.

"I'll taxi up to the building that looks like a temple, or whatever. You want to get out there, or the end of the main avenue?"

"Near the temple building, I think," said Price.

"Can hardly hear you. Switch on your suit radio, and we'll monitor from here. We'll keep in touch with you every second. Might as well keep up a running commentary of everything that happens from the moment you meet them."

"Right. I'll do that." Price's voice came clearly from the speaker in the roof of the plane, and also from a grill covering a small speaker on the front of his helmet.

"Start your camera running," said Connor. "We'll check the monitor screen."

Price activated the tiny TV camera built into the front of his suit, and on the monitor screen a small, sharp image of the interior of the cabin appeared, with Connor and Harn clearly recognizable.

"Now," said Connor, "the back camera. We'll be able to see if any of those things are creeping up behind you. They'll probably think you have the proverbial eyes in the back of your head, if we have to alert you about being stalked from behind."

"Don't say things like that," protested Price.

Harn started the camera on his backpack. "Turn around," he said, and on a second monitor screen he and Connor appeared again.

"Look!" Connor pointed. A number of the aliens were coming along from the end of the main avenue. This was the closest view the human team had gained of them up to now, and it was more disturbing than they had expected. The drom were about the height of an average man—perhaps a few centimeters less. Their bodies were short, upright cylinders balanced on four legs resembling stiff, tapering tentacles ending in rounded pads. They seemed to move in short, quick steps, with three of the four feet always on the ground at any one time. The four upper limbs, flexible throughout their length like the others, terminated in pincerlike claws, or fingers—they had some of the characteristics of both. The heads were round, about the size of a human head, hairless, scaly, set directly on the trunk without the intervention of a flexible neck. Their garments were flimsy, tubelike pieces of dull-colored fabric, enclosing the trunk and ending just below where the four legs began.

Harn focused binoculars on them while they were still over a hundred meters away, and suddenly he gave a sharp cry.

"Am I hallucinating? Or have those things got eyes all around their heads?"

"*What?*" Connor reached for the other pair of binoculars and focused them on the front rank of the walking figures.

"Wait until one of them turns around, or turns sideways," said Harn.

"I've got it. Yes. There seem to be four eyes, I think. Spaced evenly around their heads. It would give them all-around vision, wouldn't it?"

"Takes the steam out of our trick of putting a camera in the back of Asgard's pack. It wouldn't impress them at all. They can see behind them all the time''

The gray figures moved smoothly towards the temple building, keeping close to the walls, as if uncertain of the aircraft.

"Wonder how they evolved that way?" mused Connor. "Doesn't suggest a carnivorous ancestry, does it?"

"Don't know," admitted Harn. "Carnivores generally have two eyes looking forward, to focus on their victim. The typical victim has eyes on each side of its head, so it can see nearly all around it. But all the major life-forms we know evolved up from animals with two eyes. If you start with four, your modifications could mean anything."

Connor turned to look intently at Price. "Still want to go through with it, Asgard?"

"Yes."

Connor extended his hand. "Good luck."

Price gripped it.

"We'll monitor your every movement, every step of the way. And we'll be listening to every word you say, and transmitting your words and pictures back to Red Lake. If you feel uncertain of anything—anything at all—let us know right away."

"Where will you be?"

"I'll park the plane on the other side of this level area, but I'll keep the engines idling all the time you're with them. At a second's notice I can open the throttles and be right near you. But take care!"

A final handshake with Harn, and Price climbed down out of the plane and began walking steadily towards the nearest group of drom, who were now standing motionless, waiting.

"He's game. I'll give him that," said Harn.

"There's a difference between courage and plain damned stupidity, Charl. Sometimes the line's hard to define. I just hope my gut feeling is wrong about this."

"They still haven't made any move," said Harn, looking over the top of his binoculars. By now the white-suited figure had covered half the distance to the waiting drom.

"This reminds me of something," murmured Connor. Suddenly his voice sharpened. "I know! The first time one of the kesrii interrogated me. He wore a totally enclosed suit like that. Even the same color. White."

"I remember that. Same with Jiro and me. Suits like white nylon. All you could see was their eyes."

"That'll be about all the drom can see of Asgard. Well, we know how they feel, eh? After being on the receiving end in the same situation."

"Look! They're moving!"

Price's voice came over the radio. "They're moving aside as if to let me through between them. They don't look hostile to me. I'm going to keep on walking at the same speed. I'll give them a signal."

Price slowly raised his right arm, holding his gloved hand open with the palm towards the drom.

"I think that's a universal symbol of peace, isn't it?"

Connor seized the microphone. "I wouldn't be too sure of that. I don't think it applies to a carnivore-evolved species like the kesrii. When a cat raises its paw, claws forward, it's not a gesture of peace. It's a threat of violence."

"What's the kesrii greeting?"

"I think it's both hands upward and outward, elbows not bent."

"You mean . . . like this?"

"Ah. They seemed to react better to that, didn't they?"

"It got some result, yes." Price's voice sounded strained.

"Are you letting your voice go through the external speaker?"

"No. Just on the radio. I'll switch to external." A click, and then they heard Price's voice say "Greetings!"

"They won't know what the hell he means," muttered Harn.

"Hey, look at this!" It was Price's voice, on the radio only. The drom in front of him had moved aside to form two parallel columns, leaving an open space leading up to the broad, gently sloping ramp that gave access to the templelike building with the blue dome.

"They want me to go inside. Think I should?"

"I wouldn't, if you can get out of it. Stay where we can see what's happening to you."

"I'll try. They look friendly enough from here. Can't read their expression though. Their eyes are round, with no lashes, like a fish's eyes. All the same color. Light amber. We were right—they have four of them, evenly spaced around their heads, so they can see in every direction at once. Except straight up."

"It seemed to take the ones on the beach a long time to realize the plane was coming," said Harn thoughtfully. "Perhaps two eyes, looking straight ahead, concentrate your vision better, or see farther than four set to take in the full circle."

"Can you see one that looks like some sort of leader?" asked Connor into the microphone.

"No. I've been looking for one. They seem very much on the same level, as if they've gone overboard to be equal."

Price was now walking between the two files of drom, and his cameras gave Connor and Harn a very good view of what he was seeing.

"God! They're like nothing I've ever seen," whispered Harn.

"Watch they don't start to close in behind him."

"Some of them are, I think. Yes!"

"Here," said Connor. He took two objects out of a locker and handed one of them to Harn. "Stick that in your belt. Hope we don't need them."

"What is it?"

"Solenoid pistol. Explosive bullets. Don't shoot at anything close to you."

"Did Nordstrom okay these?"

"He doesn't know. Nobody knows. I don't think the council would have agreed, and I didn't feel like coming up here unarmed."

"Did the kesrii let us have these from the ship?"

"No. Made them in the workshop at Red Lake. Just in case of emergencies. There's some odd wildlife in the delta."

"Take a bit of explaining if we have to use them."

"I hope we don't—but hang on to it."

"Price's voice came over the radio again. "They seem to want me to go into the building. Are you monitoring all this?"

"Sure. We can see everything in front of you, and behind you."

"What are they doing behind me?"

"Just following at a respectful distance."

"All right. I'm going in."

Price walked up the long, sloping ramp that led to the interior of the building. "It's fairly dark in here," he said, "Like being underwater. Bluish light over everything. Daylight coming down through the blue dome. Would have been brighter if they'd kept the dome clean. As it is, it's got a thick layer of dust, especially higher up, where it's a more horizontal surface.''

"What's inside?''

"Can't see too well yet. Just came in out of the daylight. Lot of dust on the floor, as if the place hasn't been used much and is never swept out. Columns all around the circular walls, leaving a round, clear space under the dome. There's a statue on some sort of pedestal, towards the far side, facing the door. Wait a minute. I'm seeing a bit better now, as my eyes adjust to the light. . . . It's like the statue of a man, but—but . . .''

"But what?''

"Hold on.'' There was silence for a few seconds. Turning the sound up to the full, they could hear Price's footsteps on the dusty floor, and the ragged sound of his breathing.

"Look,'' he said suddenly. "Both of you have seen kesrii. What do they look like exactly?''

Connor exchanged glances with Harn. "Bit taller than a man, velvety fur all over. Tails. Big, rounded heads, ears pointed like a cat's. Big eyes, a bit like a cat's, too, and—''

"That's enough!'' snapped Price. "That's the thing I'm looking at. That's what the statue represents. A kesri! Standing in their temple, facing the door.''

"I can see it now,'' said Connor. "But what's happening in there?''

"Not sure,'' said Price. "They want me to stand alongside the statue. Up on the pedestal.''

The cameras showed little in the dim light—only a milling crowd of gray drom bodies. They seemed to be all around Price now.

Suddenly his voice lifted in a short, inarticulate cry.

17

"Price! What's happening?" Connor shouted into the microphone.

Price's voice came in broken sentences, mixed with the sound of fast, convulsive breathing. "Gone mad . . . bastards . . trying to get my helmet off . . ."

The monitor screens showed little, except close, out-of-focus views of struggling bodies. Abruptly the sound from the loudspeakers increased, a complex rustle of sound that suggested Price's helmet had been removed, giving external sounds more access to the microphone within his suit.

"Voices of the drom," said Connor. The sound was like the rustle of wind through dry leaves. "Let's go!"

He opened the throttles of both engines, used the wheel brake to pivot the aircraft around and roared across the bumpy ground towards the temple. A number of drom near the entrance scattered, either moving along close to the exterior walls of the building or disappearing within it.

Connor swung the machine around near the bottom of the ramp, cutting the engine speed down to idling and locking on the wheel brakes.

"Stay with the plane, Charl," he shouted, and sprang down and ran towards the temple, drawing the solenoid pistol from his belt and pulling an antiseptic mask over his mouth and nose. As he ran, a voice suddenly crackled from the speaker in his suit—Nordstrom's voice. Harn must have patched the radio through.

"Con! Don't shoot any of them, whatever you do!"

Connor could have replied through his radio, but some instinct told him not to. He ran up the ramp and into the entrance to the temple. He couldn't see Price—only a solid wall of eight-limbed bodies.

He pulled down the antiseptic mask, shouting "Asgard!" But there was no answer.

He lifted the solenoid gun above his head as he ran. The effect on the drom was electric. They seemed to recognize the thing as a weapon, even if they didn't know what effect it produced. Perhaps the kesrii had used a similar-looking device. Whatever the explanation, the barrier of bodies in front of him quickly dissolved into two groups scrambling apart.

Ahead of him he could see the statue of the kesri on its raised dais, but there was no sign of Price.

"Asgard!" he shouted again, but there was still no answer. He mounted the dais, about one meter above the floor, with ramps, not steps, leading up to it. He glanced briefly at the statue. Life size, it was exquisitely made of some dark metal, its surface marked in representation of the kesrii fur, its eyes yellow and shockingly alive.

The last of the drom were vanishing through doors at the sides of the temple, but Connor was sure Price hadn't gone that way—from the moment he'd entered, he had been able to see both sides of the great circular room. He turned.

There was a door in the wall behind the statue, a few centimeters less in height than a standard human-designed door. At once he sprang down from the rear of the dais and ran to it. It was a sliding door, partly closed, and he pushed it open with difficulty against the resistance of some opening or closing mechanism.

Beyond was a long passage with doors and transverse passages opening to either side of it. This part of the building was low, single-storied, and the passageway was lit from a number of dusty skylights at intervals.

Connor reached one of the transverse passages, but there was no clue to the whereabouts of Price. As he turned he saw the door sliding across the end of the passage where he'd entered.

"Hey!" he shouted.

The door continued to slide until it had almost closed the opening. Connor edged behind the angle of the wall between the intersecting passages, sighted his gun at the door and fired, pulling his head back at the same instant—he did not know what power his explosive bullets had.

In the confined space of the passage the explosion was a thunderclap. Fragments of splintered metal or plastic flew past the junction of the passages, clattering along the floor. When he looked around the corner again, the door was hanging askew, partly shattered.

He ran towards it, kicking enough of its remains out of the way to break through into the circular room again. The drom were nowhere in sight.

He ran out through the main entrance again, and once in the open he turned, his weapon still held ready to shoot.

"Con! What the hell's happening?" It was Nordstrom's voice again.

"Can't find him, Chief. They nearly trapped me. Had to shoot a door to pieces to get out."

"Come back to base. To Red Lake. I'll meet you there."

"What about Price?"

"It's his own damned fault, contacting a race of beings we know nothing about."

"God, Chief, I can't simply leave the idiot!"

"We'll mount a properly equipped rescue. What do you think happened?"

Harn had already climbed aboard the plane, and Connor joined him, slipping into the pilot's seat and opening the throttles so the roar of the engines thundered into the temple.

"I think he made the mistake of climbing onto the dais alongside that statue of a kesri. Remember, up to then he had a helmet on, and an airtight suit. I think they thought he was a kesri. That's why they gave him special treatment—almost the sort of treatment you'd expect them to reserve for a god. Then, when he stood alongside the statue, they had doubts. Once they got his helmet off, they realized they'd been fooled, and it was important to them. They went ape."

"What happened when you went in?"

"I was holding a gun."

"That's another thing! Where the hell—oh, never mind now. How did they react?"

"Couldn't read their expressions, but I think they were

scared witless. They must have seen some weapon in the hand of a kesri that looked enough like mine.''

"This was before you fired the thing?"

"Yes, before. After I fired, they melted away like smoke."

"Don't underestimate them, Con. You caught them by surprise. They may be coming back with weapons of their own. Take off right now! We'll meet you at Red Lake."

"We'd lose time that way, Chief. Have you got my maps?"

"Can get a copy on the screen . . . Yes."

"See the place I've called Sandstone Point?"

"Ah . . . I have it."

"There's a flat, hard area just behind it. I'll see you there. Can we ride back here with you in the other plane? I won't have enough fuel left for the double journey."

"Right. Meet you at Sandstone Point. Out."

The whole city of the drom was ominously silent. Connor swung the plane into the wind, opened the throttles wide, and took off.

He reached Sandstone Point before the flier from Central, because he had a considerably shorter journey to make.

For all they could see from here, they might have been the only life-forms on the planet. The suns, linked by the golden lance of the gas torus, were low in the west, and the waters of the Equatorial Sea slapped lazily on the brown rock.

"Here he comes," said Harn at last. The silver dot of the battery-powered flier came straight towards them, not along the line of the coast, but in a great circle route from Central. Nordstrom was obviously working from Connor's maps, and doing it very efficiently. Connor wondered how many skills a man could pick up by the time a cybernetic system assisted him into his third century.

Nordstrom had come alone. "Show me your gun," was the first thing he said to Connor. Reluctantly, Connor handed him the solenoid gun.

"Ingenious," commented Nordstrom. "But use this." He handed Connor another weapon. "It stuns. Doesn't kill."

"From the supplies?"

"No. I made a few at Central. Just in case of unforeseen trouble."

He handed another of the weapons to Harn, taking away the solenoid gun. When his eyes met Connor's, it almost seemed to Connor that Nordstrom showed slight embarrassment. Then they both smiled.

Nordstrom gave Connor the job of flying his machine to the city of the drom, leaving the twin-engined aircraft at Sandstone Point. He ran inland about a hundred kilometers west of the city and approached it from the side towards the mountains.

"There's the temple," he said.

"Impressive," said Nordstrom. "Land in front of it, on the level ground just below the ramp."

The flier made far less noise than the methanol-burning aircraft, but even so, Connor had expected to attract more attention when he landed. There were none of the drom in sight, over a large area of the city surrounding the temple.

"Where are they?" asked Harn.

"I don't like it," said Connor.

Connor and Harn had both added helmets to their suits, Nordstrom a protective helmet only. Nordstrom waited with the aircraft while Connor and Harn went into the deserted temple, keeping in constant radio communication with them. The only thing that showed the previous visit had taken place was the shattered door in the wall behind the statue.

"They can't trap us with this again," said Connor, kicking aside a few more shards of broken plastic from the door. "Let's see what's behind it."

They walked down the passageway to the intersecting gallery. Nothing moved. They went on to the next intersection.

"Look!" said Harn, pointing to the right. Price's helmet lay along the passage about ten meters away, against one wall, as if dropped by someone in a hurry. They walked over to it, and Connor picked it up.

"Look at this. Blood." He ran his gloved finger along the edge of the helmet.

"His? Or theirs?"

"Don't know what color their blood is. It's the right color for his."

There was no one in the rooms nearby, most of the doors of which opened freely. There were objects that might have been of interest in the rooms, but they could spare no time for them. Harn carrying Price's helmet, they went out through an external door, around the temple on the outside, and back to the front.

They were walking back towards the flier when a crashing roll of thunder brought their eyes up to what appeared to be a clear sky. Something flashed across above them—something black, massive, unbelievably swift. It vanished behind a close horizon of buildings.

"What the hell was that?" Nordstrom got out of the flier, looking around.

Suddenly they spun around at the thunderous sound of a kesri voice. The gigantic figure of a kesri seemed to tower above the nearer buildings, and although they knew it was some kind of magnified hologram, the sight of it chilled them with an atavistic fear of the unknown. The figure pointed down at them, roaring some command in a language they did not know.

"Only fireworks, of a sort," said Connor. "Let's spread out."

He ran back towards the corner of the temple while Nordstrom returned to the flier. Connor didn't have time to see where Harn went, because only a few meters around the corner of the temple he stopped sharply as the black shape of a kesrii aircraft glided into view only a hundred meters ahead of him from behind a building. Two kesrii sprang out, dressed in black airtight suits with helmets. They shouted at Connor in their own language, and one of them waved something that might have been a weapon.

Desperately, Connor lifted the stun gun that Nordstrom had given him, but the kesri's reflexes were like a flash of lightning. Connor felt a jolt like a heavy electric shock from his shoulder all the way down his right arm, and his gun clattered to the ground.

He staggered, and the other kesri ran towards him in great, bounding strides. Six or seven meters away, he sprang high in the air, his three-toed feet lifted in front of him. One of them landed on Connor's chest, and he found himself flying backwards, the impact with the ground almost stunning him.

Then one of the kesrii was bending over him. His right arm still felt numb. He lifted his left fist, but the kesri blocked it easily and slapped him hard across the side of the jaw. He couldn't get his senses together until they had him inside their machine.

They tossed him into a low, bench-type seat that ran across the back of the cabin. One sat behind the controls, the other

faced him across the back of a seat, pulling off Connor's
helmet and then its own. It snarled at him in its complex,
rapid language.

He couldn't understand a word it said, but its anger came
over like a tangible force. The flattened ears, the blazing eyes
that stared unwinkingly into his—all these suggested that the
thing had been on the verge of killing him, and might at any
second, with the slightest change of its mood.

He got out of the situation, for the moment, by feigning
unconsciousness. A hand seized him, shook him violently,
then abandoned him.

For the moment . . .

Eyes closed, Connor tried to get his shaken thoughts into
order. He was in trouble—that was a certainty. He did not
feel the machine lift off, yet when he risked looking through
almost-closed eyelids, he saw high-level cloud whipping past
the large windows of the aircraft at a speed he would not have
believed possible within an atmosphere.

There was no sensation of movement in the cabin. Theoretically, with the acceleration they had used, the force of inertia
should have spread them all like jam across the back wall of
the cabin, yet something was obviously counteracting it.

Connor lay still for a while, and after a few quick glances
back at him the kesrii ignored him, speaking between themselves and occasionally into a microphone.

Once, they passed high mountain peaks with white snow that
was red-tinged here and there in places where only the secondary
sunlight reached. Lifting his head slightly to see out of one of
the low windows, Connor saw that they were traveling due east
along the irregular band of the Equatorial Sea between the two
continents. He was much farther east than he had been before.

Soon the coastlines of both continents receded, and they
ran out over a vast ocean sprinkled here and there with chains
of islands that looked of volcanic origin. The suns, high
above the horizon when they had taken off, were now almost
setting, so they had traveled an appreciable distance around
the planet's equator.

Abruptly the machine dived steeply down, and Connor was
able to see through the forward windshield a mountainous
island with an arm of the sea twisting between two jagged
ranges. They swept down between the ranges—again with no

physical sensation of movement—and leveled off on a broad area of green moss or grass in front of a number of metallic and crystalline buildings of outlandish design.

Connor was dragged out of the machine and walked towards a building by one of the kesrii, who gripped both his wrists in an unshakable grasp by the two large digits of one seven-fingered hand. Connor made no attempt to struggle, weighed down by the depressing realization that the kesri was keeping the other hand free for his weapon. He had already had enough indication of the kesrii's hair-trigger fury.

He was taken inside a bronze-colored building that looked as if it had been made from a single enormous metal casting, with a roof of different metal fitted to it. He was marched along a passageway, then thrust into a room about five meters square. A large window gave him a view outside, but it didn't appear capable of being opened. The door closed behind him.

The room was devoid of furniture. The floor felt soft, but when he looked down, he saw that it was of apparently unseamed metal, with an invisible, resisting field a centimeter or two above it, giving the feel of unseen carpet or foam.

His shoulder and arm still felt a certain numbness, but it was gradually wearing off, so that he felt stabbed by innumerable needles when he moved. Wearily he sat down on the floor, his back against a wall, and looked out through the window at the fantastic buildings. One looked strangely reminiscent of something. A tall, triangular tower bearing at its summit something that whirled in such rapid movement that it appeared as a spherical blur. The memory fell into place. It was like one of the very first artifacts of kesrii engineering he had ever seen—back on the planet where he thought he'd found an outlying human settlement. He recalled again the chilling feeling of horror when he realised the things he was looking at were of alien origin.

He wondered what had happened to Zella. Her child could arrive any day, and a great bitterness suddenly came to him as he realized he could not get to her.

Without warning the door opened, as if a section of wall had instantly vanished. A kesri stood outside, dressed in a totally enclosing suit. Connor scrambled to his feet.

"Kralg," he said. "Get Kralg."

It was the only individual kesrii name he knew. The kesri

in the doorway stood looking at him for a few seconds, and duplicated the name Kralg. Then an idea seemed to come to him, and he repeated a much longer name, unpronounceable to Connor, which seemed to begin with the syllable Kralg. Abruptly he was gone, and the wall where the door had appeared seemed unbroken. Connor walked across to the wall and slapped his hand on it. Where the door had appeared, it made a slightly different sound, but it felt just as solid as the rest of the wall.

Nothing happened for a considerable time. It was dark outside now, except for the glow of what he at first took to be moonlight, although its greenish-white color was different from that of the moonlight here. Also, it did not shine on the dark mountains opposite. Moving closer to the window, he saw it came from a number of glowing, luminous disks that seemed to float in the air high above the buildings—how high, he could not estimate, because he did not know their size.

His arm was now feeling almost normal. He risked a few tentative exercises without ill effects, then sat down against the wall to rest awhile. He must have slept, for when he looked out of the window again, he saw an aircraft taking off, although he had not noticed its arrival.

Stretching, he walked to the window. There were three aircraft parked neatly outside. Two of the black kesrii craft and—his breath suddenly seemed to stop of its own accord. The third machine was Nordstrom's flier!

Connor tried calling Nordstrom's and Harn's names with the full power of his lungs, but the effort brought no response. He walked up and down the room for a while. Tentatively he kicked at the window, but it was as if he had kicked a sheet of boiler plate.

He must get to Zella. The thought kept coming back to him again and again. But so far he could find no way of getting out of this room. He was beginning to feel hungry. Possibly the kesrii didn't know what to feed him.

Some time not long before sunrise the door opened without warning and two of the kesrii stood there in totally enclosing suits. One of them beckoned to Connor, who followed them out along a passageway to another room, with equipment that looked strangely familiar to him. In a few seconds he realized why. It was like the sterilizing room on the kesrii spaceship, with its shower cabinet with mirrorlike walls, needle jets, and the hard violet radiation.

Resigned, he let them strip him, shower him with hot water, blast him with warm air, blindfold him to irradiate every part of his skin. Then there were the tests, running instruments over the whole surface of his body while watching the readouts on dials and cathode screens. Finally they gave him his clothing back. It felt hot, as though they had sterilized that, too.

When he had dressed, they led him into another room, where a tall kesri with black-and-white fur stood waiting.

"Con-nor. I greet."

"Kralg! I greet." He made a gesture. "Why am I here?"

"You ruined a large experiment."

"How?"

"Man you call Price, sometimes Asgard. Contacted drom. Not his fault. Drom took helmet off. Exchanged microlife from his body, from their bodies. Different."

"What happened?"

"Many drom dying. More and more, as Price microlife spreads through them. No natural enemies. No . . . what word?"

"Antibodies?"

"Ah. Yes. Wrong antibodies."

"What happened to Price?"

"Dead."

"How?"

Kralg made a lateral hand gesture that seemed to indicate he neither knew nor cared. "Drom accept we are higher form of life. They thought Price was kesrii. Found he was not." He made a violent motion with both hands, as if he had seized something around the throat with both hands, then twisted. Then he spread both hands out as if there were no more to be said on the subject.

"What can I do?"

"Nothing. Experiment was finishing, near now. Drom dying out here. Lost will to live. There are other drom, other planets."

"Your people study us, too, don't you?"

The slightest hesitation. "Yes. Have learned enough now."

"Didn't take you long."

"Small sample. Enough time used."

"What happens now?"

"We go elsewhere. Work elsewhere."

"So my people will be stuck here?"

"No. We return your ship. Large ship in orbit. We return small . . . ship.'''

"Our shuttle?"

"Ah, Shuttle. We return shuttle. You use to fly people to large ship. Then go where want."

"Our large ship was wrecked by a meteor."

"By what?"

"By rock in space. Smashed iso-drive."

"Ah. We repair. Now quite good."

"Could you let me go home? Now?"

"Home?"

"Place we call Red Lake. Dry lakebed near river."

"I know it. Why now?"

"My female is about to have a child."

Kralg looked at him penetratingly, as if he were looking through his eyes into the interior of his skull. "When?"

"Few days." Connor hesitated. "First on this planet. I'm worried. Want to be with her."

Kralg seemed to think for several seconds. It was the first time Connor had seen him show this much hesitation. "My female is expert in births," he said. "She might help. Learn, too. Your female also learn, yes?"

"My female is a doctor."

"I know." Kralg lifted his left arm, and Connor noticed for the first time a dark, segmented metal bracelet around his wrist, with a tiny keyboard. He stabbed at several of the congested keys with a sharp-pointed finger, then spoke at the bracelet in his swift, bewildering language. Then he looked up at Connor.

"Wait," he said. "Short time. We go."

He went out, leaving Connor wondering whether he had done a wise thing.

A few minutes later Kralg returned with the first female kesrii Connor had seen. Not as tall as Kralg, about the same height as Connor, she was extremely slim, clothed in a long, plain garment of what looked like very flexible metallic foil, which left her head and arms uncovered. The three-toed feet, just visible, were sheathed in similar material. The head, nearly the size of Kralg's, looked enormous above the slender body. Her fur was brown, like that of a Burmese cat, and the huge, turquoise eyes had the unmistakable cruciform pupils of the kesrii.

"Con-nor," said Kralg. "My female. Auru."

Connor gave a stiff little bow that he had learned from Jiro Kosaka. "Auru, I greet," he said.

"Come," said Kralg, gesturing to the door. The female walked gracefully ahead, Connor following, Kralg behind him. She led the way out to one of the kesrii aircraft which hovered centimeters above the ground, and they entered it, Connor sitting on a kind of bench seat across the rear of the cabin. As he entered, he noticed that Nordstrom's machine had gone.

The female had apparently brought the aircraft here in answer to Kralg's call, and she took the controls, Kralg sitting beside her and looking back at Connor. He indicated the female with a movement of his hand.

"Expert in birth," he said. "Kesrii. Other."

Connor said nothing. He wasn't sure he wanted two aliens to see Zella at the present moment, but this seemed the only way for him to reach her himself. The aircraft took off vertically, then forward at meteoric speed, with absolutely no sense of inertia transmitted to the interior of the cabin. They swept over mountains and out over the Equatorial Sea.

Connor was surprised to see that they headed south of west, so that they could be traveling almost directly towards Red Lake from the moment of takeoff.

Auru made occasional little remarks to Kralg, and he seemed to direct her, as she once made a course correction when he spoke. Soon they were flying high above the snow-covered central mountain ranges of the southern continent, and Connor saw that there was not just one range, as he had thought, but a vast, contorted complex of ranges stretching back, row on row, for a thousand kilometers.

"Big continent," he said to Kralg.

"Continent?"

"Big land mass."

"Yes. Planet nearly half land, good balance."

Kralg had apparently flown over Terranova many times before. He indicated a couple of passes that gave them smoother access through the tangled mountain ranges. Then, when they cleared them, he pointed to a spot on the distant coast. As they began the long, straight descent, he ran his hand lightly down the furred arm of his companion, the two large digits of his hand closed, only the light, slender ones making contact. The movement was extremely sensuous, and Connor was momentarily surprised at seeing another side of the complex being that had once struck primordial terror into him.

Dead ahead, the red oval of the dry lakebed appeared. They continued down at the same angle until the buildings became visible. Kralg unerringly pointed out Connor's house, and Auru brought the machine to a landing at the edge of the field, just in front of the house. The door of the aircraft opened.

"You go," said Kralg. "Explain first."

18

Connor walked over to the house and mounted the veranda. Zella came to the door in a loose wrap.

"Con! Where were you?" She flung her arms around him. "I thought you'd vanished somewhere. Con, can you get Chang for me?"

"I brought someone else. An expert in childbirth, I'm told."

She pulled her head back and her voice hardened. "Who else is there?"

He stepped aside, and she saw the kesrii aircraft. She pressed the back of her hand over her mouth.

"It's all right," he said. "They're friendly."

Kralg emerged from the machine, then Auru. When Zella saw the kesrii female, she seemed to freeze. Auru raised her long, slim arms in the kesrii greeting, then took a large metal box with rounded corners from the aircraft, carrying it in one hand as she walked straight towards the house. Kralg remained standing near the aircraft. The female halted a few meters away from the veranda. Looking at Zella, she spread her hand on her chest.

"Auru. Zella, I greet."

She had evidently learned the language from Kralg, or at least through the same indirect source.

Zella raised her hand "Auru—I greet."

Auru pointed to the front of Zella's body, then to the suns.

When she saw that neither Zella nor Connor knew what she meant, she repeated the gesture, then moved her hand from the suns down to the western horizon several times.

"A few days," said Zella. She pointed to the suns and repeated Auru's gesture four or five times.

Auru mounted the veranda and put her hand gently on Zella's arm. Zella motioned her inside the house, and they disappeared from Connor's view. He became aware that Kralg had come up beside him—the first indication was the faintly different smell of the kesrii body. Kralg put one of his furred, long-muscled arms across Connor's shoulder, and gestured towards the house with the other.

"Good!" he said. "Female to female. Females not so— aggressive, is word?"

"Not so aggressive," agreed Connor.

He glanced furtively around. If Sven came raging up here now, he'd have some more explaining to do.

Kralg walked over and stood looking down at the river, showing obvious interest in the steam-driven punt and the bulldozed roads, but making no comment. Connor walked aimlessly up and down, staying close to the house.

About ten minutes passed before Zella and Auru appeared on the veranda together, Auru carrying her metal box, Zella holding a large bag.

"Con," said Zella, "I'm going with Auru."

"You're *what*?"

"She knows what she's doing. I trust her."

"No, wait! I'll get Chang. I can fly him here within a couple of hours!"

"No, Con. Auru has better equipment. And she has wider experience to call on. Con, we're both doctors. I know what I'm doing. They have expertise centuries ahead of ours."

"They probably want to study us—through you."

"I trust her, Con."

She began to walk with Auru towards the kesrii aircraft. Connor made a move to follow, but as he took the first stride Kralg's powerful hand closed over his arm, holding him like a vice.

"Let me go!" he shouted.

"Is all safe. Good." Kralg did not release his grip.

The two women—why did Connor suddenly think of them

as that?—reached the aircraft, and Auru turned, saying something in her own language to Kralg. She stroked Zella's forehead, then slipped her hand under her knees and lifted her into the aircraft, showing surprising strength. She took her into the rear seat of the aircraft. Then Kralg released Connor and bounded over to the machine, springing in behind the controls with a single, superbly coordinated leap.

Connor rushed forward.

"Con!" called Zella. "I'll be all right!"

The door of the aircraft closed, and Connor pounded on it with his fist. Then the machine took off, and a strange pressure forced him down for a moment, as if he'd suddenly become much heavier or had stepped into a field of more powerful gravity. The effect faded quickly as the aircraft shot skyward. Air swirled around him, filling the space left by the machine as it screamed into the sky like a rocket. It leveled off, and within a few seconds he heard the sound of a trans-sonic boom. Then the machine was a mere speck dwindling towards the east-northeast. A few seconds later he lost sight of it.

Connor stood gazing around him. The four-seater, single-engined aircraft stood in front of the shed. His first impluse was to fill it with fuel and set off in pursuit of the kesrii machine. Then he realized he could never carry enough fuel to reach their island base, even if he knew exactly where to fine it in that immense expanse of ocean.

He walked back into the house just as the buzzer sounded to indicate a message from Central. Without hurrying, he opened the channel, and Nordstrom's face appeared on the small screen.

"Ah, Con! We've been trying to raise you. Thought the kesrii might still be holding you. Con, they've returned our shuttle to us! It's right here on the beach near Central, and they've put the big ship in low orbit, passing over every hundred minutes."

"That what they tell you?"

"Yes, and we've checked. Karl located it with the telescope. They tell us they've fueled the big ship and repaired the impact damage that took out the iso-drive. When can you be down here?" When Connor didn't answer right away, he went on, "I want you to come up with us to check over the ship. Say, what's the matter?"

"They've taken Zella."

"What?"

"Kralg and one of their females. They took Zella to their base. She went willingly—they said they'd help her deliver her child. Their female was a doctor, and Zella and she talk the same sort of language. Zella thinks they're way ahead of us in techniques."

"What are you going to do?"

"I don't know. I know where their base is, but it's out of reach of our aircraft. Halfway around the planet."

"We'll do something, Con. I think they've become cooperative. Come up with us in the shuttle and we'll check out the main ship."

"Right," said Connor after a short hesitation. "I'll be down."

When the connection was broken, he walked outside and stood looking east-northeast, where the kesrii craft had disappeared over the mountains. He drove his fist into his palm.

"Right," he said aloud. *"The shuttle!"*

He took off in the four-seater plane and flew down to Central. The shuttle was visible from far off, lying on the hard strip of beach. It must have made a tricky landing, and he wondered who had brought it down.

Landing on the level area behind the HQ building, he went in search of Nordstrom. He eventually located him down on the beach among a crowd of the settlers near the shuttle. Nordstrom saw him coming down across the dunes and went to meet him.

"Any news of Zella?"

"None."

"What happened?"

"I was at their base—all night, out on an island in an ocean a long way east—"

"So were we, briefly. Then they brought us here."

"I told them I wanted—told them Zella was pregnant. That it was urgent. Kralg brought a female doctor of theirs with him, and they took Zella to their base."

Nordstrom looked at him keenly. "Your aircraft couldn't reach their base?"

"No."

"But the shuttle might?"

Connor looked at Nordstrom for a long time without speaking. More than two hundred years of experience looked back at him from the pale eyes. "I thought," he said, "after I'd ferried you up in the shuttle . . ." He let the sentence fizzle out.

Nordstrom's expression was enigmatic. "We need to make a number of trips in the shuttle, Con. And did you see much of their island?"

"A little."

"Where would you land the shuttle? You need a runway. Their machines land vertically. Even if you got it down without wrecking it—which I doubt—you'd never be able to lift off again."

Connor looked at the shuttle. "I suppose you're right. But I'm not leaving while Zella's there. I'll find some way. Use one of our aircraft to fly fuel to Sandstone Point, use that as a base to go farther on."

Nordstrom put his hand on his shoulder. "When is Zella's time?"

"A few days."

"Leave it until then. I don't think the kesrii are all bad."

Connor looked down towards the shuttle again. "What's happening down there?"

"Most of us want to leave." Nordstrom looked around in the air, as if watching for the microsurveillance units they had once assumed were insects, then he lowered his voice. "We're going to head out from here, when everyone is aboard, towards Sagittarius. Lose ourselves against the star clouds. Then we head back the way we came along the Orion Arm to a human-settled area. We have to warn the rest of the human race about the kesrii. The two races are both expanding towards one another, and we can't let the eventual contact come without warning our people."

"They might follow you. Did you think of that?"

"We thought of it. Karl and I think a number of changes of course, when we're well away from this system, should throw off any pursuit."

"Be careful, Chief. They're very good. Better than I thought."

"We know that. But we're forewarned. We'll take no chances."

"You said most people wanted to leave. Do some want to stay here? I know I do, and Zella. Jiro, Charl, Sven, I think, in fact everyone up at Red Lake."

"We'll have to divide up our equipment. Actually, you'll have greater need of it than us, since we'll be heading back to civilization. But we'll organize that later."

Connor flew the shuttle on its first run to rendezvous with the orbiting ship. As he swung around the planet, seeing for the first time its pattern of continents and oceans all around the globe, he looked intently for the kesrii island base, but was unable to pick it out. There were innumerable islands in that large ocean, which seemed to occupy a third of the planet, some of them in chains suggesting continental drift, some in huge, circular patterns which implied ancient impact craters. But the base could have been anywhere in that enormous expanse. He was not even sure of its latitude.

Zella. Seeing her every day, and with the pressure of adapting to a new environment, he had not fully appreciated her. Now that she'd been separated from him, a volcano or fury and frustration within him seemed to seethe towards eruption. Because he still thought logically, the fury was not channeled. He could see Nordstrom's point in not letting him look for Zella with the shuttle. He could see Auru's point in helping Zella with her birth, even if there was an ulterior desire to learn more of human beings. Alone in the alien environment of Red Lake, Zella could have died, killed by some microorganism unknown and unforeseen. And yet, he'd been separated from her just when she needed him most. Always thinking logically, he could not put blame on anyone, even himself. So the rage within him built its pressure, seeking a violent outlet.

They matched orbit with their original ship. It had seemed colossal when Connor first saw it, but the later appearance of the kesrii ship had put it into a different perspective. As they approached the shuttle lock, the doors opened and lights showed within. There was a black kesrii craft in the shuttle bay, and they discovered there was a small, skeleton crew of kesrii on the ship.

They spoke the same somewhat mangled human language

Kralg had used. Enough for essentials. They showed Nordstrom and Connor the work that had been done on the shattered iso-drive unit, and both men were impressed. Some of the parts, replaced by kesrii parts, seemed to show an improvement on the original equipment.

"Make sure the ship's not bugged," said Connor to Nordstrom when none of the kesrii were near.

"Don't worry. I will. We'll check every square centimeter of it."

About three quarters of the people on Terranova wanted to return to what they described as civilization. Connor found that he no longer had a usable definition of the word civilization—it seemed to have become a meaningless cliché. One thing that struck him forcibly was that the majority of the people who wanted to "return," as they put it, were those more recently brought out of stasis. Of course some, like the zero-grav people who would have difficulty adapting to any planetary surface, had been left in suspended animation continuously.

One of the two other shuttles aboard the ship was made active to assist in the work of bringing people and equipment aboard. When Connor made his second flight up to the ship, he saw another kesrii craft in the shuttle bay—smaller than the first. As he emerged from the shuttle, two kesrii in airtight suits and helmets were standing in front of their machine.

One of them looked at something that might have been a card or a photograph in his hand, then began walking towards Connor a little unsteadily in the light gravity maintained by the ship's spin.

"Con-nor?" he said with the rising inflection that seemed almost universally to indicate a query. He was speaking through a grilled diaphragm in his helmet.

"Yes," said Connor, surprised.

"Come," said the kesri.

"Why?"

"Come. Your female."

"What's happened to her?" burst out Connor, but the kesri had apparently learned only a few words of the language. He was already moving back to his craft.

Connor followed, getting into the machine with both kesrii.

"Con! What's this?" Nordstrom came striding into the shuttle bay.

Connor waved. "See you, Chief."

The kesri at the controls touched a switch, and abruptly a normal planetary-surface gravity seemed to push Connor down on his seat, the floor becoming firm beneath his feet. The door of the machine closed. Then, with no internal sense of movement, they shot forward at meteoric speed out of the shuttle bay and down towards the white-and-blue globe of the planet. Connor tried to see what the pilot did. As they neared the surface of the atmosphere, he touched something that apparently threw some protective field around the machine, for it seemed to be surrounded by a filmy shell of bluish light. There was no sensation of heat buildup within the cabin, although they dived at a frightening speed into the ocean of air.

As they neared the surface below, it became obvious to Connor that they were not heading for the island base of the kesrii. Below him was the familiar coastline of the western edge of the south continent. They were heading down at a sharp angle to a red, oval marking near the green triangle of a river delta. Red Lake.

They swept around over the little settlement. Connor noticed two of their aircraft there, the four-seater and the twin-engined machine, which someone must have flown back from Sandstone Point. Near his house he saw one of the small, black, triangular machines used by the kesrii.

They landed, opening the door for him. He stepped out onto the hard red ground, feeling no change in gravity—the internal field of the kesrii machine must have been capable of very accurate adjustment.

As he hurried towards his door, the tall, slim figure of Auru appeared in the doorway. She stepped back, beckoning him inside. He rushed in, halting a moment to let his eyes adjust from the sun glare outside to the darkness of the room, because the windows had been covered with something opaque.

"Con!" came Zella's voice, subdued yet intense. "Come and look at him."

Connor moved silently over to the bed and sat down on the edge of it. "He's got his eyes open," he said. "He's actually looking at me!"

'He's going to be very bright,'' said Zella. "Perhaps the brightest human being ever to come along.''

Connor smiled, kissing her forehead. It was slightly damp, and he picked up a small towel near the bed and wiped her head, then stroked the red-gold hair. "Every mother thinks that,'' he said.

"Yes,'' she said quietly. "But this is different. Auru did some things I didn't know about.''

He felt a chill seeping into him. With an effort, he kept his voice level. "What things, Zel?''

"Oh, a lot of things. We're beginners, Con. We know next to nothing. The gases a mother should breathe, the oxygen level, the—never mind, dear. He'll be fine. And so will all the other babies born here. I've learned so much . . . so much . . .''

After a few moments she slept, smiling. Connor looked at the baby. It looked at him with a curious directness for a baby. It was smiling, too, but as it looked at Connor's face its smile faded. Quickly Connor forced a happy expression, smiling broadly. The child looked at him with a strangely intent expression for a few moments, then smiled and gurgled.

Connor rose quietly and tiptoed out of the darkened room to find Auru. But when he went to the veranda, there was no sign of her, and both the kesrii aircraft had gone.

After Nordstrom and three quarters of the population of Terranova left in the big ship, both the Central and Red Lake areas seemed quiet and uncrowded. Karl O'Donnel, Sven, and a few of their original helpers kept the engineering plant going at Central, expanding it as needed, and Connor and Mak nurtured an embryonic aircraft industry at Red Lake.

Kosaka and Harn had settled down with ladies of their choice from stasis, and were happy in their associations. Harn often joked that it was a magnificent advantage to have access to your future wife's dossier while she was still asleep.

Connor's son grew into a healthy, extroverted natural athlete who seemed unremarkable for the first ten standard years, but then began to show signs of a phenomenal memory, an intense power of concentration, and an ingenuity that sometimes left Connor staggered.

Zella prodded Connor into building a long-range aircraft that could reach the kesrii's base in the Eastern Ocean, as they called it, basing their maps on a zero meridian through Central. It took a number of sweeps over the broad ocean to find the island, which was one of thousands. As Auru had promised Zella, they found much of the kesrii medical equipment had been left there, including the atmosphere-controlled room where Connor's son had been born.

Zella had wanted to call the boy Kralg, but Connor had vetoed that. His own doubtful choice was Nordstrom, but Zella flatly objected to that, even in abbreviated form of Nord. Someone else suggested the name Terranova, since he was the first child born there. The name was almost at once shortened to Terry, which somehow stuck.

All subsequent mothers were flown to the island for the birth of their children, using the kesrii facilities. Connor at first resisted this move to enhance the intelligence of the next generation, but eventually changed his mind.

"After all," he said when Zella delivered Jiro Kosaka's first daughter, "we have someone ahead of us. Some day our descendents are going to run into the kesrii. They'll need all the brains they can get."

After fifty revolutions of the yellow and the red suns about their common center of gravity—the equivalent of more than twelve terrestrial years—the people at Red Lake had almost forgotten the kesrii.

Then one day, without warning, a black kesrii aircraft screamed down through the atmosphere and hovered above the center of the dry lake. Connor, who had been in the middle of a meal, walked out to his veranda, followed by Zella.

"They're back," he said, with a cold feeling in his solar plexus. Zella rested her hand on his arm, saying nothing.

Hovering, the kesrii machine slowly rotated, its needle nose swinging until it came to a stop, pointing straight at Connor's house. With silent, bewildering speed, it suddenly leaped forward to hover within a hundred meters of the house, twenty centimeters above the ground.

The door opened in the side of it, and one of the kesrii stepped out. Facing Connor and Zella, he flung both arms upward and outward in the gesture of greeting, then strode towards them. He was in a totally enclosing black suit, with yellow helmet, gloves, and boots. Behind him, manipulating rods were lifting something out of the machine, placing it on the ground.

"I make short visit," said the kesri, speaking through a diaphragm. "I come from Kralg. I greet, Con-nor. I greet, Zel-la."

Zella's fingers trembled where they still clutched Connor's arm, but she kept her voice steady as she echoed Connor's words: "We greet you, friend of Kralg."

The part of the face they could see within the helmet was orange yellow, the eyes green as emerald. "I see all is well," said the kesri, waving his arm to indicate the distant fields of ordered cane. He stood in front of the veranda, but his greater height brought his eyes level with Connor's.

"Our crops are growing well," said Connor. "Can you tell that to Kralg?"

"And to Auru," added Zella. "Tell her the children are fine."

"I tell," said the kesri, and he held up an instrument he was carrying. He touched something, and their last few words were played back to them. The kesri pointed to the instrument. "It tell."

The kesri turned and pointed to three different-sized boxes which had been unloaded from the machine. They were lime green, with rounded corners.

"We return some equipment of yours, which was overlooked. It may be useful to you."

"Thanks," said Connor.

The kesri strode back to his machine, halting before he entered it.

"We grow," he shouted in a powerful voice. "Together or not—we grow."

"We grow!" echoed Connor, raising his hand.

Within seconds the machine turned in the air and lifted like a rocket, whistling into the upper air until they heard the trans-sonic boom then a long roll of thunder as air fell into the hole drilled in it by the supersonic passage of the black ship.

Connor and Zella walked towards the boxes. They were of lime-green plastic of some kind, with markings in dark red, strange characters of kesrii origin. They were made with lids secured by what looked like screws with heads incised with a Y-shaped slot like a three-pointed star. A strip of adhesive tape held a screwdriverlike tool on top of the largest box.

Connor laughed. "Think of everything, don't they?"

He pulled the tape away from the tool and used it to release the screws holding the top of the largest box. When he lifted the lid away, he gave an exultant shout.

"What is it?" asked Zella, who couldn't see down into the box.

"The big electron microscope from the ship! We can certainly use it."

The second box contained the smaller electron microscope, the third a large optical microscope.

"Remember when Karl caught one of those flying spy machines?" said Zella. "The things that looked like insects? He was complaining that he didn't have a proper microscope to examine the pieces when the thing had blown up."

Connor stood back, looking at the microscopes. "We'll get these under cover as soon as I get a bit of help. You know, Kralg and his crowd, when you think of it, are quite reliable friends to have."

He turned to her, and the smile suddenly left his face. His eyes seemed to focus in an infinite distance. He turned slowly back towards the boxes.

"What's the matter, Con?"

Suddenly he gave an inarticulate shout, almost like a scream of pain.

"God!"

He slammed his fists down on the box.

"Con! *What is it?*"

His expression was wild, his eyes showing whites all around the irises. "We've lost! You realize that? *We've lost!*"

Zella shook her head. "I don't follow you. How do you mean, we've lost?"

He waved his hand, gesturing at Red Lake. "Not here. I mean the whole human race, in the long run." He pointed to the microscopes. *"Why now?"*

"I don't understand. . . ."

"Why now, after Nordstrom and his ship are gone over twelve standard years? Look—they gave us our ship back, right? By now it's well on its way to human-settled areas, and it's way, way out of our radio range. We can't communicate with it."

"So?"

"So why is it only *now* that they give us the microscopes they took *from the ship*?"

Slowly her eyes seemed to darken, and her face paled. "You mean, the ship must be full of their microspy instruments?"

He nodded. "And Nordstrom and the others will never suspect it. The kesrii probably have another ship shadowing them all the way back to human settlements. They can make spy instruments too small to see, perhaps picking up everything that's done on Nordstrom's ship, and then relaying it to a following ship or probe, and so back home."

He turned and walked back to the house, climbing onto the veranda and turning to lean on the handrail, looking bleakly out over the airfield. Zella went after him and joined him.

"At least, they probably won't kill the race off," she said. "They didn't kill off the drom."

Connor shook his head. "They didn't physically kill the drom, no. But they killed off their dreams. Which is worse?"

After a long silence Zella said, "What happened to your optimism, Con? You once said what the human race needed was a pacemaker a little way ahead of it."

Connor didn't speak for a long time. Then he looked at her and said, "Perhaps it may work that way. After all, I think the drom were already on the way downhill long before the kesrii ever found them. Our people may have a better chance."

She managed a smile. "Is that the way you'd bet?"

He put his arms around her and held her tightly against him, looking up over her shoulder at the enigmatic sky.